Castleview

"Witty, erudite, beautifully written."

— Locus

"A Lincoln-Mercury dealer opposes Queen Morgan le Fay in a small town in northwestern Illinois; the plot involves the primal rite of sacrificing the king to ransom the sun. Horses, cars, pretty women and frightened men are involved in large numbers; so are a sly dog and part-time plastic surgeon, a tough tomcat (formerly of the FBI and CIA), an occasionally French girl in training as a vampire, and an actual vampire. There are lots of chases and fights, and a good deal of shooting."

— Gene Wolfe, on *Castleview*

"Few writers other than Wolfe, with his polished, assured, persuasive style, could bring this unlikely premise to intriguing life. Clever, unusual, and disquieting, to be sure."

— Kirkus (starred) review

Tor books by Gene Wolfe

CASTLEVIEW

GENE WOLFE

TOR
fantasy

A TOM DOHERTY ASSOCIATES BOOK
NEW YORK

CASTLEVIEW

Copyright 1990 by Gene Wolfe

A Tor Book
Published by Tom Doherty Associates, Inc.
49 West 24 Street
New York, NY 10010

Cover art by Richard Bober

ISBN: 0-812-50625-1

Library of Congress Card Catalog Number: 89-25712

Printed in the United States of America

First edition: April 1990
First mass market edition: January 1991

0 9 8 7 6 5 4 3 2 1

This book is dedicated to the memory of my father, Roy E. Wolfe, and to that of Alfred, Lord Tennyson. I'd like to thank Elliott Swanson and the folk group Barley Bree for their help, and also to send my very best wishes to Cyndi Shaeffer and her colt, Urth Sun Rebel.

Whether liketh you better, said Merlin, the sword or the scabbard? Me liketh better the sword, said Arthur. Ye are more unwise, said Merlin, for the scabbard is worth ten of the swords, for whiles ye have the scabbard upon you, ye shall never lose no blood be ye never so sore wounded, therefore keep well the scabbard always with you.

—Sir Thomas Malory

1

THE HOUSE AT THE EDGE
OF THE FIELDS

TOM HOWARD stood at the edge of the loading dock and stared out across the storage yard. It was raining, raining hard, and that made it hard for him to see. The first shift had already gone; there was no second now that summer had gone, too. The yard was clamorous with rain, cold drops that pounded the steel drums.

Yet he was certain he had seen something.

When he went down the dock steps, the rain pounded him as well, drummed upon the shoulders of his yellow slicker, drove hard against the brim of his rubberized hat. It was not dark enough yet—not quite dark enough—for him to require the black, five-cell flashlight he carried, but he switched it on just the same.

No one crouched between the rows of fifty-five-gallon drums. No one squatted behind the low stack of three-quarter-inch angle iron. As Tom splashed toward the scrap heap and the dumpsters, there came a sudden jolt that halted all thought. He fell face down onto the flooded gravel, but he never felt it.

Joy Beggs, "Your Real Estate Lady," regarded the old Howard place with an admiration that was not entirely feigned. It was by current standards much too large, and it had not really been modernized to the degree Joy would have liked. And it was wood, true. But it had been repainted in August, white not some crazy color, and its roof was only two years old. "A lovely old home, Mr. Shields," she declared with enthusiasm. "Didn't I tell you? *And*," she let her voice drop, "you can get it for a song. He's been promoted, and they have to move."

Leaning forward so that her mouth was at her husband's ear, Ann Schindler whispered, "Look at those flowers, Willie." Ann had retained her maiden name.

Her husband answered firmly, "We're not going to pay sixty thousand for flowers." He added, "No matter how wet they are."

Ann murmured, "But it shows they care."

Joy nodded approvingly. "You're absolutely right, and let me tell you, Mr. Shields, you're lucky to have this rain. Most folks looking for a home won't go out when it rains, but there's nothing sillier. With rain like this you can go up in the attic with a flashlight—I've got one—and look for leaks. Then there won't be any surprises the next time it rains."

Shields nodded and rubbed his jaw. He was a long lank man, and it was a long lank jaw that he rubbed.

"Aren't we even going to get out and look at it?" Mercedes Schindler-Shields griped from her place beside her mother in the rear seat. Mercedes was sixteen.

"Of course we are," Joy told her. "There's a black-topped drive around here somewhere, and I've got enough umbrellas for everybody."

They were golf umbrellas, striped orange and brown; Joy and Mercedes shared one, Shields and Ann the other. There was, very fortunately, a spacious front porch with a roof; Joy pressed the bell button. Above the pounding of the rain, Shields could hear chimes tolling slowly and almost sadly, somewhere far beyond the door.

Keeping her voice down, Joy said, "It's an old farmhouse. There's more than three acres still. Let me tell you, we call properties a lot smaller than this 'estates' in the real estate business."

"Room for a tennis court?" Mercedes wanted to know.

"Absolutely."

Shields folded their umbrella and banged the ferrule on the porch to shake the water out.

Joy told him, "When the subdividers get interested in this area—and they will—you could sell off a couple acres for more than the down payment on the house."

Seth Howard opened the door. "Come on in," he said. "You can leave your umbrellas in the hall."

"We'll leave them on the porch," Joy told him. "They'll be okay." They trooped inside. The hallway was wide for a private house, high-ceilinged and dark.

"Mom's in the kitchen. You want to see her? Dad's not home yet."

Joy said, "That won't be necessary. I'll show the house. Just don't pay any attention to us."

Seth followed them anyway, mouse-quiet in athletic shoes. He was seventeen, nearly eighteen, tall already, and dark, with his father's blue Norman eyes. Mercedes lagged somewhat behind her parents, and soon she and Seth were walking side by side, neither speaking until she asked, "Where does this little door go?"

"To the turret—want to see it? It's kind of cool, but it'll be cold up there."

"Sure," she said. "I noticed the turret from outside." I am, she thought, ohmyGod, a *twelve*. What the heck would he want with a pig like me?"

"Okay." He opened the door, disclosing a steep and narrow stair. "All the rest of the house is two stories, but this's three. There are windows, and you can see pretty far." He led the way, to Mercedes's infinite relief.

High in the attic, Joy Beggs apologized. "I'm afraid it's terribly cluttered right now. They'll be moving a lot of this out.

Anything they leave will belong to you folks, and you can do whatever you want with it."

Shields nodded absently, staring around. He looked first at the underside of the roof, because it was where Joy played her light; but reason suggested that she would not have been so eager to bring them here if she had thought there was a chance of a leak, and he transferred his attention to the contents of the attic, mostly boxes, old trunks, and stacks of books. He had a sudden premonition that the Howards would move none of it. All this would be theirs, if they bought this house—his to explore slowly, on rainy Sunday afternoons.

"You could convert this into more bedrooms," Joy suggested. "There are eight of these big dormer windows, and they let in plenty of light when the sun's out, even with all this junk in front of them."

Ann murmured, "Or a study. Willie, I could write up here—I know I could."

"Oh, you're a writer!"

"Only cookbooks," Ann told Joy.

Shields said, "She's had three published so far. Arkin and Patris in New York—they're her publishers." Proud of her, he wanted to say that it was not just some church group printing a few hundred, though he did not know how to do it without giving offense.

"*Cooking with the Lake Poets*, that was my first one. And then I wrote *Cooking with Abe and Mary*, and *Cooking for George Bernard Shaw*. That's Irish-English vegetarian. What are you looking at, Willie?"

Shields had been peering through the grimy glass of the nearest attic window. "Nothing," he said. "Nothing at all."

Rain drummed unceasingly on the roof.

In the turret, Mercedes looked out of each gray window in turn. "Boy, I *like* this," she said. "Wonder if my folks will let me have it."

Seth asked, "Are they going to buy the house?"

Mercedes shrugged. "We've got to live someplace."

"You're just moving to Castleview?"

"My dad's bought a dealership here." There was a window seat, and Mercedes sat down, careful to leave room for Seth if he wanted it.

"Motorcycles?"

She shook her head. "No, cars. He's been the manager at a Buick agency ever since I was a little kid. Now he's bought his own agency here."

"Oh, yeah. I know the one. It's been for sale." Seth did not sit down.

"You don't mind that we're maybe going to buy your house?"

"What for? We've got to sell it. We're moving to Galena. My dad's been promoted, and he says we can't afford two places. Only my great-grandfather built it, and I've lived here my whole life. See that little picture?" He pointed toward a watercolor framed behind glass, the only decoration in the small, hexagonal room. "My grandmother painted that."

"No kidding?" Mercedes rose to look. "Where's Galena? Is it very far from here?"

"About thirty miles."

The watercolor showed a line of rugged hills, fringed with scarlet-and-gold maples. Slender stone towers, faint and even ghostly, loomed above the treetops.

"Then you could come over," Mercedes told him. "I mean, if you wanted to see the house again. That is, you could say you were coming to see me. We could walk around, and you could tell me about stuff."

Seth nodded.

Down in the kitchen, Shields and Ann shook hands solemnly with Seth's mother, Sally Howard having first wiped her flour-powdered hands on a dish towel, and Shields having washed his somehow-dusty hands at the sink.

Ann said, "We didn't feel it was polite to go all through your home without ever meeting you."

5

"Besides," Joy added practically, "they ought to see the kitchen."

"It's a lot of steps," Mrs. Howard said, sighing, "but I'm going to miss it when we move. The kitchen in the new place is a lot smaller."

Ann smiled. "And I'll bet it doesn't have an avocado-green phone, or half as much cupboard space."

"No, it doesn't. Have a look inside if you want to. You folks aren't from around here, are you?"

Shields shook his head, and Ann said, "We're from Arlington Heights. It's northwest of Chicago, about twenty miles from the Loop."

"I see. Well, this kitchen was meant to feed the farmhands and such, as well as the family. At harvest, there'd be three or four women working in here and ten or twelve men eating at a big table outside."

Ann spun around. "*Cooking for the Harvesters!* That'll be my next one! What was in season, and how it was prepared."

Joy said proudly, "Mrs. Shields writes cookbooks."

"By Ann Schindler," Ann corrected her absently.

From Ann's expression, Shields knew she was already deep in the planning of her new book. He said, "I've been wondering why this town's called Castleview."

Mrs. Howard glanced toward a kitchen window. It was quick, no more than a flicker of her eyes; yet Shields felt sure he had seen fear.

Joy stepped in. "It's really quite romantic. They say you can see a castle in the distance, sometimes, just at sunset. I have to admit *I've* never seen it, and I've lived here seventeen years plus. But lots of people have, or say they have. It's an illusion, not a hallucination—a few people have taken pictures, although they don't usually turn out very well."

"We're looking east here, aren't we?" Shields asked. He crossed to the window.

Tonelessly, Mrs. Howard said, "That's right."

"Technically, they call it a Fata Morgana," Joy told him.

"Heaven only knows what that means, but my kids had to study about it in school."

"It means 'Morgana the Fairy,'" Shields explained absently. "Morgan le Fay." He was staring out at the rain.

Ann said, "Willie was a lit. major. It was very handy when I was doing *Lake Poets* and *Cooking for Shaw*."

"Anyway," Joy continued, "it's supposed to be some kind of funny atmospheric effect that takes something way off and makes it look close. My guess is that people are seeing the skyline of Chicago. That would look like a bunch of towers and things, because it *is* a bunch of towers and things."

"When was this town settled?" Shields asked.

Sally Howard said, "In eighteen-fifty. We're really pretty historical here. My family—I'm a Roberts, and we were with the first group, the pioneers. Tom's family, the Howards, came here in sixty-six, after the Civil War."

"And was it originally called Castleview?"

"I believe so. You might find out something about that at the County Museum."

Ann said, "It's charming, isn't it, Willie? Like having a family ghost. Should give me some lovely touches for my book."

Turning to face the three women, Shields nodded. "What did you say the price was, Mrs. Beggs? The asking price?"

Joy shot Mrs. Howard a swift look. "It's not ethical—"

Mrs. Howard said, "It's not up to me. Tom will have to decide."

"Perhaps if we went into the living room. . . ."

Ann nodded agreement. Shields followed them down the wide, shadowy hall and into a big, high-ceilinged room nearly as dark, where Joy switched on a floor lamp with an old-fashioned fringed silk shade. "This is what they called the parlor when the house was built. Your friends and acquaintances paid calls on Sunday, and this was where you received them."

"After church," Ann said eagerly.

"Yes, I suppose so."

7

The women were still standing, so Shields remained standing himself, fidgeting and listening to the rain. After a minute or two he heard feet on the stair; the tall boy who had admitted them came in, with Mercedes close behind him.

"There you are," Shields said. "I've been wondering what happened to you."

Mercedes threw herself into a leather armchair. "Seth's been showing me around. I like it. Can I have the tower?"

Shields nearly said, "If you're still a virgin, Merc." He decided it would not be funny and substituted, "We haven't made an offer yet."

The telephone in the kitchen rang, one long peal.

Seth shrugged. "No phone in here. Just in the kitchen, and across the hall in Mom and Dad's room."

Another peal, this one cut short. Shields could visualize Mrs. Howard wiping her fingers before picking up the handset.

Joy said brightly, "I hope that isn't another buyer. I'd hate to see you lose this place."

Ann hissed, "It's just sixty thousand, Willie. That's all they're asking."

They could hear Mrs. Howard's voice, faintly, as she spoke in the kitchen, the click when she hung up, then her slow steps in the hall.

Seth said, "I bet it is another buyer, Mrs. Beggs. Mom's coming to get you."

Her face was not precisely white when she entered the room. Makeup takes care of that, Shields thought afterward; even women baking, in the big kitchens of old farmhouses in little country towns, wear makeup now while they work.

She glanced at him first, for some reason. Then at Joy and Ann, and last of all at Seth. She did not look at Mercedes, or perhaps did not notice her.

She said, "There's been an accident at the plant."

2

CASTLEVIEW

JOY RETURNED Shields, Ann, and their daughter to the real-estate agency, where they transferred themselves wetly into their own car. Mercedes grumbled, "I sure hope it doesn't rain like this all the time."

"Of course not, darling. It's fall—it always rains in the fall."

"It's dead here, Mom. It's absolutely dead."

Ann snorted. "How many people would you see on the street back home in this rain?"

"I asked Seth about this high school," Mercedes continued. "You know how many kids go there?"

"I've no idea."

"Two hundred and seventy-three. That's the whole darned school—freshmen, sophomores, juniors, and seniors. Just two hundred and seventy-three kids."

"I think that's perfectly marvelous, darling. You'll get to know everyone. It'll be just like a little club."

"And Seth won't even *be* there!"

Shields muttered, "I wouldn't be too sure of that, Merc." He turned a corner. The Red Stove Inn was on Old Penton Road, and he thought he might have glimpsed a sign for it, though in the downpour it had been impossible to be certain.

"On account of the accident, you mean, Dad? Mr. Howard's just hurt. He's not dead."

"Dead or dying," Shields muttered.

Ann turned to look at him. "Willie, what're you saying? Willie, I want that house!"

Mercedes leaned in, her head between her parents'. "Well, she said he'd only been hurt."

"I saw her face," Shields told his daughter. "Do you think she'd tell that boy his father was dead in front of a bunch of strangers?" He caught sight of the fiery neon through the rain, a small electric-blue VACANCY flashing below it.

Ann lowered her voice, a signal to Mercedes that she would be expected to behave as though she had not heard. "This is my money, Willie—mostly mine, anyway—and I want that house. They put it on the market, and we made them an offer in good faith."

"Which they haven't accepted," Shields said practically. "Until they do, there isn't even an oral agreement."

The dark figure of a horseman appeared on the road before them as though it had fallen with the rain. Shields hit the brakes. The Buick skidded, its rear axle slewing left. He steered into the skid, pumping the brakes, his body braced for the crash.

Back at the Peak Value Real Estate Agency, Joy Beggs hung up her dripping raincoat and ducked into the tiny toilet to try to do something about her hair. A glance in the mirror showed her it was hopeless, and it was close to quitting time anyway. She put on a little powder and touched up her lipstick.

Fred Perkins, who owned the agency, inquired, "Were you showing?"

Joy nodded wearily. "The old Howard place."

"How's it look?"

"Good, at first. But—" The telephone on Joy's desk rang, and she picked it up. "Peak Value, Joy Beggs speaking. . . . The house in Galena? Don't worry about it, Sally. Nobody's going to force you to move if you don't want to. . . . Oh, Sally! Sally, I'm so sorry. God, how tragic! . . . How awful for you. . . . What can I say? . . . Is there anything I can do? Anything at all? . . . Well, technically, I suppose financial counseling's out of my line, but a lot of the work I do involves financing. . . . No, certainly it's not too late. Sally, you're a friend. . . . Stew and dumplings will be fine, whatever you've fixed. I take it there isn't much of an estate? . . . What about life insurance? . . . Sally, you don't have to worry, you're sitting in the middle of sixty thousand dollars; compared to that, paying off the car's chicken feed. . . . I'm on my way."

She hung up.

"It's starting to look good again," she told Perkins.

Ann studied Shields sympathetically. "You're itching to get back to your dealership, aren't you?"

"I don't want—"

"Willie, Mercedes can watch TV just as well with you gone. And I can read just as well—better. Did you like that Chinese place where we ate last night?"

He nodded, hoping, yet not daring to hope.

Ann glanced at her watch. "You go out to the dealership. We'll meet you at the Golden Dragon at seven thirty."

He had already risen, but he said, "How will you get out there?" A moment too late, remembered to add, "Darling."

"Call a cab. I know this is a small town, but it's sure to have a cab or two. The woman here at the motel should be able to tell me who's reliable."

Shields was through the door before she finished speaking. It was not until he closed it behind him that he realized he had left his sodden raincoat dripping in the closet. It really did not matter, he decided. A raincoat that had soaked through was not much protection, and the rain was letting up a little now, anyway.

Fortunately, the car was right in front of their room. In one wet bound, he had the door open; and in half a minute he was tooling back up Old Penton Road. There was no sign of the rider he had so nearly hit, no mounted figure lurking in the shadows, not even a trail that Shields could see.

The lights of downtown Castleview appeared, and he began to sing.

Mercedes asked, "Where're you going, Mom?"

"Up to the motel office," her mother said, shrugging into her raincoat.

"To ask about the cab?"

"That's right. Want to come?"

Mercedes shook her head; she had already turned back to the TV. "I'll stay here."

Ann grinned to herself as she picked her way along the flooded brick walk; Mercedes only wanted to come when she knew she was not wanted. Hadn't she herself been like that at Mercedes's age? It was necessary, after all—it was precisely the things from which girls were excluded that girls had to learn if they were to become women.

"Evenin'," the white-haired woman behind the counter said. "Everything all right in Number Ten for you folks?" She had been reading *The Weekly Castle View*, and laid it in her lap as she spoke.

"Everything's fine," Ann said. "I just wanted to ask you something."

"Be glad to help, if I can." The older woman studied her over the tops of her glasses.

"We very nearly had an accident coming here tonight."

The older woman nodded. "Rain makes the road slick. Must be near to freezin'."

"It was somebody—a big man, I think—on a great big horse. He didn't have any lights—" Ann paused, feeling foolish. Who in the world would expect lights on a horse? "And they crossed the road right in front of us. My husband tried to stop, but we almost hit him."

"But you didn't?" The older woman was still staring over her glasses.

"I don't believe so. We would have felt it, wouldn't we? Wouldn't there have been a bump?"

"Hittin' a horse? I'll say there would. Wreck your car if you were goin' fast."

"Then I don't think we did," Ann said. "But it seemed like we ought to have. Do you know what I mean?"

The older woman said nothing; the paper rattled in her lap.

"I was wondering if you knew who it might be—who'd be out riding in the rain like that."

The older woman nodded slowly. "Kids. There's a summer camp down the road 'bout five miles, only it's only five miles by the road. If you walk or ride a horse, maybe three."

"And they have horses?"

"Sure. Sometimes when they're supposed to be asleep a kid will sneak out and get a horse and ride into town. They'd ride in the rain—do any crazy thing."

"I'd like to go down there and have a word with whoever's in charge," Ann said.

"The name's Sullivan or something like that. Just follow the road till you see their sign. Meadow Grass, they call it. Gate won't be open now, though."

An elderly man in an undershirt looked in through the door behind the counter. "She see the white lady?"

"Course not!"

Ann ventured, "What's the white lady? Is that a local legend?"

The man in the undershirt chuckled and nodded as he stepped into the narrow space behind the counter. "Thumbs for a ride at night."

His wife muttered, "No, she don't."

"Please. I'm a writer—that is, I just write cookbooks, but they have lots of local color, little stories, you know? I'd love to hear about the white lady."

"Do you really write cookbooks?" the woman asked. "I might have a receipt for you." She said *receipt*, Ann noticed, instead of *recipe*. "You like pear jelly?"

"Really good pear jelly," Ann answered carefully, "jelly that actually tastes of fresh pears, is very—is *extremely*—difficult to find."

"Then you got to get a taste of mine. Alfred, open up the gate for her."

Alfred lifted a hinged section of the counter so that Ann could pass through. "It *is* good," he told her. "Wins the fair 'most every year."

"*Every* year," his wife declared firmly. It was not until Ann was on the other side of the counter that she realized the woman was in a wheelchair.

There was a small apartment behind the door. Pushing his wife's chair, Alfred led Ann through a cluttered living room and into a tiny kitchen.

"Sit down," the woman said. "Bread or toast? I've got a little zwieback too, if you care for that."

"Whatever you're having." Ann seated herself in a bright yellow kitchen chair. A big jar of greenish-brown jelly and a big pat of butter were on the table already. Alfred brought in a chair for himself from the living room.

"We've got one of these electric hot water things now—it gives you hot water right away. Like some instant coffee? Or tea?"

"Tea, please."

While the woman busied herself making tea, Ann whispered, "Aren't you going to tell me about the white lady?"

Alfred chuckled again. "Emily don't like me to talk about it. She's afraid it scares customers away."

"It won't scare *me* away," Ann declared. "I slept here last night, and I'll sleep here tonight. We'll probably sleep here tomorrow night, too."

"Well, the white lady's just a ghost some sees around here. I never seen her, and neither has Emily."

Three feet away at the low drainboard, Emily interjected, "Don't nobody see her, if you ask me."

"She's pretty, they say, and just a little bit of a thing. Sometimes people that see her think she's a kid. She wears a gown like a nightgown that comes clear to her feet. It's white, and she's got long blond hair. She waits by the road, generally over here on the west side of town, and tries to get people to give her a ride. Only she don't really thumb, like I said back there—"

Emily asked, "Sugar?"

"Yes, please."

"She sort of stands by the road and begs. Holds out her hands, and so on."

"Begs for what?" Ann asked. Emily set a sugarbowl and a spoon before her, rapidly followed by a plate heaped with homemade bread.

"For help, I guess. She wants them to take her someplace or help her find somebody. Sometimes she's cryin'."

"Has anybody ever picked her up?"

Emily said, "Long Jim *said* he did. I didn't believe him then and don't now."

"Long Jim?"

"Jim Long, his real name was. He was about as tall as the flagpole in front of the post office, so everybody called him Long Jim. He stretched the truth to his own size, too."

Alfred protested mildly, "Don't do good to speak ill of them that's gone. Jim wasn't so bad."

"Jim's dead?" Ann asked.

Alfred nodded. "Ten years. I'd went to school with him, though he was a couple years younger than me."

"What happened to him?"

Emily said, "You haven't touched that bread or my pear jelly. Try some."

"He was run over, that's all. Hit-and-run driver."

Ann spooned sugar into her tea and stirred. "What did he tell you about the white lady?"

Alfred shrugged. "She was real pretty and spoke with some kind of foreign accent. He said he tried to talk to her two or three times, but mostly she wouldn't answer. Kept tellin' him to go faster, and starin' out the window at people they passed. Said when he saw that, he knew she'd gone past him a time or two when he was walkin' himself. He recollected that white face at the window."

Emily sniffed, and Alfred added, "Understand now, I don't swallow all this. I'm just tellin' you so you can put it in your book if you want to."

"And I appreciate it," Ann assured him, spreading butter on her bread.

"Then there's the black rider." Alfred chuckled, and took a sip of his tea. "The high-school kids tell that he's the one chasin' the white lady, and if you see his eyes, you die."

3

CARS AND HORSES

THE DEALERSHIP was downtown, as old dealerships in small towns often are, its lot sprawling across most of a block that would make someone a great building site, when and if the town began to grow. It had entered into Shields's calculations, with many other things; late at night, as he lay in bed beside a snoring Ann, he imagined Chicago inching toward Castleview, closer and closer, until at last it had become a remote suburb.

Awake, he knew it would not happen—not in his lifetime and not in the lifetimes of Mercedes's children; the distance was too great.

There were a couple of parking spaces under the overhang at the front of the building, but Shields pulled around to the back and dashed through the rain to let himself in by way of the rear door. Better to leave those dry front spots for customers. The back, the service area, was closed; the mechanics went home at five. Two cars awaited their return on the lifts: a three-year-old and a four-year-old model, Shields noted, both nearly ready for replacement.

His salesmen were sitting in the showroom drinking coffee. There were no lookers, and certainly no buyers (thus the vacant spaces); still, the salesmen were honor-bound to remain at their posts until the stroke of nine. It was Friday night, after all—the big shopping night in Castleview. Speaking as one, they said, "Evenin', Mr. Shields."

He answered, "Good evening, boys," and smiled, though in truth he was pleased with neither.

The younger one, Teddy, said, "Not much action on the new models tonight."

There was an implication that this was Shields's fault, and as it happened it was one with which Shields agreed. "We'll be kicking off our winter ads soon."

Teddy shook his head. He was going bald, and the movement caused the showroom lights to play across the bare spot as if it were polished glass. "Winter's the worst season there is."

"That's why we need an advertising campaign then."

Bob Roberts, the older salesman, said, "Mr. Hotchkiss used to close for January. He'd always go to Fort Lauderdale."

And you got a month's vacation, Shields thought. Aloud he said, "I might do that too—if November and December sales are good enough." Roberts was the better of the two, he felt sure, but Roberts was old, over sixty-five.

Teddy asked, "What's the winter angle?"

"Wait until you see it." Shields winked; if he told Teddy about the price cuts, Teddy might advise his favorite customers to wait until they were in effect.

Roberts was at the coffee machine. "Like some coffee, Mr. Shields?"

"Sure." One of the salesmen would not be replaced, Shields decided. He would fill that slot himself, and replace the other with a woman. Women bought cars nearly as often as men did, and women liked to deal with a woman.

The telephone rang. Teddy answered it with alacrity: "View Motors, Ted Camberwell. How can we help you? . . . Yes, he's right here." He held the handset out to Shields, saying, "Your wife," under his breath.

"Ann?"

"It's me, Willie. Willie, I just had an idea. Now you don't *have* to do this, all right? It's just a thought."

"What is it?"

"I want you to lend me a car. You've got a bunch of used ones, so couldn't you have that salesman drive one out here for me? Then I'd bring him back. It would save paying for the cab—we may not be able to get one anyway—and then I'd have a car to run errands and things while you were there."

Shields nodded to himself. "I've got a better idea than that. I'll have him bring our car to you. I can take one of the trade-ins when we close."

"Oh, Willie, would you?"

"Sure. He'll be there in ten minutes."

"Willie, I love you very, very much."

There was a click. Shields hung up, handed Teddy his car keys, and explained what he was to do.

"There's some real nice machines out there," Roberts told him after Teddy had gone. Shields nodded, noticed the coffee Roberts had set before him, and stirred in powdered whitener. "It's your agency," Roberts said. "You might as well get the good out of it."

Shields shook his head. "Mostly the bank's, I'm afraid."

"Okay, if they want a car I'll let them have a loaner."

Shields chuckled appreciatively. "Bob, could you tell me where the County Museum is?"

"The Castle County Historical Society Museum? Sure can." Roberts pointed. "Willow Avenue, three and a half blocks down. You can't miss it—a big two-story brick with a red, black, and white sign out front. I painted that sign myself."

"I didn't know you were a sign painter," Shields said.

"Sarah paints a little. Pictures, you know, and she got me to dabbing in it. I've done a few posters for the agency, not printed-up posters, just one-of-a-kind things to stick in the window. So when they decided they needed a sign, I said I'd do it. I'm a trustee, and I feel obliged to save our money when I can."

"I don't suppose it's open now?"

Roberts shook his head. "Thursdays and Sunday afternoons

is all. We have trouble getting somebody to come in and look after things. Usually you sit there for your hours and nobody comes. Were you wanting to go tonight? I could take you."

"I'd appreciate it," Shields said. "I really would."

"Be glad to do it."

Shields was in the little office going over the books when he heard the Buick splash up outside. Through the window, he saw Teddy jump out and run for the door. Shields waved to Ann, and was rewarded with a smile and a blown kiss as she drove off.

From the rear of the building, Shields and Roberts looked out across the brightly illuminated lot. "Since you haven't got a coat," Roberts suggested, "maybe you could just tell me which one you want. I'll get the keys and drive it around." Roberts himself wore the black oilskins favored by farmers.

"Okay." Shields nodded.

"The blue and cream Linc's real nice."

Shields shook his head. "It's too nice, let's keep it here and sell it. What's that sticking up at the far end?"

"Eighty-six Cherokee. The outside's pretty beat up, but she runs good. Got four-wheel when you want it."

"I'll take that." Suddenly conscience-stricken, he added, "If you don't mind walking—"

Roberts grinned, showing perfect teeth Shields felt certain were false. "I won't melt, and this slicker's about new anyway. Hold on a second." He vanished into the building.

Alone at the edge of the rain, Shields tried to recall the attic of the Howard house, the window, the driving rain that had sometimes spattered its glass, and what he had seen through it. I'm chasing a phantom, he thought, an illusion. I may need that four-wheel drive.

Roberts reappeared and hurried off into the rain, moving among motionless vehicles with white-numbered prices on their windshields and in their windows: $12,999; $9800; $8750; $6900. After a minute or so, Shields heard the engine of the Cherokee start, cough, die, and start again.

There was a pause as Roberts let it warm up, a long pause in which Shields could not be certain it had not died a second time. At last it roared forward, headlights glaring, out onto Dixon—hurried down Dixon, and turned the corner to Main.

In a moment more it was braking in front of him, Roberts having circled the building so that the passenger's door was before Shields. Shields opened it and climbed in.

"Figured I might as well drive," Roberts said. "I know where it is."

"Sure," Shields told him. They pulled away; and suddenly, insanely, Shields felt that he had been standing before the gate of a fortress. This gray-haired man—an old squire or a master-at-arms, perhaps a master-of-horse—had just led up the charger he was to ride.

And it was not young and elegant, or even very clean, but a big, rough, rust-colored stallion with flashing eyes.

The next question, Ann felt, was whether to take Mercedes. She would have liked her company, but Mercedes would not want to come, and would not understand in the least why Ann herself was going.

Would not, that is, unless Ann explained, which she had no intention of doing. She drove past the motel without stopping, forcing herself, actually, to slow down to take the mileage at the sign. Five miles, Emily had said, by road. What was it called? Meadow Gold? That sounded like butter.

An antlered buck stepped daintily onto the road and halted, spellbound by her headlights. Icy-footed mice scampered up and down her spine as she stopped. Not only because she might have hit the buck (though that would have been horrible) but because for a fleeting instant the graceful buck had seemed an object of supernatural dread.

Like the horse and its rider.

She blew the horn, and the buck bounded away—no more than a common deer, a deer to be shot in all probability on the first or second day of hunting season. Or had hunting season already begun? Perhaps it was over already. Who would want to hunt in this rain?

She had started forward again when she saw a dark something in the rearview mirror. It swelled and roared around her, tires screaming and throwing up combs of rainwater, a rusted-out sedan without lights. Already it was gone, leaving Old Penton Road as dark and silent as before.

According to the odometer, she had gone exactly three and three-tenths miles since passing the motel. Five miles by road, Emily had said. Abruptly, the road dipped. A sign: TRUCKS USE LOW GEAR. Not a bad idea for her either, Ann decided, shifting the transmission into second. What had the sedan done? It must have been going eighty when it hit this section.

Around every bend, Ann expected to see the orange flames of its demise.

She wished—very much—that she had brought Mercedes after all. Any companionship would be welcome, even that of a sulky sixteen-year-old. And Mercedes would— The radio! How could she have forgotten?

She switched it on. "*—all along Old Penton Road. Flash floods may also—*"

Off again. What was the good of a radio if it just scared you? What had Goethe said? Willie would know. "Nature reacts not only to physical disease, but to moral weakness: when danger increases, she gives courage." Something like that. Well, come on, Nature, get busy.

Cooking with Goethe.

Cooking for Nature.

An infant waterfall appeared out of the darkness far above her, tumbling down onto the already-drowned asphalt. Ann gunned the Buick and crashed through it. This road must have dropped several hundred feet in the last quarter mile, she thought. Or was it a quarter mile in the last several hundred feet?

The engine sputtered, caught again. Something inside had

gotten wet; Ann knew that much about engines. It had dried out again because the engine was good and hot. Willie had told her, and Willie used to race—Willie should know. If it stopped, she would be stuck here until the police came, or the rain stopped, too. Maybe all night. Damn!

Meadow Grass—that was it. And there was the sign, big but old, flaking a little now.

Ann stopped the Buick, got a flashlight out of the map box, and lowered the window half way. MEADOW GRASS SUMMER CAMP, with a picture of a cowboy—no, a girl—on horseback. A girls' camp, then; she should have guessed. Nobody would call a boys' camp Meadow Grass.

"When they're supposed to be asleep," Emily had said, "a kid will sneak out and get a horse and ride into town." Girls for sure. Boys would ride at night, but not into town. Boys would jump fences or something.

Hearing the thud of hooves, Ann redirected her flashlight. Someone was riding toward her, galloping down the curving road on the other side of the gate. Through silver rain, the light glinted on the oiled barrel of a rifle.

Mercedes had decided to get a shower two minutes before the knock. Hurriedly she hooked her bra again and slipped back into the pink sweater she had taken off. "Coming! Just a minute."

When she opened the door, Seth was standing outside in the rain. "Oh," she said. "Come on in. Get out of that."

"Thanks." He shook himself (rather like a wet dog) before stepping inside.

"You can hang your jacket in the closet here." Tentatively she extended one of the motel's plastic hangers.

"Where's your mom and dad?"

"Gone off someplace. Mom'll be back pretty soon."

"Too good." He was wearing a Castleview High letter jacket. The blue wool showed indigo spots where drops of rain had soaked the fabric; others rose in crystalline warts from the nearly new green leather sleeves. He unzipped it and hung it up.

"Listen," Mercedes said, "I'm really terribly sorry about what happened to your dad."

A sudden spasm twisted Seth's features. "So'm I."

"How's your mom taking it?"

He shrugged. "Not so good, I guess."

"He's dead, right?"

"Yeah, he's dead. How'd you know?"

"We guessed, or Dad did. I thought he was probably right."

"He fell. That's what they say."

There were brown vinyl chairs beside the little table that held Ann's abandoned book; Mercedes sat down in one and motioned toward the other.

"Hey, would you like to go out and get a Coke or something? You could leave a note. I've got Mom's Olds."

"How many legs on a horse?"

Seth stared at her for a moment. "Four?"

Suddenly decisive, Mercedes stood. "I'd love to. We just about—I'm a little shook, to tell the truth. I need to get out and do something."

"Too good. Me, too." Seth sighed. "Rain's quitting, so maybe we can chase the castle, after. You ever done that?"

4

THE VIEW AT NIGHT

ROBERTS UNLOCKED the door, stepped inside, and switched on the lights. The County Museum had been a private house once, and they stood in what had been its foyer; there was a desk for an attendant, a few cabinets against the walls.

Roberts said, "What was it you wanted to see, Mr. Shields? I can take you right to it."

"The castle," Shields told him.

"We've got a whole exhibit on that. Over this way. You believe in it?"

Shields nodded. "I saw it."

"Really? I guess that would make a man interested. Right through here, this was the music room when old Doc Dunstan built the place. About the castle's in the next room, the studio."

Shields nodded. The music room held coins, mostly, and a few sad-looking violins. He stopped for a moment to peer at the faded pages of a diary.

"My great-grandpa's," Roberts told him proudly. "He was a Wells Fargo agent for a while. Saw some interesting things, and had some interesting things to say about 'em."

Shields nodded. "I'll bet."

"They were after me to donate it, but if I did, what would happen to it if they close this place? So it's just loaned."

Shields said, "You should keep it in the family. Got any children, Bob?"

"No more Robertses—I'm the last. Two daughters, though, and two grandchildren."

Shields straightened up. "They'll value this, when they're older."

"I hope so. He had a theory of his own about the castle—thought it was rocks out in Arizona. A mesa, he called it."

"He'd seen it, too, then."

"Oh, sure. He'd grown up right around here. Everyone that does sees it. It doesn't really stand to reason that the kids should see it more than the grownups, but that seems to be the way of it. You'd think that kids wouldn't see it so much 'cause they're shorter, nearer to the ground."

Shields said, "Grownups don't climb trees."

"That's a fact. Could I ask where you were when you saw it, Mr. Shields?"

"In the attic of a two-story house with high ceilings. The Howard house—we're thinking of buying it."

Roberts nodded. "I know about that."

"I guess it's true, what they say." Shields bent over the diary again, trying to decipher its florid, faded handwriting. "News travels fast in a small town."

"Sure does," Roberts confirmed. "Specially if you're Mrs. Howard's father."

Shields turned to look at him. "That's right, she said her maiden name was Roberts. I never put two and two together."

"That's my daughter Sally."

Shields hesitated. "Do you know that your son-in-law got hurt this afternoon, Bob?"

"Tommy? Lord, no. Was it serious?"

Shields nodded. "I think so."

"Sally should have called me. Maybe she called Sarah—no, Sarah would have called and told me."

"Maybe you ought to call her."

Roberts nodded. "If you'll excuse me just a minute, Mr. Shields."

"Of course."

Roberts hurried back to the hall. Shields could hear the dial of the old-fashioned telephone spin, then Roberts's muted voice. Somewhat embarrassed, he bent over the diary once more.

The page to which it lay open began with the continuation of a sentence: "—a shock? Why, I would not have gone to the door to see a ghost after that, nor suffered anyone to speak to me of it. To find someone from home out here, homesteading on the Santa Cruz, beat seeing the elephant."

Roberts said, "Sarah's with her. Sarah says she's taken something and gone to bed. She didn't want to wake her up."

Shields nodded.

"Tommy's dead—I guess you knew. You wanted to break it to me easy. I appreciate that."

"I thought he probably was," Shields admitted. "I didn't know it."

"Sally called Sarah, didn't say what was wrong, just asked her to come over. Naturally, Sarah came. After she found out, she tried to phone me. Teddie told her you and me were already gone."

"If you'd like to go there, Bob. . . ."

Roberts shook his head. "Not right now. Sally's asleep, and there's nothing I can do. Seth's off someplace—Seth's my grandson. He'll be all right, he's Tommy's boy."

"I'm sure he will," Shields said.

"Tommy was a tough one," Roberts told him. "Tommy was a fighter."

Shields nodded again, not knowing what else to do in the face of the older man's controlled grief.

"You were wanting to see the stuff about the castle. It's in that room there. That's the studio. Switch is on the wall, to your left as you go in."

"Thanks," Shields said. He went into the studio and turned on the lights. Behind him in the music room, he heard Roberts blow his nose. Bob wasn't tough, Shields reflected. Bob wasn't a fighter. Or perhaps, he was.

The rider reined up, his horse stopping so abruptly that it appeared to crouch. He pointed his rifle at Ann like a pistol, keeping the reins in his left hand. "Get out of that car."

Ann nodded, opened the door, and stepped out into the rain. It was no longer falling quite so fiercely as it had been, Ann decided. She thought of her body sprawled on the wet grass, the last gentle rain tapping at her upturned face. The gun was the kind you saw in cowboy movies; it seemed strange that such a gun could fire anything but blanks. Its muzzle followed her like a menacing eye.

"Come over to the gate."

Ann did as she was told.

He tossed her a bunch of keys. "Unlock it."

The big padlock was drowned in darkness. Ann clamped the flashlight beneath her chin, found a key that looked as though it might fit.

Freed from the hasp, the gate swung toward her. The horse tossed its head, watching her sidelong through the rain; its rider's eyes were lost beneath the brim of his rain-soaked hat.

"You get back in that car. If you think you're real smart, you'll cut the lights and throw her in reverse. And I'll have six or seven bullets in her before she's thirty feet back down the road."

Ann shook her head. "I'm not going to do that."

"Then you ease her by the gate. Go real slow. When you're through, get out and lock the gate."

She nodded, saw him try to peer through the windshield when the domelight came on. It seemed odd and almost unnatural to be inside the car once more, away from the rain. She shifted into drive and let the Buick creep forward.

When she opened the door, the rider said, "Kill the engine.

Give me my keys back, and the keys to the car." He dug a heel into his horse's flank; the horse turned obediently, presenting its left side to Ann. He dropped his reins on the horse's neck, took both sets of keys with his left hand, and stuffed them into the pocket of his jeans. "Open the doors of that car," he told her. "All the doors."

"All of them?"

For an instant she thought he was going to shoot, leaning from the saddle, his left hand grasping the wooden part of the gun in front of the trigger. She turned quickly, opened the rear door on the driver's side, trotted around the car to open the other doors.

"Open the trunk," he said.

"I can't," Ann told him. "You've got my keys."

He dismounted. "Shut that gate and lock it."

She did so. The lock was large and shiny, well-oiled. He wasn't really much taller than she was, Ann decided.

"Get into the car on the other side. I'm goin' to drive." He put his rifle flat on the rear seat, slammed the doors, raced the engine as he started it.

Ann closed the other rear door and got in beside him. "I could have grabbed your gun," she said. "I could've turned it around and shot you."

"I know," he said. "But you're not goin' to do that." He tapped the horn to get his mount off the road, and wrestled the shift lever in a way that showed he was accustomed to a stick.

Ann clutched the armrest as the Buick rocked around a sharp curve. "What about your poor horse?"

The rider chuckled. "Buck'll be along. Wants to get back to the barn, get his saddle took off. You very wet, ma'am?"

"Not as wet as you are," Ann said.

"I guess that's right." He was driving the gravel road much faster than she would have, but he obviously knew every twist and turn of it. "If they hadn't of busted my jeep, I wouldn't have had to take him out in this."

Ann said, "I'm sort of sorry I went out in it myself."

"That's somethin' I was wonderin' about, ma'am. You come to see one of the kids?"

Ann shook her head. "I just wanted to talk with whoever is in charge."

"In charge of the kids, or in charge of the place?"

"I hadn't thought about that," Ann said. "In charge of the horses, I suppose."

"Then you got him. You want to go through our barn? Maybe you'd like a chance to dry off first. We got a big fire goin'."

"That sounds good," she said. Actually, it sounded heavenly; she imagined a red-hot pot-bellied stove in a bunkhouse, cowboys spinning tall yarns (or was that sailors?), while a battered old stoneware coffeepot bubbled. Despite the heater, her teeth were chattering.

Triumphantly, the Buick roared to the top of a small, steep hill; at the bottom, under a brilliant light on a tall pole, in a valley that seemed separate from the rest of the world, stood a big white barn and a red-roofed rambling fieldstone building.

"This is a girl's camp, isn't it? I'd have thought you'd be closed by now."

He nodded without speaking as the Buick rattled over an old wooden bridge.

When he had switched off the engine and returned her keys, he got his rifle from the back seat. "I guess you ought to open up that trunk, ma'am. Just to be sure."

Ann did, and he glanced inside. She closed it again and made certain it had latched. "Just what are you so frightened of, anyway?"

"I don't rightly know," he told her. "Come on in."

She followed him into a wide rustic room, one wall of which was mostly fireplace; it held a bigger, redder, hotter fire than Ann could ever have imagined. Four young women were sitting on a long sofa dividing the room, not so much watching a television set as talking above the noise of it.

The rider said, "We got company, Miss Lisa."

All four looked around and stood up.

Wearily, Joy Beggs opened the front door of her own little house on Willow and hung her coat in the hall closet. Her son Todd called, "That you, Mom?"

"Uh huh."

"You've got company."

"Who's—" Joy began, as she came into the living room. She fell silent as her visitor rose.

He was a very dark man with a thin, pointed, black beard and oddly penetrating eyes. There was something odd about his clothing, too, Joy decided—about the long brown tweed overcoat he drew tight despite the warmth of the room, and his pointed, shapeless shoes.

"Per'aps I should introduce myself," he suggested. "I am Liam Fee, and I am an archdeacon." He extended a business card.

Joy accepted the card. "I'm afraid Todd and I aren't very religious, Mr. Fee, and I'm terribly tired. Maybe if you could come some other time, when it's not quite so late . . . ?"

"I will," he told her. "Oh, indeed I will. I trust that you will have good news for me then."

Joy recalled having heard someplace that *gospel* meant "good news." She repeated, "We're not very religious," and added, "we don't have much money."

Fee smiled, displaying small and crooked teeth that did not look white even in his swarthy face. "That is a misfortune that may be remedied, Mrs. Beggs, and one that I hope to remedy. You sell houses? Buildings?"

Todd said, "He wants to build a church, Mom."

"I see. Yes, I do." Joy took her favorite chair, the big wingback with the green and gold Chinese pheasants. "Won't you sit down again, Archdeacon Fee? I'm sorry if I seemed a little brusque, but it's been a long day."

"Then I will not keep you. We have several postulants here in your town—you may be unaware of that, yet it is so. We wish to provide them with a suitable place of worship."

"You need a building lot in a good location, with space for parking." Mentally, Joy flipped pages in the big black register back at Peak Value.

Fee shook his head. "More, per'aps, than that. We cannot build at once for so few. For the present, we wish a house—a capacious residence. It should be near the site where we will build, so that the congregation may assist in the construction after services."

"I see."

"And it must not be too much in the town. A country place not far from the town, per'aps, or a home on its outskirts. You have told me that you are not inclined to religion, Mrs. Beggs. May I take it that you are not prejudiced against faiths other than the Christian?"

"Of course not," Joy declared. "As a matter of fact, I've got quite a few Jewish friends."

"Then I should inform you that we do not worship the God of your Jewish friends. He cares less even for us than for you." Fee waited for her to object; when she did not, he continued, "A commission will, as I understand the matter, be paid your agency by the seller. You will share in that. In addition, we offer to pay a finder's fee, directly to the individual who arranges the sale. To yourself, assuming you are that person."

He paused again. Joy could feel him weighing her with his eyes, estimating her price.

He said, "We would pay you a finder's fee of three thousand dollars."

Joy smiled. "Isn't it strange? I was showing a home that would be perfect for you just today."

5

MARAUDERS

THE OLD doctor, Shields thought, had held some lofty ideas about art. His studio was long and by no means narrow, with six large windows. The brushes and the tubes of pigment were gone now; so were the easels and the artists—his daughters, presumably—who once had toiled before them, and perhaps received callers here. The paintings themselves were not.

Or at least there were a great many paintings and drawings in the room, and not a few photographs. Shields began to study them, and was still studying them when Roberts came in.

"Pretty various, aren't they, Mr. Shields?" Clearly he had himself under control now.

Shields nodded. "At least I thought so at first."

"Well, you look for yourself. Most see a castle—it's what somebody's told them they're going to see, so they see it. Some see something more like a city—maybe it's St. Louis, maybe some other place. And what some of 'em see, don't even the Good Lord know. Look at that one there and tell me what it is—buildings, trees, or rocks?"

Shields said, "Suppose they're all seeing something nobody has ever seen anyplace but here, a unique thing?"

Roberts was silent for a moment, stroking his jaw. "You do have some ideas, don't you? Bet our winter sale's going to be a whiz-bang."

"I hope so."

"What sort of thing would this be?"

"I don't know," Shields told him. "If I did, I'd be back at the dealership."

"I guess so. Well, you saw it. What did you see?"

Shields shrugged. "I saw the castle of Castleview—let's leave it at that. You've had a lot more time to look at these than I have, Bob. Have you come to any conclusions?"

"Only that people are seeing three or four different things and calling them the same thing. See the pinkish one over here? Got five points on it—towers, or whatever you want to call 'em. Now look at this one. The towers aren't pink any more; they're black. Over on that one, they're gray. The black one," Roberts waggled a finger, "it's got one, two, three, four, five, *six* of them. The gray one's got three. Sure, things will change color with changes in the light, 'specially if they're some ways away. But they don't change their shapes."

"Some things do," Shields said.

"Clouds, maybe."

"And cars. Airplanes."

Roberts stared, then turned to look from picture to picture. The old house groaned in the silence, icy tears dropping from its eaves.

At length Roberts said, "You think it's moving."

"There's a chart of sightings over here," Shields told him, "you must have seen it. Most are east of town; but there are a lot that are almost due west, one north, one northwest, and so on. We've been saying it has towers. Imagine somebody back in the Middle Ages looking out to sea and catching sight of a big warship. He'd think he was seeing a floating castle, wouldn't he? And he really wouldn't be very far wrong."

"The stacks and masts and so on, you mean."

Shields nodded.

"And if it was headed right at him, he'd see just the one tower, 'cause all the rest would be behind that one. But if it was sideways to him, he'd see three or four—however many stacks and whatnot it had."

Shields nodded again. "Let's look at the photos; paintings and drawings are pretty subjective. None of the photos are very clear—whatever it is doesn't photograph well, it seems, and no one had a long enough lens—but all of them show something." He pointed from picture to picture. "Three towers here, and three in the next one. Then that one shows five—one of them rather indistinct. The next shows three again, and the one after that four, with one a good deal wider than the other three. Would you mind going back to the desk now? It's on our way out, anyway, and there's something I want to show you."

But Roberts was no longer listening to Shields. "Did you hear a sort of scraping just then?"

"No," Shields said. "Did you?"

"Thought I did. Probably just a car going by. Sure, we can go back out to the desk. You want to make a call?"

Shields shook his head. As they passed the glass case that contained the Wells Fargo agent's diary, he asked, "Have you got a transcription of that, Bob? I'd like to read it."

"I can loan it to you. The keys ought to be in the desk."

Shields hesitated. "All right. Thanks." He thought that he, too, had heard something, though the stealthy sound (if it had been a sound at all) had come and gone so swiftly he could not be sure.

He had noticed a tape dispenser on the desk, and in one of the drawers he found what he had hoped for: blank paper. "Look here," he said. Roberts watched as he rolled a sheet of paper into a cylinder, taped it, and stood it on end on the desk. In rapid succession he added four more, forming a rough circle.

"Crouch down, Bob." Shields demonstrated, squatting on his heels. "Count them, and tell me how many you see. Not how many you know are there, but how many you can see."

Roberts bent, his palms on his knees. "Five now. Only if I

move over a little, it's only three, because two are behind two others. When I move back a little—you're right—it looks like four. Only one's thicker, because it's really two, one peeking out behind another one."

Somewhere nearby, glass broke with a crash as precipitate as an explosion.

"Perhaps I should introduce myself," Ann said. "I'm Ann Schindler."

One of the young women walked briskly around the end of the sofa, hand extended. "Lisa Solomon—wonderful to meet you! I'm afraid that we're closed for the season," (the other young women giggled) "but I'll be very happy to tell you anything you want to know about Meadow Grass. Is your daughter between the ages of fourteen and twenty?"

Ann nodded. "Yes, but I— I don't know, maybe we could. You see, we're moving here, moving to Castleview, and I—"

The three young women shouted in unison, *"A townee!"*

"Her name's Mercedes," Ann finished weakly, accepting the outstretched hand. "I'm afraid—I really shouldn't say this— that we named her after the automobile."

The three young women attained hysteria.

"We really shouldn't have. But that was Willie's favorite car back then—though it isn't any more, of course—and the man who named it, named it after his daughter." She turned to the rider. "You know, I don't think you and I ever met—properly, I mean. I'm Ann Schindler."

He took her hand and nodded. "Wrangler Dunstan, ma'am. I hate to leave so quick, but I ought to get his saddle off Buck and get him bedded down. You want to see our barn, Miss Lisa or one of the girls can show you."

When he had gone out, Lisa Solomon smiled. "You'll have to excuse Wrangler—he's terribly shy. Won't you sit down?"

Ann nodded. "Over by the fire, if that's all right with you."

"Certainly. Do you know, I read just today that open fires don't actually heat a building? It seems they draw in more cold air than they warm; just think of all those ignorant people who froze themselves to death, and never realized it, for thousands of years. Would you like something hot? We don't allow alcohol, but one of the girls could make tea or cocoa."

"Tea, please."

They were crowding around. The blonde said, "I'm Sissy—I'll do it."

"And this is Lucie d'Carabas. Lucie's from France."

"*Normandie,*" a raven-haired young woman sketched a curtsy.

"And Sancha Balanka, from Rio."

The darkest of the three smiled shyly.

"Sissy's from Cleveland," Lisa added. "Her name's really Cecilia Stevenson."

Ann said, "I'm not sure I understand. If you're closed—"

Sancha told her softly, "My parents are in Europe, you see. They are delayed. They—"

From the other end of the room, Sissy called, "Nobody wants us, Mrs. Schindler. So since we haven't got anyplace to go, we stay here."

Lisa said, "That's not true, Sissy," in the tone of one who has repeated the same words many times. To Ann she explained, "These are girls whose parents haven't been able to come for them yet. We—Wrangler and I—live here year-round, so we're *in loco parentis.*"

Sissy added, "For extra money. I put the kettle on. Tea and cheesecake in half a minute."

"Thank you." Ann dropped into the leather armchair behind her. "Won't all of you sit down?"

Lisa pulled up another leather chair for herself. "That's right, for extra money—which we need quite badly. You didn't really come to talk about sending Mercedes here next summer, did you?"

Ann shook her head.

"But conceivably you will, so I may as well be honest with you. We're underfinanced, and we've had problems this year."

Sancha muttered something evil-sounding under her breath.

"Two horses have been killed, and now somebody's sabotaged our jeep. It's hoodlums from town, I suppose."

Ann said, "So that's why he was out at night with a gun."

"Yes. Things seem to happen in bad weather, mostly. That doesn't make sense to me, but that's the way it's been. Lately Wrangler hardly sleeps at all when the weather's nasty."

"Wrangler's not his real name, is it?" Ann asked.

The young women giggled, and the older young woman looked at them with such humorless severity that Ann realized she was hardly more than a girl herself. "No. It's a perfectly nice, perfectly *beautiful* name, but for some reason he's embarrassed by it, so we call him Wrangler. I could tell you what his real name is, but the girls would tease him to death, so I'd better not. He's really a wonderful guy, and he's worked his head off for this place."

Ann said, "He pointed a gun at me."

"Sissy, go make the tea—I can hear the kettle whistling from out here. Mrs. Schindler, I'm awfully sorry about that. Where were you?"

"When he pointed the gun? At the gate. I'd turned off Old Penton Road."

Lisa nodded. "We've had problems down that way, and it's not our main entrance. The main gate is on Sixty-eight, about two miles after it leaves the interstate."

Sancha murmured, "There have been much, much bad troubles. Twice they start fires, when it was more dry."

"That's right," Lisa said. "And Wrangler's scared to death they're going to burn the barn. He's got smoke alarms all over it, and when he sleeps, he sleeps in there with a gun and a fire extinguisher."

Sissy came in with a teapot, teacups, a sugar bowl, a milk jug, and a thick slice of cheesecake on a big tray. Sancha and the other young woman—Ann had already forgotten her name—found a small table and set it in front of the fire.

"I'll pour," Sissy announced. "Mrs. Schindler, one lump or two? Do you like milk? We don't have any lemons."

"No sugar, please," Ann told her. "Just milk. Lisa—Ms. Solomon—can't whoever owns this place help you? Hire guards or something?"

"We're the owners," Lisa said. "And no, we can't. We're doing all we can already."

"You and Wrangler?" Ann accepted a blue willow-pattern cup from Sissy.

"It belonged to an elderly lady named Sylvia Baxter," Lisa explained. "She was an old dear and quite a sharp businesswoman, but it never made much money for her. I was head counselor, and Wrangler saw to the horses; he's related to the Baxters somehow. At the time that Miss Baxter passed away, the camp owed us both a good deal in back wages, so she willed it to us in lieu of all debts. We were delighted—the land alone's worth at least forty thousand. But we've lost those horses, as I told you, and had a lot of damage. I had to sell my Cherokee—" She broke off to take a cup from Sissy.

Ann drank from her own. The tea was fragrant and flowery, enormously warming and comforting.

"But you don't want to hear our problems. And if you were ever going to send your daughter here, you're not going to now. I sincerely apologize for Wrangler, and no doubt he's apologized for himself already. But it was late and dark, and we've had a great deal of trouble, and you were on our land. Now what can I do for you to make up for it?"

"I'm not certain. How many horses do you have?"

"Right now? Twenty-one. There are stalls for thirty."

Sissy said, "Can I show them to her? I want to make sure Lady's okay."

"If she wants to see them," Lisa said. "Do you? Wrangler mentioned it, I think. What for?"

"Because I—we, my husband, our daughter, and I—saw a man on horseback tonight. I thought it had been Wrangler at first, but it wasn't. It was a much bigger man, on a bigger horse."

Lisa nodded. "I see."

"Besides, Wrangler wouldn't walk a horse out into the road in front of a car. I really can't explain it, but I talked to him a bit, and he isn't that sort of man—he doesn't have that kind of arrogance."

Sissy nodded. "You're right. He wouldn't do anything that might get a horse hurt unless there was a good reason for it."

"It frightened me," Ann continued, "more than I would admit at the time, even to myself; and things that frighten me make me angry. Besides, I was told that it was some kind of spook, and I refuse to believe in spooks."

6

THE CASTLE CHASERS

"ARE WE really going to see the castle?" Mercedes asked.

"Maybe," Seth said. "You never can tell. Sometimes it's easy, sometimes you never see it at all. The best time's when there's lots of stars and no moon. Rain like this is the worst, or fog. But the rain's letting up, and when you do see it in rain or fog, it's up really close, and that's a trip. You can practically always see it if you go up to the scenic view after one and really look hard, but sometimes it's way far away. You know those pictures they have?"

Mercedes sipped her Coke. She had asked for the Super Size to see whether Seth would object, and had more than half of it left. "You mean like your grandmother painted? That's the only one I've seen."

A black on yellow sign displayed a sharply curved arrow and warned: 40 MPH. Seth took it at sixty. "No, that's people who just happened to catch it and drew it from what they remembered. Like, Grandma Roberts was pulling weeds and looked up, and there it was, sticking right up out of the trees on the other side of the cornfield. So she watched till it was gone—she says maybe ten minutes, but I think more like a minute—then she set up her art stuff and started the picture."

"You mean she saw it in the daylight?"

"Damn straight. That happens sometimes too. I saw it like

41

that when I was a little kid. Take it from me, that's something you remember. But the photos—"

"I didn't know they had any."

"Sure they do," Seth told her. "Look, we're going up there right now—suppose we see it. Okay, if we had a camera we could take a picture, but it probably wouldn't be a very good picture."

"I've got a pretty good camera," Mercedes said, "only it's back home. We haven't moved our stuff yet."

"What kind? An Instamatic?"

"An Olympus. You know, the clamshell?"

"Sure, I know them. It's not a bad little camera, but it's got almost a wide-angle lens. Say you want to get a picture, so you buy some really fast film and take your little Olympus up to the scenic view on a good clear night, around one or one-thirty. There's the castle, ten or fifteen miles away. *Snap!* Back home you turn in your film at the drugstore, and you get back this little thirty-five neg, and the castle's a tiny little speck in the middle of it. Then you get somebody to blow it up to some humongous size and cut off all the stuff around it, and there's a lot of shimmer anyway from the distance. That's if you were smart and set your camera on the stone railing they've got. If you held it in your hands, forget it."

Mercedes took another sip. "You really do know a lot about photography, don't you?"

"Sure. I worked in Burke's Photo Supply this summer. Mr. Burke says he's going to get me to come in after school whenever he needs me. He's thinking about staying open evenings one day a week during the winter, just to try it out. The deal would be that I'd come in after, so he could go home and eat dinner. It would be Friday night, if he does it. I've got a camera with me right now, a Pentax. I took it in on trade, and he let me keep it. It's an old model, but it's got damn good glass."

"Can I see it?"

Seth nodded. "I'll get it out as soon as we stop. It's in the trunk." He hesitated, suddenly embarrassed. "Listen, you don't have to get out to look if you don't want to. I mean, if it's still raining. You can stay in the car."

"I want to. I've got a plastic thing to put over my hair. Is that where we're going? The scenic view?"

"That's the best, you can see three counties. Not tonight, but on a clear day. Sometimes you can see the river, and into Iowa. I thought this rain was going to stop, you know?"

"It's not raining as hard as it was."

"Sure. But it's still raining."

"That's all right," Mercedes said.

She was watching the black, wooded hillside reel past; it seemed to her that the road they drove was an intruder in the same way that the blade of a saw would have been an intruder, vulgarly revealing the secret, almost silent life of the trees. You were supposed to see things in dark woods like this: bears, wolves, or witches. For the first time it occurred to her that people talked about such things to end the awful stillness, the age-old quiet of wood and stone. A wolf or a witch would be one heck of a relief, she thought.

She said, "It's not one o'clock now—it's not even anywhere near midnight. It's only six-fifteen. At seven-thirty, my mom and I are supposed to meet Dad for dinner at the Golden Dragon."

"That's the good thing about a night like this. It doesn't have to be after one. You might see it anytime. They come in a lot closer in weather like this, right? They think we won't see them."

"Who comes in closer?"

"The people in the castle. There have to be people, right? It figures. They're watching us."

"Why should people in a castle watch this one little town?"

"How should I know?" For an instant Seth seemed irritated, then he laughed. "If we meet some we'll ask them, okay? Maybe there's a weak spot right here where they can sneak through. Or maybe this reminds them of someplace else."

"Aren't there ever any other cars on this road?"

"Not this late," Seth told her.

He had no sooner spoken than she saw one, not really on the road but pulled off onto the shoulder: an old rusted-out sedan, dark and silent. In a second it was past, no longer in their lights, lost, vanished, disappeared into the darkness, the mist, and the rain.

The road angled sharply to the left, and there were no more trees on her side, only unending empty night. Seth twisted the wheel again, more sharply still; the car slowed as he tapped the brakes. A low stone wall rose from the rain dead ahead. "Here we are," he announced.

"Yeah. I don't see how we can see anything out there."

"After I turn off the lights and our eyes get used to it."

The Olds crept toward the wall. Mercedes wondered how fast they would have to hit it to go right through and over the cliff she felt sure was on the other side. Hadn't anybody ever done that? Seth wouldn't, Seth was being careful—though not really as careful as she would have liked—but what if she came up here sometime with somebody else? Maybe with somebody who was drunk or something. She pictured herself in another car, the old dark car she had seen beside the road, plunging over the cliff, down, down, down, until at last it hit the rocks and burst into flame. Some guy was in that car right now making out with some chick, Mercedes thought. Bet on it.

They stopped; Seth put the car in Park and set the parking brake. Mercedes was glad he had done that; most guys, she knew, would not.

"Now," he said. He switched off the headlights—two quick clicks—and turned off the ignition.

She edged nearer him. "You know, it's kind of scary, way up here at night in the dark." She put her Coke on the floor, between her feet.

"Not really," Seth said. "It's not like Chicago, where you have muggers and so on. Pretty safe here."

"I don't think it's muggers I'm afraid of—mad slashers or something. I don't know."

"Well, don't worry." He put his arm around her shoulders, as she had hoped he would.

"I bet you're on the football team."

He nodded—she felt the motion of his head. "Wide receiver. But I was only second string last year. I still got to play a lot. I lettered."

"Maybe they'll want you where you're going, too. Galena? Maybe they need a really good wide receiver, somebody with good hands who can run." Mercedes did not know much about football, but she knew what a wide receiver did; she congratulated herself on that now.

"We're not moving," he said. "Not since my dad died."

"Oh," she said. "Oh, gosh." She felt good, and she felt awful. What kind of a person was she, feeling good because his father was dead? Yet she did.

"I mean, there isn't any reason to, any more. It was just because of his job. We might still sell the house. Grandpa and Grandma Sary, they're here, so we might move in with them."

"Would you mind?" She leaned against him.

"I guess not. Only Aunt Kate's living with them already, with her little girl, Judy, and Judy's rotten tomcat. It would be kind of crowded."

They kissed, and it was not (as Mercedes had always heard it was supposed to be) before she knew what was happening. She knew perfectly well what was happening—that a whole world, new and strange, terrible yet wonderful, was unfolding for her. She understood, when their lips touched, exactly why Snow White and Sleeping Beauty had been awakened by a kiss, knew what those old grandmothers of eight hundred years ago had been trying to tell her, and knew that they *had* told her, their coded message coming clearly across the years, and that those dear old grandmothers—the bent crones at the firesides—had triumphed, their words not lost with the crackling of the sticks in their fires. That she and Seth or some other like Seth would someday ride on one white horse, laughing in the sunshine.

After a very short interval during which whole ages of the world reeled past he muttered, "I guess our eyes are used to it now, and the rain's let up a little. Maybe we ought to get out and take a look."

She said, "Okay," feeling warm and out of breath and badly in need of cold night air. She got out on her side, hitching up her strap without letting him see, and he got out on his. And the shutting of the car's doors was not the noise of denial (as it usually is) but the sound of consent, like the note struck by the door of a room when two people go into that room and shut it behind them.

He was correct, the rain had stopped. They stood hand-in-hand at the wall and looked out across the countless hills and valleys spread before them, the hilltops at times nearly clear when they were touched by roving rays of starlight, the valleys drowned in mist from which each hill rose as if from an ocean.

"Maybe we won't see it tonight," Seth said. "Sometimes you don't."

"That's okay," Mercedes told him. "Maybe we could come up here some other night and look."

"Yeah. You'll be at the motel?"

"For the next couple days, probably."

"I could give you a call there."

"Uh huh. This is pretty, even if you don't see the castle—all those trees, and hardly any houses."

Someone coughed some distance behind them, and both looked around. A tall, lean man was walking across the parking space. He coughed again, as if to make certain they had heard him, and said, "Pardon me, folks."

Seth said, "Sure. You need a ride?"

"I guess I do. We were comin' up here, but my car conked out. I saw you go past, so I got out and started walkin' after you.

Hope you don't mind too much. There wasn't much else I could do."

Mercedes said, "No, of course not."

"If you could stop where my car is, and give me and my date a lift . . . ?"

Seth nodded. "We were going back to town now anyway, sir. She's got to meet her folks at the Chinese place."

Mercedes said, "I'll ride in back. He can show you where his car is better that way." For some reason she did not want the tall man sitting behind her; she opened the door and got into the car before Seth could protest.

"Goin' to get your upholstery wet a little," the tall man said. "Guess it can't be helped."

She studied him in the light from the dash as Seth backed and turned the car. He was as old as her father, she thought, and perhaps older; but a perfectly ordinary man until she shut her eyes. She kept them open, wide open, after she discovered that, staring sometimes at him, sometimes at Seth or the rain-wet trees.

It must have been a long walk for the tall man, Mercedes reflected, up the dark, steep road; but it was only a short way, less than a mile, for them. Seth stopped beside the rusted car, and the tall man got out and peered through the window. His car looked so ancient, so abandoned, that Mercedes was surprised to see the dome light come on when he opened the door. "She ain't here," the tall man said, looking surprised himself.

Seth nodded. "She probably got tired of waiting, sir, and started walking back to town."

"Guess that's right." The tall man pushed his damp felt hat back on his head. "We ought to see her in a bit. But you don't have to sir me, son. Name's Jim." He held out his hand.

Seth shook it through the window. "I'm Seth Howard. This is my friend Mercedes Schindler-Shields."

"Pleased to meet you, Miss," the tall man said, pulling down the brim of his hat once more. "I'm Jim Long."

7

BROKEN GLASS

"THIS IS Wrangler's territory," Sissy explained, flourishing her flashlight. "He doesn't really like having us in here even when we come to help him. But we have to—how to take care of horses is one of the things they're supposed to teach you here."

Ann said, "I see." The barn seemed huge, cavernous, in the darkness. Somewhere a horse stamped twice, its sleep disturbed by their voices.

"The main switch for the lights is in the tack room."

It was full of bridles and saddles, mostly big comfortable-looking cowboy saddles. Until Sissy found the switch, it seemed cobwebby; when the overhead light came on, everything was clean and well oiled.

"What's that, a pack saddle?" Ann pointed to a contraption that appeared utterly unsuited to human hips.

Sissy laughed. "No way—that's an old U.S. Cavalry saddle, a McClellan saddle. If you really screw up, you have to use it on the ride next day."

"My God!"

"It's a real pain," Sissy admitted, suddenly serious. "But it's very easy on the horse—easier even than an English saddle. That was the idea. When the cavalry was chasing Indians, the horses wore out a long time before the men did. Besides, after you've ridden that thing for a couple of hours, killing somebody looks like a whole lot of fun. That's my own idea; the other I got from Wrangler."

Ann was examining the McClellan saddle. "I wouldn't have thought he'd know that sort of thing."

"He does. He knows just about everything there is to know about horses. You wouldn't think it, but he's smart. You know what the conquistadors shoed their horses with?"

Ann shook her head. "I can't imagine."

"Solid silver, when they could get it. Rawhide when they couldn't. Come on. Is there any particular horse you wanted to see?"

"The biggest," Ann said.

They went out into the main bay of the barn, brilliant now with fluorescent lights. Sissy pointed. "Boomer's the biggest. He's a jumper, and a pretty good one. Lisa won on him this year at the state fair."

"Can you handle him? I don't understand horses."

"Oh, sure." Sissy opened the stall. "Hey, boy, did we wake you up?"

Ann looked in. Boomer was lying on clean straw, blinking sleepily up at Sissy; he did not look dangerous. "Can I touch him?" Ann asked.

"Go ahead. As long as you're not rough with him, he won't mind."

Ann edged cautiously into the stall, and Boomer extended his muzzle toward her.

"He wants you to pat his nose. That means you're friends— gently, just like you'd pet a cat."

Ann did, surprised to find it clean and velvet soft.

"I've got three cats at home," Sissy told her, "and horses are a lot more like cats than you'd expect."

"I never thought of them that way." Ann shifted her hands timidly to Boomer's neck. It too was clean and smooth—and dry. Completely dry. "It wasn't this horse," she said. "Not unless he's been blow-dried. Is there another big one?"

They looked at eight horses in all, progressively smaller horses, as well as Ann could judge. None of them were damp.

"Where's Buck?" she asked at last.

"I thought you'd already seen Buck, and it wasn't him."

Ann nodded. "I have, and it wasn't, but Wrangler said he was going to take the saddle off Buck and bed him down. Where is he? Where's Wrangler, as far as that goes?"

Sissy appeared startled. "Gosh, I don't know. He probably thought he ought to make another circle—riding fence is what he calls it. I mean, really, he's up half the night."

Ann relaxed and glanced at her watch. "And I ought to get going myself—I have to meet my husband. Thanks for showing me around, Sissy."

Together they went out to the Buick. The rain had stopped. Ann got in and started the engine, waving to Sissy before making a slow turn in front of the barn and heading back up the gravel road.

It's been quite an afternoon, she thought, and a very, very large day. Should she tell Willie about Wrangler and his rifle? To get her thoughts in order, she began to review Emily's recipe for pear jelly: "Let your pears ripen right on the tree, not on the windowsill; and don't pull leaves off, it don't do any good. Wash them in soap and water—use a brush. Blanch them and skin them . . ."

The road took an ugly hook to the left, so that she had to apply the brakes harder than she liked; it had seemed straighter when Wrangler had been driving, but of course he had known every inch of it. She slowed down, and switched on the brights just in time to see a riderless horse gallop out of the darkness and disappear into the dark once more. The Buick skidded a little as she stabbed automatically at the brake pedal.

A soft voice behind her said, "I should not give attention to that, madame. Certainly you will embroil yourself in so many difficulties."

* * *

"The diary!" Shields exclaimed. Afterward, he did not know why he had thought it was the display case containing the diary that had been broken—perhaps it was simply because he had been reading it a few minutes before. Whatever the reason, he dashed into the music room. Behind him he heard Roberts's feet on the stairs.

The glass was unbroken. The tattered diary lay beneath it exactly as it had before, open to the same page.

Shields stared down at it; around him, the museum waited in silence. It seemed to him that he should have been able to hear Roberts, hear him walking upstairs. It seemed plain Roberts had gone upstairs, believing it had been from there that the crash of breaking glass had come, just as he himself had run into this room.

There were no such sounds, no footsteps—only the pattering of the rain. "Bob!" Shields called. "You okay?"

The telephone rang. He returned to the desk and picked up the handset. "County Museum."

"Hello? Dad?"

Not Mercedes's voice. He said, "This is Will E. Shields. Can I help you?"

"Oh. This is Sally Howard, Mr. Shields. Is my father with you? Robert Roberts?"

Shields hesitated, listening to the silence. At length he said, "I think so, Mrs. Howard. Mrs. Howard, I was sorry, very sorry, to hear about your husband."

"Thank you."

There was another long pause, a hesitation so long that it seemed that time was one thing to him, another to Sally Howard, for whom minutes were now but seconds, hours merely minutes.

At last Shields said, "Would you like me to try to locate him for you, Mrs. Howard? He's probably around somewhere."

"Oh. I thought you were going to. I'll wait—I'll hold."

"It might take five or ten minutes, Mrs. Howard. Why don't I have him call you? I'm sure he will."

"All right."

There was a click, and Sally Howard was gone. Shields hung up his own instrument, and stood listening; the old house was as quiet as before.

Teddy told her, Shields reflected. She'd called for Bob, and Teddy told her we'd come here. No, her mother told her, of course. Bob spoke with her over this very phone—but possibly Teddy had told someone else, possibly that was why someone had broken a glass case or a window, the reason for the silence now.

He dialed the dealership. "This is Shields, Teddy. How's business?"

"I wish I could say good, Mr. Shields."

"Anybody been in?"

"Not a soul, Mr. Shields."

"Any calls for me?"

"I'm afraid not, Mr. Shields."

"What about calls for Bob?"

"That's right, I should have told you. His wife phoned, looking for him—some kind of family matter, I believe. Is he still with you, Mr. Shields? Maybe he ought to call her."

"Didn't you tell her where we were?"

"I didn't know," Teddy said. "You and Bob just went off. Where are you?"

Shields nearly told him, biting back the words barely in time. "It doesn't matter, Teddy. Lock up at nine and go home. If I see Bob, I'll let him know."

He hung up before Teddy could protest.

Upstairs next; there was nothing else to do. With no great hope he shouted, *"ROBERTS!"* and waited, listening. There was no reply, not even a whisper of sound.

He's had a heart attack, Shields thought, sprinting up the steps. Why the hell didn't I think of that? Bob's an old man. Probably felt bad, sat down somewhere . . .

And died.

But maybe not. Maybe Bob's still alive, and if I call for an ambulance in time—

The upper floor was dark. The switches Roberts had thrown when they came in obviously did not control the lights on this floor, so that was where Roberts would have gone first: to the upstairs switches, wherever they were.

He had not reached them. Whoever had broken the glass had reached him first.

And yet they'd be right here, Shields thought. Here at the head of the stairs. They'd have to be. He imagined the doctor and his wife returning from a late dinner party. Their children would be asleep; they would probably have given the housekeeper and the maid the evening off. They would unlock the front door and let themselves in, turn on a light in the foyer, climb these stairs, and turn on another light in this upstairs hall to find their bedroom.

His fingers groped along the wall, feeling only smooth oak paneling. The rain dripped from the eaves as before; but when a second or two had passed, the house was no longer weeping alone in the silence. An instrument with a voice as deep as an organ (though it was not really an organ) sobbed, too, its notes long and throbbing, reedy and infinitely sad. Hearing them, Shields froze. Seconds passed before he identified the melody. It was the "Valse Triste" from *Peer Gynt*.

It's recorded music, he thought, it has to be. There's a speaker system, and I'm listening to a record or a tape.

Yet the wall he touched seemed to vibrate ever so slightly in sympathy with the deepest tones; it seemed that he could hear the squeak of the pedals.

There's no switch here. So it must be—has to be—on the other side of the hall. Why would an intruder play music? To cover the sounds of his movements, of course, now that breaking the glass has given him away. Most burglars wouldn't be that smart—this is no kid, a clever man, a dangerous man.

Shields's fingertips swept the paneling to his left, found a switch plate, and pushed in the old-fashioned switch.

Light flooded the hall.

It was empty save for three ill-assorted occasional chairs. "Valse Triste" moaned on and on, seeming to gather strength from the light. He could no longer hear the rain.

He had not been frightened earlier in the dark. Or rather, he had been afraid only for Roberts, afraid that the older man was dead or dying. Now it seemed that the yellowish hall light must soon reveal some abomination, showing him the naked face of Hell, or revealing that his own hands were drenched with blood. Those hands shook; so that he would not see them, he jammed them into his pockets. Sick now with fear, stomach churning and legs shaking, he went slowly down the hall.

A doorway opened into a dark room on his right. He reached inside and found the switch; the room was empty except for five display cases pushed against its walls.

And yet something prowled the old house. He wanted to run, to climb into the rusty Cherokee outside and—

The keys! The thought steadied him, giving him something to think about beyond his own terror. Bob had driven; no doubt Bob had the keys. If he ran now, he would have to run in actual fact, flee along the rain-swept sidewalks of Castleview. As he realized it, he realized too that he would not run; his fear was ebbing—he had not run when it had been worse.

He returned to the hall and strode to the next door; this time the doorway was on his left. When he pressed the switch, floodlights in the ceiling revealed a model town: red brick and shiny black asphalt streets, tiny red and white houses flanked by bright green trees, a town as charming as a child's drawing. Castleview, of course. He chuckled softly at his own fears as he crouched to look beneath the big table that held the model. The shadowy space was empty of all but dust; and yet something stealthily walked, and there was a pervasive animal reek, faint but distinct, throughout this upper floor.

As he straightened up, he felt illogically sure that Bob was no longer in the building. He would find Bob, dead, behind the wheel of the Cherokee, perhaps. Or never find him at all.

From the floor below came the sound of breaking glass.

8

HITCHHIKERS

THE HEADLIGHTS seemed merely to polish the oily black road that wound through the tunnel of trees. Mercedes studied its asphalt surface obsessively, afraid to close her eyes and equally afraid to look squarely at the back of Long's rain-soaked hat. Black-and-yellow signs crowded by trees warned of steep descents and abrupt curves ahead, yet it seemed to Mercedes that it was the trees themselves that moved, skipping lightly by the motionless car: rapt in their secret dance, they twirled left, then right.

Something inky and shapeless crouched by the road, its eyes glowing green in the headlights.

Seth hit the brakes hard, and the Olds spun in a sickening skid. It was as though the giant on the horse were back again, as though she were in the Buick again; she implored God that it be so, that Mom and Dad be with her as before, in their own car on the way to the safety and warmth of a motel.

It was not. The Olds stopped, angled diagonally across the narrow road. "That's her," Jim Long said. "Damn, but I'm glad we found her."

The dark, shapeless thing rose, became a human figure with a pale blur of face. Long left the car, edged around the front bumper (it was among the trees) and hurried over. They did not embrace, though they joined hands; for a moment they talked, or so it appeared—Mercedes could not hear what was said, and did not want to hear. "Seth, let's get out of here."

He glanced back at her, surprised. "We can't just go off and leave them."

"Please."

He rolled down his window. "Everything all right?"

Turning toward them, Long said, "Sure. She's just a little upset, is all."

Seth switched off the ignition and got out. Mercedes heard him through the open window: "I'm really sorry. I didn't expect you to be in the middle of the road."

Mercedes opened her door and got out, too; it seemed to be the only thing to do. The white-faced figure was a woman, very blond, whose pale hair fell to her waist. Mercedes said, "Are you okay?"

The blond woman nodded. "Yes, I am fine. It was too quick for me to be frightened." She dabbed at her eyes with something that looked like a rag.

Long told Seth, "Dead animals—dead things in the road get her upset."

"It was a mother and her baby," the blond woman explained. Her voice was low and sweet. "What do you call the babies? Her cub, her kitten. They killed them both."

Mercedes looked. Her eyes had adjusted to the darkness now that they no longer followed the headlights. A large raccoon lay dead. Near it, almost touching, was a much smaller raccoon; it, too, was dead.

The blond woman said, "They drive so fast, even when they cannot see. They never think that there may be little ones in the way."

Seth nodded slowly. "Yeah. Well, we can't help them now." He sounded embarrassed.

"We can weep for them, as I do. It is a terrible thing, to die as this little one did, with no one to mourn."

Long put his arm around the blond woman's shoulders, then drew it away as though afraid she would object.

Seth cleared his throat. "I better move my car. Somebody coming up this road might hit it."

Long said, "Sure."

Seth went back to the Olds; Mercedes wanted to go with him, to get into the front seat beside him again and beg him to drive away; but the blond woman was speaking to her. "It is very kind of you to take us. Jim told me. It is not where we wish to go, but perhaps we may get a ride there. If not, we will walk. We shall manage in some way."

"Okay," Mercedes told her. "That's okay." The blond woman was half a head shorter than she, but Mercedes felt she must be a good deal older—twenty or twenty-five at least. Even so, she seemed far too young for Long. Awkwardly, Mercedes held out her hand. "I'm Mercedes Schindler-Shields."

The blond woman clasped it briefly; her slender fingers felt hot, almost burning, as though she were running a fever. "Viviane Morgan."

Her breath held the pensive sweetness of a spring morning; Mercedes found it an effort to speak. "I'm happy to meet you, Ms. Morgan."

"Call me Viviane, please."

The hoarse grinding of the Olds's starter interrupted. The engine sputtered and fell silent. Mercedes walked to the open window. "Won't it start?"

Hunched over the wheel, Seth shook his head angrily. He twisted the key and pumped the accelerator. The starter motor snarled on and on, but there was no answering sound from the engine.

Long peered over Mercedes's shoulder. "You oughta turned off your lights."

Seth told him, "The battery's good. It just won't catch." There was a faint smell of gasoline.

"Oughta turn 'em off anyhow. Won't do no good to run the battery down."

"I guess not." Abruptly, the lights were gone. Darkness

dropped like a snare from the overarching trees, and Mercedes shivered.

The starter snarled again, perhaps a trifle less strongly.

"You got her flooded now," Long said. The gasoline smell had grown pungent.

Seth's voice floated out of the night, astonishingly near. "I guess so."

"I thought that mighta been what was wrong with mine. If that's what was wrong, she mighta fixed herself by now. They do that—they dry out. Gas dries up pretty fast."

Mercedes said, "We can wait. I suppose we'll have to."

"We oughta push it outa the way, Miss." Long spoke from some unknown place in the darkness. "There might come a car up this way and slam into it."

Seth muttered, "That's right. Mercedes, would you steer? We'll have to push—Mr. Long and me."

"Okay," she said. The dome light came on as Seth got out, a too-brief reminder of the world of day. She got in, shut the door, and switched on the headlights.

"Maybe you ought to leave those off," Seth suggested.

"What's the use of having somebody steer if she can't see where she's steering?" Although Mercedes had no license, she understood steering well enough, she thought.

Seth and Long got in front of the Olds, bent their backs, and pushed with all their might. "Straighten out the wheels!" Seth shouted.

Mercedes tugged at the steering wheel, finding it extremely hard to turn.

"That's the way! More!"

Slowly, inch by inch, the Olds crawled back onto the road again. Its lights picked up Ms. Morgan, still standing beside the dead racoons, a slight smile on her face.

"She could do something," Mercedes whispered to herself. "If she helped them, it would be that much more."

"Okay!" Seth shouted, and they stopped pushing and stepped

aside. The Oldsmobile crept down the steep slope until Mercedes stamped on the brake pedal.

Seth came to the window. Tiny drops of water on his lashes gleamed like diamonds in the dash lights. "Now just let it roll slow, okay? Park it off out of the way."

"We could coast! Seth, we can coast to the bottom of this hill. Get in!"

He shook his head impatiently. "I wouldn't want to try it—it's got power steering and power brakes. Get it over to the side like I told you, and I'll see if I can find out what's the matter with the engine."

It was a bit easier to steer with the car rolling forward, but Mercedes had to force down the pedal with both feet to stop.

Seth called, "A little more off to the side."

She edged the Olds over until both right wheels were well out upon the road's soft, narrow shoulder, wondering whether it would not be stuck there even if Seth got the engine running.

"Okay!"

Thankfully, she put the transmission into Park and set the parking brake.

"Fine," Seth called. "Pull out the hood release."

She had to look for it, but it was not hard to find, a knob with a picture of a car with its hood up.

"Turn off the lights."

Mercedes did, and left the car. There was a small light on the underside of the hood; Seth bent over the engine, prodding here and there. Long mumbled, "Could be the distributor's wet," and wandered away.

Seth glanced up at Mercedes, shaking his head. "This has a solid-state distributor. He's out of it."

She smiled sympathetically. "He's probably used to working on old cars like his."

"Sure." Seth had turned back to the engine too quickly to catch the smile.

The night was dark and wet, and there was nothing to do but watch Seth. Mercedes got back into the Olds and looked for her Coke. It had spilled on the floormat, its paper cup crushed by Long's feet; she cleaned up the mess as well as she could in the dark.

Seth called, "Slide over onto the driver's side, will you? I want you to crank it for me."

She guessed that meant she was to turn on the starter. She did, producing a feeble groan.

"Again. Pump the gas."

The grinding of the starter trailed away to silence.

As though lit by lightning, the road and the mist, even the black trees, sprang back into existence. A car was coming down from the scenic view, a silent old sedan with a single headlight, though at that moment that headlight seemed like the sun.

Seth jumped into the road in front of it, waving his arms. It slowed and stopped. Mercedes knew there was only one car it could be before she heard Long's voice. "Got mine runnin'," he said. "Hop in. Boys in front, girls in back."

Seth exclaimed, "Great!" He opened the front door and got in, presumably beside Long. "Come on, Mercedes."

Slowly, she left Seth's car, thinking about Seth and Seth's dead father; she wanted her own father as badly as Seth no doubt wanted his, wanted his hand on her shoulder, wanted very badly to hear him sing his crazy Irish song.

She opened the rear door of the rusted-out sedan. Viviane Morgan was a faint sheen in its cavernous, musty interior. "Sit down," she said. "There is plenty of room."

Mercedes did, reluctantly, shutting the door; she did not intend to speak, but she said, "You know, the other time, when Mr. Long opened the door of this car, that light up there came on."

"Indeed?" Ms. Morgan sounded amused. "But I was not here then, was I?"

With a clank from the universal joint, the old car lurched ahead.

"No, you weren't. This is a setup, isn't it? Some kind of a setup. This car would always run."

Ms. Morgan laughed.

"Who sabotaged Seth's car while we were talking to you?"

Ms. Morgan had a soft laugh, a truly attractive laugh; and it was accompanied by breath that seemed perfumed, as a garden does after a warm rain. It continued for so long that Mercedes grew uneasy, and at last frightened. Ms. Morgan's hand was on her thigh, stroking its soft flesh through the threadbare blue denim. A seam had given way for an inch or so; burning fingers found the spot and crept through.

"Stop that!" Mercedes hissed. The low laugh and fevered exploration continued as before. She groped for Ms. Morgan's wrist to force her hand away; but there was no wrist or so it seemed, no wrist and no arm—only five burning fingertips and the pinching, tweaking thumb.

Long slowed the old sedan and wrenched its wheel, swerving off the pavement and onto a narrow dirt road that wound among a thousand trees. "Too good!" Seth exclaimed. "I never noticed this. Where's it go?"

"Goes where you're goin'," Long told him. "It ain't very far."

Seth nodded, trying to mark mentally the exact place where the dirt road turned off. Long's girlfriend was giggling about something with Mercedes in the back seat. She had a nice laugh, Seth thought.

9

THE STOWAWAY

Ann hit the brakes as hard as she could, nearly catapulting the girl in the back seat into the front. "Who are you!"

"One who has hurt her poor nose, madame. You must be more careful how you drive."

Ann shoved the transmission into Park and stared into the rearview mirror, which showed nothing at all. "Damn it! You just about scared me into a heart attack." Turning the knob of the headlight switch lit the dome light; she loosened her seat belt and twisted around to look back at the girl huddled on the floor. "I've seen you before someplace."

"We have been introduced, madame," the girl said. "Now, again, I think. *Sang!* I bleed!"

"Here." Ann fumbled in her purse for her handkerchief. "Back there. At that camp. You're one of the foreign girls. Here, take this."

"*Merci.* My name, it is Lucie. You are Madame Schindler. You are German, I think. At least you have a German name, no?"

"My grandparents. What are you doing in the back of my car, Lucie?"

"Begging that you will please take me to the town with you, Madame Schindler. That is all. It is so very important that I go, and that woman, that Lisa at the camp, would not permit it.

63

Because of the rain and the many things that have occurred—
such terrible things, madame, they did not tell you the worst—
and I should have to ride a horse."

"I don't blame her," Ann declared. "I'll have to take you
back."

"Oh, madame . . ." As agilely as a monkey, Lucie was over
the back of the front seat and seated beside her. "You must not
try to turn your large auto about here. You will be mired,
madame, truly you will. The road, it is so very narrow and the
ground now a paste." She had wide, dark eyes, which were
fixed upon Ann's own in a disconcerting stare.

"I suppose you're right, but I can turn around when we get
to the gate." Ann pushed the Buick into Drive. The road itself
was getting soft; she could sense its give beneath the tires.

"That is wise, madame. That is very wise indeed. Let us go
far from this terrible place. But I must find someone. It is so
urgent, and he is in the town."

Ann nodded, keeping her eyes on the gray strip of road. "A
boy?"

"No, madame. A man. A gentleman, *un homme comme il faut.*
You think him my lover? No, no! Only a man who does not
know me, or only a little, though I must speak with him."

"All right. If Lisa Solomon says you can go, I'll take you with
me."

"But she will *not*, madame!" Lucie's soft voice rose to an
agonized whine. "She will say, how shall you return? No! You
may not go."

"I doubt that you should go myself, if you haven't any way to
get back."

"You might drive me, madame, in this auto. Or perhaps your
husband? Then all should be well. Do you not have to meet
your husband? So you said as you left the barn. I was there
behind, and overheard you."

Ann glanced at the dashboard clock; it was seven-fifteen. "I
can't do that," she said. "I'd like to—I'm going to be late as it

is—but I really can't. We're just going to have to turn around and go back when we get to the gate." It seemed to her that they should have reached it already, but no gate showed in her brights. The road wound down a narrow little valley, hardly more than a gully, that Ann did not remember at all. She asked, "How much farther is it?"

"Two kilometers, perhaps."

How much was that in miles? About a mile and a half, Ann thought, maybe.

"It seems longer, does it not, by night?"

"It certainly does," Ann agreed. Almost against her will, she added, "We went across a little bridge—Wrangler and I, when he was driving the car. You and I haven't gone over that bridge yet."

"And we will not, *Dieu le veuille!* There is no bridge this way. It was old this bridge, and of wood? One which shook much as you crossed? I fear always that it shall fall with us."

Ann nodded grimly.

"Then you have taken the wrong road from the lodge, madame. You arrived by the back, which is nearer the town and now locked always by Wrangler before the light has gone. This road that we take, it marches to the main gate."

"Is that one open?" Ann had forgotten about the padlock; she berated herself for it now. "Can we get back to town that way?"

"Oh, yes. It is farther, but that is all. You must turn to the right when we reach the big road—the high way, is that what you call him? Then it is—" Lucie grabbed at the top of the dashboard.

"What's the matter?"

"The water! Don't you see it? Be careful!"

Born of the rain, an infant stream formed a waterfall over a miniature cliff and cut a dark path across the road. Ann let up on the accelerator, then decided the water could be no more than a couple of inches deep, if that. The Buick's wheels sent up

65

geysers left and right, as she drove through it with a scarcely perceptible pause.

"I am sorry, madame. Once nearly I drowned, when I was a little child—thus I have the fear of waters. I do not know the name in English."

"Aquaphobia, I suppose. But the water didn't really hurt us, now did it?"

Lucie shook her head. "It terrified me, madame, and that hurts me very much. I would rather I pricked the finger."

"Well, let's hope we don't have anything worse than that to cross," Ann said.

The road wound out of the tiny valley, considerably rutted in places, and crested a small hill. Ann's dashboard clock read 7:21. Unconsciously she drove faster, until they were rattling through the wet night at nearly thirty miles an hour. Something long—something that was not white but lighter in color than the mud and wet grass—lay beside the road. She slowed and stopped.

Lucie murmured, "It is nothing, madame. Drive on, please, I beg you."

It lay outside the beams of her headlights, a dim hump that might almost have been a small log. Ann rolled down her window and peered at it.

"Madame, you do not know this place. Terrible things may occur. Go on, for both our sakes."

Ann said, "That's somebody hurt." She got out, turning on her flashlight. The rain had stopped, leaving behind it a mist and a sense of vague disquiet. When she touched the prone man's face, her fingertips came away warm and sticky with blood. *They got him,* she thought, *whoever they are. They got him, and they may still be nearby.*

Just as she had once or twice felt that a roast was burning before she could smell it, she felt now that Lucie was about to drive away in the Buick. She had left the keys in the ignition and the engine running. She glanced up; but the French girl was only watching her, her face taut and expressionless.

"It's Wrangler," Ann told her. "Come here, you'll have to help me."

"I was supposed to meet my wife and daughter here," Shields told the hostess at the Golden Dragon. "I'm afraid I'm a little late. Have they been looking for me? I'm Will Shields."

The hostess shook her head.

"My wife's a little taller than you. Reddish-brown hair, blue raincoat?"

The hostess said, "I'm afraid not, sir. Actually nobody's been here looking for anybody. It's been a slow night, because of the rain."

"Maybe they just came in and got a table?"

"I'm afraid not, sir," the hostess repeated. "But you can look for yourself if you like."

He did. Only three tables were occupied, and none of the diners at any of them resembled Ann or Mercedes in the least.

At his elbow the hostess asked, "Would you like a table, sir? You could wait for them."

Shields shook his head. "I'd better call. Do you have a public phone?"

"Certainly, sir. Down those steps. It's just outside the lounges."

Shields went down the stairs as quickly as he could. Tired and ravenously hungry, he felt as if his knees might give way on every step. The "lounges" were restrooms, of course, with a pay telephone on the wall between them. He groped in his pocket for change.

"Red Stove Inn."

It was the old woman; he had to rack his brain for the room number. "Cabin ten, please."

It rang and rang again.

She's in the bathroom, Shields told himself.

A third ring.

But they couldn't both be in the bathroom; if Ann was in there, Merc would be in the bedroom watching TV or reading.

A fourth ring.

If Mercedes was in the bathroom . . .

A fifth ring.

Ann had said something about running errands. She must've taken Merc with her. They were stuck somewhere, or some errand had taken far longer than Ann had anticipated. What were those errands anyhow? They were probably on their way right now.

A sixth ring.

He glanced at his watch. Ten minutes past eight.

"There's no answer," the old woman said. "I think probably they went out."

"Are you certain you were ringing ten?"

"Sure was. Is this Mr. Shields?"

"Yes, it is."

"Well, your wife came up to talk to Alfred and me earlier. She asked me about the camp down the road. You think she might have gone there?"

"An army camp?"

"No, for kids," the old woman said. "They teach them how to ride and swim and so forth. Some just stay a couple weeks, but some all summer—mostly teenagers. Belongs to Syl Baxter, or it did. She's gone now."

"And Ann asked about this place?"

"She asked where do they have horses, and that's the main one. Some folks have a horse or two, but that's the main one."

"Could you give me their number?"

"I can look it up for you. Hold the line a minute."

"If you would, please." Shields leaned against the wall, waiting, suddenly aware of the silence of the place, the smell of food from the dining area above. There was no one, he felt sure, in either restroom. If there had been, they would have come out by now, would have flushed a toilet or run the water. Very faintly, he heard the murmur of the diners' voices; they faded until it seemed to him that he waited alone, in an empty building, in an abandoned town.

At his ear, the old woman at the motel said, "Here 'tis. Got something to write with?"

"I'll remember," Shields assured her, wondering whether he would. Whether he could.

"Three nine one—all the numbers 'round here are three nine ones. Maybe you've noticed."

"Yes," Shields said. "Three nine one."

"Eight eight seven eight."

"Eighty-eight seventy-eight. Thank you."

"Happy to help," the old woman said, sounding as if she meant it; she hung up.

He hung up as well and groped in his pocket for more coins. Another telephone, no doubt on another line, was ringing faintly upstairs, ring after ring.

He pushed two dimes into the slot. Three nine one, eighty-eight seventy-eight. A pause, then somewhere—at the camp where they had horses, presumably—a third telephone rang. Two rings. Three.

"'Ello?" It was a young woman's voice, not Mercedes.

"Is this the camp?" He berated himself for not knowing its name.

"*Sim.* Thes' Meadow Grass."

"I'm calling about my wife—Ann Schindler? Is she there?"

"Sheeler?" (A second girl's voice, more distant from the mouthpiece: "Let me talk.")

"Schind-ler," Shields repeated hopefully. "Ann Schindler. Or our daughter, Mercedes. Have they been there?"

"This's Sissy Stevenson," announced a new voice. "Are you looking for Mrs. Schindler? Who are you?"

"Her husband, Will Shields."

"Did you say Shields?" The distant voice sounded doubtful now, yet excited.

"Yes. Will E. Shields."

"Wait a minute!"

A *thunk* as the handset fell, and a babble of girlish voices from a distance.

"This is Sissy Stevenson again, Mr. Shields. Do you by any chance know a Mr. L. Robert Roberts?"

The hostess's voice came from the top of the stairs. "Sir, there's a Mrs. Schindler on the phone. She says that she's your wife."

10

Shots in the Night

There was a knock, soft and almost furtive.

Not Seth. Seth would've come straight in, and she had not heard the car.

Another neighbor with another jar of soup, another covered dish. Sally wished, suddenly and detestably, that Tom had died a year ago, that Tom was already buried, that healing grass had grown and been cut over his grave all summer.

Tap, tap, tap?

Whoever it was could see that the lights were on inside—old Mrs. Cosgriff from across the street, probably. Old Mrs. Cosgriff had not come yet. Old Mrs. Cosgriff would know that she, Sally Howard, was still up. Wearily she rose and went to the door.

It was a small, swarthy, thinly bearded man in a long coat. In place of a casserole he carried a worn leather briefcase like a lawyer's.

"Yes, what is it?" Somebody from the company, she thought. They've sent him from the home office.

"I hope I'm not disturbing you." He spoke softly, with an accent she could not quite place. For no reason she could have put a finger on, she thought of the Deep South and of its coast—of desolate, muddy beaches that lay below Washington but were much further from Washington than the moon.

"I'm sorry?" she said.

He bobbed his head. "Wouldn't want to disturb *you* . . . saw your light—" From the back of the house there came the sound of breaking glass.

Sally stiffened. "What was that?"

The dark stranger smiled. "Only a glass, I think. Someone dropped a glass, or knocked one over."

"My mother's gone home," Sally said.

He looked at her blankly.

"I'm alone in the house."

"Per'aps your cat?" He reminded her of a cat himself.

"We don't—I'd better see what it was." She turned away.

"Per'aps it would be better if a man accompanied you."

"Oh! Oh, yes." He was not large and did not look strong, yet she knew he was right, that two people would be more apt to frighten away a prowler than one. "Thank you very much. Won't you come in?"

Somehow he was across the threshold and past her, walking noiselessly but swiftly down the hall toward the back of the house.

Then he was gone.

She called, "Is it all right?" and hurried after him. The rooms were dark, and he did not know the house—he was probably groping for the light switch, and the prowler might attack him, might even kill him, while he groped.

And yet she felt certain she was wrong; that there was no small, dark, briefcase-carrying stranger, and no prowler; that she was alone in the house, save for Tom's ghost. "Tom," she whispered. "Don't leave me. Don't hurt me like that, Tom."

She turned on the light. There was no one in the kitchen, but the window above her sink had been broken. Shattered glass had fallen into the sink; more lay upon the brown vinyl-covered floor.

"*Sir!*" she called. "Mister? Where are you?"

There was no answer. She went from room to room, switching on the lights in the pantry, in the dining room and the bathroom and the big master bedroom; but she was alone in the house save for Tom's ghost. When she sat down on the bed, she felt certain that the ghost was sitting in Tom's chair, smoking one of Tom's pipes; but when she went back into the living room, eager to see even a ghost if the ghost was Tom's, she could not see it.

Someone pulled up outside; she heard the car door slam. It was strange, she thought, that she had not heard the small dark stranger's car. Had he walked, or come in a taxi? Wouldn't she have heard the taxi's engine, the closing of the taxi's door?

The doorbell chimed, slowly and almost sadly. It struck her that she hated those bells, and had hated them for years. They had sounded so fine in the store, so elegant when she and Tom had picked them out; the clerk had never warned them, never told her how dismal they might sound in an empty house at night.

They chimed again, and she went to the door.

This man was very different from the first, a big burly man—bigger even than Tom had been—with a wide-brimmed hat that he pulled off as she opened the door. "Mrs. Howard?" He held up a small leather case, like a wallet; there was a star-shaped badge in it. "Deputy sheriff."

"Thank God you've come," she said. "I should have called. How did you know?"

"Know what, ma'am?" His voice was bigger and deeper than Tom's, too, Sally thought. But it wasn't as smart. This man couldn't manage a factory, would never be asked to take over a bigger one in Galena.

"There's somebody in my house. Somebody's broken in," she told him.

"Broken in, ma'am?"

"Yes, I'll show you." Sally hurried off. She was always hurrying tonight it seemed, now that there was nobody to hurry for. She heard the deputy's slow step behind her.

Foolishly she had feared that the broken glass would be gone, the window whole again—that she had dreamed everything and would look a fool; but the triangular shards still lay in the sink and on the vinyl flooring she always wanted to call linoleum as her mother did. Everything was just as before.

"See?" Sally said.

The deputy grunted, nodding. "You got any notion when this happened, ma'am?"

"About five minutes ago."

"Five minutes?"

"I was in the living room, and I heard it—heard it break. There was a caller, a man at the door. He said he'd look, and he went back there. Then I went, too, and turned on the lights, but I didn't see anything."

The deputy had drawn his gun. She had not noticed it, but it was in his hand, its barrel pointed at the floor. "Where's he now?"

"The man who was at the door?"

"Yes, ma'am."

"I'm afraid I don't know. I haven't seen him since he went back here."

"You go through the whole house, ma'am?"

Sally shook her head. "Just downstairs. Not even all the downstairs rooms."

"I've got to report this. All right if I use your phone? Then we're going to go through your whole house and make sure nobody's in here. You didn't hear this fellow go out the front while you were checking the back?"

"No. He could have, of course. I wouldn't necessarily have heard him."

"That's right—but he might not have, too. That's why I'm going to look."

Half an hour later, the deputy seated himself heavily in Tom's favorite chair, right on top of the ghost.

Sally asked, "Can I get you something? There's coffee, and there's Coke and beer in the refrigerator."

"Coffee will be just fine, ma'am."

She went back to the kitchen, feeling there that something

was going to spring out at her. Broken glass still lay in her sink and on the floor. She picked up the largest pieces and put them in the garbage; they tinkled and clashed like wind chimes.

Seth was still gone. Sally wondered briefly what Seth was thinking about, going out like that with his father dead today. Only today. Probably, she decided, he wasn't thinking at all, just driving aimlessly nowhere, perhaps alone, perhaps with some friend. She hoped he was with a friend. It wasn't really late yet anyway, only half past eight.

She poured coffee, remembered she had forgotten to ask if he took cream and sugar, and put the little blue sugarbowl and cream pitcher on the tray, hesitated, then poured out a cup for herself.

"Thank you, ma'am," the deputy said, as she had known he would. He picked up a cup and sipped. Black.

"You're very welcome." She set the tray on the coffee table and sat down on the sofa.

"Let me tell you, ma'am. I don't think anybody came in through that window."

"I hope you're right."

"I believe I am, ma'am. That window's just awfully small, and the hunks of glass that stayed in the frame are still right there. They'd cut hell—I beg your pardon. They'd cut anybody who tried to crawl through, even a kid. But maybe this man who was at the door had a friend hit that window with a stick. You catch my drift, ma'am?"

Sally nodded. "I think so."

"First thing I thought of was a rock, but there wasn't any rock on the floor. He could've picked it up when he went back there, but you said he didn't turn on the lights, so that's not too likely. Doesn't matter, really. You don't have a dog, do you, ma'am?"

"We used to," Sally said, "but Rexy was hit by a car. We didn't want to go through that again."

"You ought to think about it, ma'am. Specially now, with Mr. Howard gone. A dog's awfully cheap protection."

"All right, I will."

"I didn't get much chance to say how sorry I was about Mr. Howard. One of the other officers investigated, and he told me about it. I am sorry, truly." The deputy swallowed coffee.

"Thank you. Did you know Tom? Is that why you're here?"

"I wasn't a friend or anything. I knew who he was because I've got a brother-in-law that works at the plant. Fred Davis?"

Sally sighed. "I don't—I didn't know many of the people who worked for Tom. Mostly just the office people."

"I suppose. Well, ma'am, you asked why I was here. Have you heard about Mr. Roberts?"

"Dad?" An icy hand caressed Sally's heart.

The deputy had pulled a battered little notebook from his shirt pocket. "Mr. Leonard Robert Roberts. That's him?"

Sally nodded mutely.

"I guess you haven't heard from him in the past few hours? He hasn't come over to tell you how sorry he is? Or maybe help about the funeral?"

"No," she said. "Has anything— Yes! Wait—yes, he did! My mother told me. My mother was here with me, and she made me take a sleeping pill, and before she went home she told me he'd just heard and he called. She talked to him."

The deputy nodded heavily. "Yes, ma'am. We've talked with her and your sister already."

"She said he was at the museum—he's on the board—so when she'd gone I tried to call him. Mr. Shields was there; he's the new owner where Dad works. He said Dad was with him, and he was going to ask Dad to call me back. Then I went back to sleep for a while. I suppose I missed his call."

"That's a shame," the deputy said, "if you did, ma'am."

"So Dad was all right. That was—I don't know—six-thirty or a quarter to seven. Something like that."

The deputy nodded again. "We've talked with Mr. Shields, too, ma'am. He was the one that called us."

Sally waited in silence, staring at him.

"When he went looking for your pa for you, he couldn't find him anyplace. They'd gone over to the museum together, and the car was out front with the keys in the ignition. It was raining on and off. Mr. Shields says he figured your pa wouldn't go off without saying something, and he wouldn't walk through that rain when there was a car right there he could use."

Sally said, "Dad wouldn't take somebody else's car."

"This was from View Motors, ma'am. They were just using it because Mrs. Shields had Mr. Shields's car. Anyway, Mr. Shields couldn't find your pa anywhere. The calliope started playing, and I guess that shook him up. You know the big calliope they've got out in the old carriage house?"

"Of course," she said. "I've played it. I play the piano, a little, and the organ at church."

"Do you, ma'am?" The deputy drained his cup. "That's very interesting."

Sally looked down at her own untouched coffee. "You think it might have been me. Do you know how that calliope works?"

"Yes, ma'am. It's got a switch on it—not like an electric switch, but a big lever. Push it one way, and a person can play it just like you play the organ at the church. But if you push it the other way, it reads off a roll, like a player piano. The thing is, ma'am, that Mr. Shields knew the tune. It was the Sad Waltz—he called it some foreign name, but he says that's what it means—from a piece called *Peer Gynt*. There isn't a roll for either one, so what he heard was somebody playing. Your ma says your pa's not musical. You were asleep in bed then?"

Sally shook her head. "I was asleep, yes. Not in bed. I was lying on that sofa."

"And there wasn't anybody with you?"

"No." Sally sipped her coffee: tepid and bitter. "My son had gone out earlier. Seth was terribly upset about Tom, and so was I, I suppose. After Mom left, I was alone."

"They got him over at Fouque's, ma'am, if you want to see him."

"I know," she said. "I'm going tomorrow morning."

"And you don't have any notion where your father might be?"

"Not if he isn't at home or at View Motors."

"We've been there, ma'am. The man there—Mr. Camberwell—was getting ready to lock up. There wasn't anyone there except him. Did your father have many friends, ma'am?"

"Hundreds." Sally shrugged. "Maybe thousands. If we're going to get into that, I'll make us some more coffee."

The deputy nodded in his slow, heavy way. "That might be a good idea, ma'am."

She had left the lights on in the kitchen, and now she was glad of that; she rinsed the cups and filled them with steaming water from the teakettle, adding a teaspoonful of black crystals to each. Outside, but quite close to the house, a dog barked—joyfully, Sally thought. She glanced through the jagged opening that had been her kitchen window. Something much larger than a man was moving out there, its crooked legs outlined against the white fence that separated the yard from the cornfield; its eyes gleamed red as it turned to stare at her.

Sally screamed and dropped the instant coffee jar.

Quite suddenly, the wall pressed hard against her back; she heard the deputy's pounding strides and the crash of the door as he dashed outside. The first shot was a sharp crack, like a big board breaking. He shouted something; she recognized his voice, though she could not understand the words. There were two more shots close together, like a carpenter pounding a nail.

From upstairs came the sound of breaking glass.

11

THE IMPERIAL DINNER FOR TWO

"POT STICKERS!" Ann exclaimed. "Good for you, Willie. I love pot stickers."

"So do I. Go ahead, I've had my share."

There had been a dozen small, fragrant steamed dumplings in the big bamboo steamer. He had eaten five, and felt that he had eaten nothing. Had he really had lunch at some other restaurant with Ann and Merc before driving to the real estate agency? If so, what had that lunch been? It had vanished into the darkness that lies behind Egypt and Sumer, if it had ever existed—though he could not imagine either Ann or Merc consenting to skip lunch or any other meal. Breakfast had been buckwheat cakes. Or cold cereal, Grape Nuts or Grape Nuts Flakes.

No, the pancakes had been back in Arlington Heights, whole centuries before; and the cereals had been served by his mother, quick breakfasts before school. Breakfast? "An equal time hath shoveled it/'Neath the wrack of Greece and Rome./Neither wait we any more/That worn sail which Argo bore."

Ann chewed a steamed dumpling darkly laden with the Golden Dragon's own homemade soy sauce. "What'd you say, Willie?"

"Nothing. Just mumbling to myself."

"About your adventures? From what you said on the phone, you've had Adventures."

"I suppose I have. I hadn't thought of it like that." He poured jasmine tea for her.

"Then let me tell you, Indiana Shields, you haven't seen *a thing*. You haven't done *anything*. It's me, Calamity Annie, the Queen of the Frontier, who—" She forked in half a dumpling.

He asked, "Do you want to tell me about it?"

Chewing ecstatically, Ann shook her head. "I'm going to be too busy eating, Willie. Besides, it's best to save the really juicy stuff for the end. You've ordered for both of us, haven't you?"

Shields nodded.

"Duck? This place is supposed to have great duck."

He nodded again. "And a lot of other things."

"Then have them trot it out quick, and give me all the gory details. You and this salesman went to that museum because the woman in my house said they've got stuff about the castle? And he scooted? That's what you said on the phone."

Shields sipped his tea. "I said he disappeared. Maybe on his own—that's what the police think. Maybe—" He sought the right words. "Maybe because someone else—or something else—got hold of him. That's what I think. Instead of the police, I should have said the sheriff's deputy. Castleview doesn't have a regular police force, according to him. There's a constable who rounds up stray livestock and supervises the school crossing guards."

"One pot sticker left, Willie. Sure you don't want it?"

"Go ahead."

In a trice it was on her plate. "I wonder what they really put in these things. It's supposed to be spiced pork, but it's much too good for that. Leftover duck, maybe. Why did you want to find out about the castle here anyway, Willie?"

"Because I saw it."

Ann laughed, nearly choked on a large bite of dumpling, and washed it down with tea. "Come on! As Mercedes says, get real. You saw the castle?"

Shields nodded. "I didn't say anything because I knew you wouldn't believe me."

"I believe you thought you saw it, anyway. People do, I suppose, and everybody's been telling me we saw a ghost. That man on the horse, remember? You damned near hit him."

"I don't think that was a ghost."

"Neither do I, but I'll tell you about all that stuff by-and-by. Horses and cowboys—one cowboy, anyhow. When did you see the castle?"

"While we were up in the attic of the Howard house. I saw it through one of the attic windows."

"They were pretty dirty."

"Yes," Shields admitted. "They were."

"And it was raining hard."

"The eaves kept the rain off the glass, mostly. I happened to glance out, and there it was—a big, solid-looking building with towers, not more than a quarter mile away. Sort of gray or grayish-pink. Is there a name for that color?"

"Dusty rose. Willie, it was an illusion."

He nodded slowly. "Or an hallucination. I looked at it—I stared right at it, Ann. And suddenly it was gone. You wanted to know what I had been looking at, and I said it was nothing." He paused, afraid she was going to be angry. "That didn't seem to be the time to go into it."

"That's right, you asked her about it while we were looking at her kitchen."

Shields opened his mouth and closed it again. There was no means by which Ann could be made to understand what he wanted to say, ever.

He was saved by the arrival of their waiter, who took away the big bamboo steamer and the small plates from which they had eaten their dumplings.

When the waiter was gone, Ann said, "It bothered you quite a bit, I can see that. Was this museum still open?"

Shields shook his head. "Bob Roberts had keys. Bob's on the board of directors, it turns out, and he told me about it when I asked him about the castle. That's when I decided to go—I wasn't even thinking about it when I left you and Merc at the motel. Where did you park her, anyway?"

"Just left her there," Ann said. "She didn't want to come. She's probably gone out to get something to eat."

As if on cue, the waiter returned with a tray of covered dishes. He put clean and much larger plates in front of them before ceremoniously setting out the biggest. "Peking Orange Duck. Very fine."

Ann said, "I certainly hope so," and the tip of her tongue made a brief patrol of her lips.

"Also have shredded beef oyster sauce, fried bean curd and plenty rice. Szechwan double-cooked pork, got very hot spices. All very fine. Imperial dinner three—plenty food! Other one come soon?"

"I don't know," Shields told him. "You weren't born here, were you, waiter? Born in this country?"

Ann said sharply, "Willie!"

"No, sir. Born Hong Kong. Have many cousin here, bring me, own Golden Dragon."

"So you've been in Castleview for . . . ?"

"Two year, almost."

Shields nodded encouragement. "And have you ever seen the castle?"

The waiter turned away. "No see."

"*Willie!*" Ann paused in the act of ladling duck onto her plate.

Shields watched the waiter's retreating back, shrugged, and turned to lift the cover of the Szechwan pork.

"Willie, what sort of service do you think we're going to get after that?"

He shrugged again. "I wanted to find out if he'd seen it. Whether someone from another culture would see it."

"And you didn't find out a thing."

"Certainly I did. He's seen something. If he hadn't, he would have laughed and said so. But he's seen the castle, or anyway he's seen something; and he was fascinated and frightened, just like I was. I'd love to know exactly what it was he saw—whether he saw the same thing that I did, or at least the same sort of thing."

Ann chewed and swallowed. "Well, it can't be helped now, I suppose. If we need service, I'll shoot up a flare or whatever. Was the museum nice?"

"No," he told her. "No, it wasn't." He seemed to feel the chill of its lofty rooms once more, a freezing dampness that had left him feeling that he had been in a cavern beneath the ocean. "It's an old house, almost as old as the Howard house, that was built by some doctor. Dark wallpaper in all the rooms, or oak paneling; a lot of carved moldings stained black. Lots of dusty glass cases—one got broken, did I tell you that?"

Ann shook her head and sipped tea. "Are we going to have to pay for it?"

"I don't think so. I think it was broken by whoever took Bob. It was very strange."

Ann had been tasting. "They probably use mandarin oranges, or maybe tangerines. Not Valencia oranges—they'd be too sweet. Do you know about Valencia oranges, Willie?"

He shook his head and spooned Szechwan pork onto his still-empty plate.

"Well, what we Americans think of as 'oranges' are really Valencia oranges, just that single variety out of a hundred or so. It's just like we think of lager as 'beer.' Practically all of the oranges anybody grows here are Valencias—that's in Florida and California too. The reason California oranges are different, less messy, is the climate; they're really the same variety. How's the pork?"

He chewed and swallowed, hungry again, and took a sip of water. "Hot spice, like the man said. Don't you think we ought to call the motel?"

"I wouldn't," Ann decided. "She probably walked into town to get a hamburger when the rain stopped. It's really not very far. She will have eaten, and your food will get cold."

"All right."

"You're worried about her, Willie. I can see you are. But how many times have you been every bit as worried when nothing's happened? Tell me about the glass. It wasn't a window?"

"No, it was a display case. There was an old diary in it, and somebody took it. It belonged to Bob."

"Then maybe he took it."

"That's what the police said, the sheriff's man. But why would Bob have broken the case? He had keys."

Ann added an eggroll to the heap of duck and rice on her plate. "Then if somebody got him—Willie, do you really mean they kidnapped him? One of our salesmen?"

He nodded. "Something like that."

"Then they'd have the keys, too. So why would *they* break the glass, either?"

"God knows. The funny thing was that I'd heard glass break before they broke into the case. That was an upstairs window in back, as it turned out. But I thought it was the case with the diary in it, and I ran to look. Bob ran upstairs—he'd heard it right—and that was the last I saw of him."

Ann grinned. "Willie, do you know you've eaten about five mouthfuls of that pork without drinking? You must be hungry."

"I am. Maybe being scared does it. After Bob disappeared, I was all alone in that old house—except that I wasn't actually alone, there was somebody in there with me, maybe more than one. Did I mention the carved wood? There were carved heads over the fireplaces in a lot of the rooms—tough-looking men, and women with smooth oval faces. It felt as though they were trying to talk, trying to warn me about something that was creeping up on me." Shields shivered, and drained his little cup of tea. The pork was nearly gone; he took some beef and a few wontons.

Ann told him, "The scarier you say this place was, the more interesting it sounds. What were the other carvings?"

"Horses. Swords and daggers and lances, and shields with

blazons. At first I thought it was just because of the name of this town—Castleview. Later I realized it was all Malory. The sword in the stone was carved over the fireplace in the parlor, downstairs."

"Malory?"

"He was an English author, Sir Thomas Malory. He wrote *Le Morte d'Arthur*. The old doctor must have loved it, or maybe his wife did. Then the calliope in the stable started playing. Did I tell you about the calliope? It's sort of like an organ."

"Willie, you're making all this up. You're embroidering."

"No, I'm not." The shredded beef was delicious.

"You know you are. You were never in any real danger—not at all like me. I've been through living holy hell, and believe me there wasn't a drop of fantasy involved. And the car—"

He looked up sharply. "What happened to it?"

"Well, Willie, I went up to talk to that nice old lady who runs the motel. I wanted to ask about the horse you almost ran into—the big man who rode across the road, remember that? It had seemed sort of uncanny—"

"No fantasy, you said."

"But Willie, it isn't. I thought it might be somebody in the neighborhood, somebody who might ride at night in the rain, and if there was, I thought the old lady would probably know all about it. And she did, but she had this recipe for pear jelly—I've got it in my purse, and Lisa's cheesecake too—and so we got to talking, and that delayed me. I met her husband; he's a nice old guy. Anyway, she told me—"

A soft voice at Shields's elbow inquired, "What was it you said to Hwan? The poor man's terrified."

Shields looked around.

12

THE BUYER

THERE WAS a knock at the door, soft and almost furtive—
Seth! This had to be Seth, Sally Howard thought, come home at
last. She ran to the door and threw it open.

"Sally, darling, I just heard," old Mrs. Cosgriff said; she was
holding a casserole.

"Oh, I'm so sorry . . ." Sally paused, wondering what she was
sorry for, then realized it was for the way her face had fallen
when she saw it was old Mrs. Cosgriff, who must surely have
seen it, and not Seth. "I thought you were my son."

"Ah," said old Mrs. Cosgriff. "That's who's got your car. I
saw it was gone while I was making the cobbler. He's probably
down to the funeral parlor."

There was a distinct implication that Sally herself should
have been there. She said, "No, I don't think so. But he took
my car, and I'm waiting for him to bring it back. Please come
in."

Old Mrs. Cosgriff crossed the Howard threshold with a tiny
hop.

"It smells absolutely heavenly," Sally said, accepting the
casserole; then the obligatory, "Won't you have some with me?"

"Why, I wouldn't mind one bit—it does smell awfully good,
doesn't it? You just sit down, dear, and I'll make us some tea and
dish up some."

Sally said, "Mrs. Cosgriff . . ."

"Yes, dear?"

"I don't know how to explain this. . . ."

"Then don't you try, darling. Just tell me what it is you want, and I'll see right to it. No explaining necessary."

"Mrs. Cosgriff, I don't want to be left alone—not as long as someone else is in the house and I can have company. Would you mind very much if I went with you? I could fix the tea, and you could dish up, and we could talk a little."

With the wholly unfair abruptness of sudden illness, Sally was crying. She had not cried, not really cried, since she had been told of Tom's death; she had raged and wailed and screamed at her mother, but she had not wept. Now, thus abruptly, she was a small girl again, a child; and this crotchety, gossipy old woman was her grandmother, was beloved Grandmaw Chattes herself, though Grandmaw Chattes was so long dead that her very face, her poor face, was nearly forgotten.

"There, there." Old Mrs. Cosgriff sighed. "There, there." And took her casserole back, and set it on Sally's coffee table on top of *Good Housekeeping*, and held her (though so bent by age that she was a head shorter than the child she held), and patted her back.

It came to Sally, at the crisis of her agony, that for the first time since Fourth Grade she was crying as she had when she was small, coughing and choking on her sobs, her nose running as much as her eyes. She was ashamed of it, horribly ashamed, but it did no good to be ashamed; she only cried the more for shame, though she managed to wipe her nose on the apron she habitually wore in the house before weeping again.

This, then, was why she had wept in childhood, although she had not known it. Then there had been only the unfocused sense of loss—the unplumbed knowledge that in the end the world would take away everything, even the worst things, so that at the end, when she had nothing left, she would miss even them; and surely it would take all the good things, all the best things, the good things first of all. That her most beautiful

87

dresses would turn ugly, hideous and foolish, merely by hanging in the closet; and that all the people, all the most beautiful people, the ones she loved best, would fall to rags.

"I'm all right now," she said. "I remember."

To which old Mrs. Cosgriff said, "We both need a nice hot cup of tea, dear. Let's go in the kitchen."

Meekly Sally followed the old woman, still wiping her nose on her apron while old Mrs. Cosgriff bustled ahead, switched on the light, and refilled the teakettle at the sink.

"Why, your window's broke," old Mrs. Cosgriff said.

"Yes," Sally admitted. "Somebody broke it tonight."

"You better get that fixed." Old Mrs. Cosgriff shook her head. "This weather isn't going to last forever."

"Tom always took care of those things. I suppose Mossby's would send somebody?" (Mossby's was the hardware store.)

"You tell them I said they better." Old Mrs. Cosgriff got down three dessert plates, three cups, and three saucers.

Why, she knows exactly where everything is, Sally thought. Everybody keeps everything in the same place, believing they've invented that place for themselves; but when you're old enough, I suppose, you know that, know where the woman across the street keeps her tea, and her teapot, too. "Maybe we should put Seth's in the oven," she said. "I don't know when he'll be home."

Old Mrs. Cosgriff turned to look at her. "Seth? Why Seth can hot up some whenever he wants to. Don't take but a minute. Does the gent care for tea? He might prefer coffee—I saw you had coffee cups out before."

"Oh." Sally remembered to breathe again. "He's gone. It was a deputy sheriff. You probably saw his car."

Old Mrs. Cosgriff was silent for a moment, putting the cups onto the saucers. "I guess you didn't want me to know, Sally. You might've thought I'd make more of it than's there, what with Tom not in his grave."

"Are you saying there's a man in this house? Right now?"

Old Mrs. Cosgriff spoke to the broken window. "I saw him when you were crying. He looked in, and I looked up and there he was, but he put a finger up to his mouth, the way you do, and tippytoed off. I figured he had the right idea. There's times, and then there's other times. He's in your parlor this minute, I imagine—that's where he was going when he saw us, and he must know we're out."

Sally had left the kitchen before she knew she was leaving; it seemed almost that the hall had appeared in front of her and swept her up. She was neither frightened now nor angry, simply incredulous and in some fashion compelled.

It was the dark stranger, as she had known it would be. He was sitting in Tom's chair smoking a long dark cigarette. Sally said, "I didn't think you were still here."

He rose as though he had not known she had come in until he heard her voice, though she knew that was not true. "You asked me to search for a prowler," he reminded her mildly. "I looked in here and upstairs. In your basement and attic also, and in your little tower room. You have mice. A rat, too, I believe." He chuckled. "But I found no prowler except myself."

Sally began, "You can't—you're not—"

"A prowler? Oh, but I was. I am! All through your house I prowled in the dark. That was so as not to disturb the other one, should there be another. When I entered one bedroom, I saw the intruder I had been seeking. How fiercely I sprang at him! You would have been proud—such courage, so much determination! Alas, he was merely my own reflection. I've broken a mirror, I fear, and that means seven years of bad luck."

Mechanically Sally said, "Would you like coffee or tea?"

"Tea, please. My cigarette doesn't offend you? If it does I can open a window."

"It doesn't matter," she told him. "You'll be going soon."

She had expected to find him gone—hiding someplace in her house—when she and old Mrs. Cosgriff carried in the tea things and the cobbler. He was not. He rose from Tom's chair like any ordinary visitor, and even helped with the plates, the teacups, napkins, and forks.

"I should have taken the tray back to the kitchen to carry those," Sally apologized to old Mrs. Cosgriff.

And old Mrs. Cosgriff said, "It was no trouble, dear," then looked from her to the dark stranger and back, plainly expecting an introduction.

Sally murmured, "I don't think we've really met, Mr. . . . ?"

"Fee." He gave her a card. "You are Mrs. Howard, I know. And you, dear lady?"

"Almah Cosgriff," old Mrs. Cosgriff said. She smiled and held out a wrinkled hand, which Fee kissed.

"Mrs. Howard does not wish me in her home," Fee said. "It is something I understand perfectly. Yet I am necessary. Are you aware of the situation, Mrs. Cosgriff?"

"Why, no," old Mrs. Cosgriff said, sitting down on Sally's sofa. "No, I'm not, Mr. Fee."

"Then permit me to explain. Mr. and Mrs. Howard planned to sell this house; they were to move, and felt that they could not afford two. No doubt you've seen the sign on the lawn."

"Oh, yes," old Mrs. Cosgriff said.

Sally sat down beside old Mrs. Cosgriff as Fee dropped back into Tom's chair. "Then," he continued, "only today, Mr. Howard unfortunately passed beyond mortal ken."

Old Mrs. Cosgriff nodded. "He went to a better world, I'm sure."

Fee smiled approvingly, drew on his cigarette, and puffed pale smoke through his nostrils. "Behold Mrs. Howard's un'appy situation now. She no longer need leave this pleasant village, where she grew to womanhood and where her much loved parents yet reside—the removal had been dictated by her departed husband's employment. But she believes she cannot retain her home without his income."

Sally stared at him. He tapped ash from his cigarette and

huckled. "You think me possessed of supernatural insight, Mrs. Howard. Believe me, you are quite mistaken. The truth is that I am rather a stupid person, far less astute than your lamented husband. It is only that I have spoken to Mrs. Beggs, who told me all these things. She was to arrange a time at which I might tour this house, but we were passing and I noticed your lights. I hoped that you would not object to showing it to me, and now that I have seen it, I realize it is ideal for our purpose, just as I supposed when Mrs. Beggs described it. You may say, if you like, that I intruded upon your grief, and be entirely correct. But I have found that such intrusions are frequently welcome—a little distraction can be a very good thing at such times."

Sally told him, "I've been distracted enough, thank you."

Old Mrs. Cosgriff said, "There was shooting, even, when the sheriff was over here. I was just about afraid to come. I was! Then he went away, and there didn't any ambulances come, or the firetrucks or anything, so I thought it would be all right."

"He told me he'd seen something out back." Sally weighed her words. "An intruder or a prowler. He shot at it—at him—and he jumped the fence and ran into the field. He shot twice more, but said he thought he must've missed. He said he didn't understand how he could have, especially with the first shot, but he looked around with his flashlight and couldn't find any blood. He had to phone in and report everything. It was a big man with a dog—that's what he said on the phone."

Old Mrs. Cosgriff asked, "Would you like to come over and sleep with me, Sally? What if he comes back tonight? What if you're here alone?"

Sally shook her head. "It would be better if there were somebody in the house. Seth will be back soon, so there'll be two of us."

"Seth's her son," old Mrs. Cosgriff explained to Fee.

He nodded without looking at her, frowning at his cigarette and adjusting its position in his fingers. It was an extraordinary cigarette, Sally thought, with something in it far stronger than ordinary tobacco; its smoke seemed pungent, and as heady as the smell of moonshine.

Old Mrs. Cosgriff tried again. "You've come to see about buying her house?"

"I have," Fee affirmed. "In fact, I intend to make her an excellent offer as soon as we're alone."

"Oh," said old Mrs. Cosgriff. "My goodness!"

Suddenly frightened, Sally begged, "Please don't go."

"No, I'd best be leaving—let you get on with your business talk. Thank you for the tea, Sally."

Sally rose and helped old Mrs. Cosgriff up. In the doorway old Mrs. Cosgriff said, "You be careful—life for a widow woman isn't the same as for a married lady. I know."

"I will," Sally promised. "Thank you again. Thank you for being so patient with me."

When she shut the door, Fee was rummaging in his briefcase. His hand emerged with a checkbook. "Mrs. Beggs tells me you are asking sixty thousand dollars," he said. "It seems a reasonable price for such a large house on three acres, even out here."

"It's old," Sally said, "although it's in good condition. Tom was always very careful about things like that—keeping up the house and the cars."

"Then we need not fear that your son has had car trouble."

"No," Sally agreed. "I don't think so."

"Which is comforting indeed. Such a promising young man—and his mother's support now. Per'aps I ought to add that Mrs. Beggs also told me she thought you'd accept fifty."

"I'd have to think about that."

In the kitchen, the telephone rang.

Fee said, "You didn't tell that woman that your father was missing."

The telephone rang again.

Slowly Sally replied, "I didn't think you knew about that either, Mr. Fee."

"Of course I do. I overheard you and that—"

The telephone rang a third time. Fee asked, "You do not wish to answer it?" Sally shook her head.

A fourth ring.

"You should, you know. It might be your son. It might be good news concerning your father."

Another ring.

Sally said, "It can only be bad news, and I don't trust you alone in my house." But she stood as she spoke.

She had lost count of the rings by the time she lifted the handset from the hook. There had been ten, perhaps, or a dozen. "Hello?"

"My name's Rothbell D. Patterson, Mrs. Howard—this is Mrs. Howard, isn't it? I'm on the *Chicago Sun-Times*, and I'm calling you from Chicago. We've had a tip that you've sighted something out there, a yeti or a sasquatch, like the Big Muddy Monster—a big, smelly, ape-like thing covered with hair. Is that correct, Mrs. Howard? Will you confirm it?"

Sally moved the earpiece away from her ear and stared out the broken window.

Faintly, the reporter's voice pleaded, "Mrs. Howard? Mrs. Howard?"

The draft coming through the broken window was icy; Sally shivered, thinking that it must be freezing or nearly freezing outside. "You have the wrong number," she told the telephone, and hung up.

As she had expected, Fee was no longer in the living room, though the smoke of his cigarette still hung in the air. The cigarette itself smoldered in the ashtray on the table by Tom's chair. One corner of a piece of brownish paper protruded from beneath the ashtray, and she pulled it out.

It was a check for sixty thousand dollars.

13

FORTUNE COOKIES

"WHAT DID you tell Hwan?" It was the hostess, willow-slender in a red silk dress.

Shields said, "I didn't tell him anything. I asked him a question." He rose. "Won't you sit down, Miss . . . ?"

"Sun. Phyllis Sun. I'm not supposed to, but—" Her eyes swept the almost-empty restaurant. "This late I don't think it can hurt."

Ann asked, "Tangerines? Is that what you use in the orange duck?"

Miss Sun shook her head. "Really, I don't know. I suppose it may be, or oranges and tangerines together; but our cooking's done by men—my brother and my uncles—and they don't like women in their kitchen. What was your question, Mr. Shields?"

"You remembered my name," he said. "That's flattering."

"I thought it odd that a Mrs. Schindler would say she was Mr. Shields's wife."

"I have a right to my own name," Ann told her.

"Certainly you do. What was the question, Mr. Shields? I don't think you asked Hwan about tangerines."

Shields shook his head. "I simply asked whether he'd ever seen the castle—the illusion or hallucination, or whatever you want to call it, that Castleview's named for."

"That's odd. Why should that frighten him?"

94

"Why don't you tell me, Miss Sun? Have you seen it?"

The hostess shook her head. "Never."

"How long have you lived here?"

"Since I was three. I grew up here. A lot of kids saw it when I was in school, and some of the teachers said they'd seen it, too—you study about it in Middle School. It's a mirage, or at least it's supposed to be, caused by a density inversion in the atmosphere." She paused, but neither Shields nor Ann spoke.

"In high school we kids used to run around at night looking for it. You're supposed to be able to see it better at night or in bad weather. I went a few times, but I never saw it."

Shields asked, "Did you want to?"

"Yes, as a matter of fact I did. It was something that you boasted about. Frankly, I think some of the people who claim to have seen it are lying. I was tempted to lie about it a time or two myself."

Ann said, "Mr. Hwan is lying, too. He said he'd never seen it."

"That bothers me," Miss Sun admitted. "He isn't a liar—he's just the other way, in fact. I'm going to have a talk with him the first chance I get. If I find out anything, I may tell you the next time you come in."

Shields grinned. *"May?"*

"It depends on exactly what I find out, doesn't it?" Miss Sun glanced at her watch. "I should go—the doors are supposed to be locked already. You take your time and enjoy your dinner. Hwan will put anything you want to save in cartons for you."

"Thank you," Shields said. "You've been very helpful." He rose as she did and seated himself again when she was gone.

Ann said, "You're right, she was. Oranges *and* tangerines—that's it, of course. Both are cheap, both easy to get even in a country place like this. If it's too tart, use more oranges. If it's too sweet, more tangerines."

"That isn't what I meant," Shields told her.

"Do you know, Willie, I didn't really think it was. What *did* you mean?"

"That seeing the castle doesn't depend on what culture you come from. Hwan saw it and that girl didn't, even though he's still Chinese, culturally, and she's culturally American. It doesn't seem to depend on desire, either. She wanted to see it, but she didn't."

"Okay, I'll play Devil's Advocate," Ann said, swallowing a mouthful of duck. "Have you considered that it might depend on credulity?"

"Rejected," Shields told her. "I saw it, and I've been in the automobile business since we got out of college. You don't have much credulity left after the first few years. Besides, I saw it when I wasn't expecting to, or even thinking about it." He helped himself to fried bean curd. "Now tell me about your adventures. Did you say you met a cowboy? What happened to the car?"

"It's got blood on the upholstery in back. And yes, I most certainly did. I told you I went to the office to ask that lady about the man on the horse, remember?"

Shields nodded.

"She told me there was a summer camp down Old Penton Road—it's called Meadow Grass. They have a lot of horses there, and sometimes the kids ride them at night, although it's against the rules." Briefly, Ann described her encounters with Wrangler and Lisa. "So I got this scrumptious recipe for cheesecake that the counselor's mother got from her friend. Then one of the girls, Sissy Stevenson—do you know her, Willie? When I said that, you looked as though you did."

Shields nodded. "I was just talking to her on the phone. She and another girl, a foreign girl, I think, are taking care of Bob."

Ann stopped chewing to stare at him. "You're kidding! How in the world . . . ?"

He waved the question away. "I don't know. I don't know much about it at all, but I should know a lot more after I go down there and pick him up, which I'm going to do as soon as we finish. What was your connection with Sissy?"

"She was the one who showed me the horses, that's all—all except Buck, because Wrangler was still out on Buck. They were all dry and seemed rested, so if it was one of those horses it had to be Buck, but I don't really think it was. The horse we saw was a lot bigger than Buck, for one thing, at least as big as Boomer, the biggest horse there. But it wasn't Boomer, and the man on him certainly wasn't wearing a hat like Wrangler's, if he was wearing a hat at all. Do you think he was, Willie?"

Shields shook his head. "I have no idea."

"If he was, it was a cap or something like that, something close-fitting." Ann sipped tea while she considered the matter. "Anyway, I thanked Sissy and got in the Buick, and off I went."

"How did—"

"*Please* don't interrupt, Willie. I'm trying to tell you. Well, the first thing was that I took the wrong road. I mean, it was the right one, the road to the main entrance. But it wasn't the one I'd come over before, the road I knew. Pretty soon I was sure I was lost, but there wasn't any place to turn around, so I just kept driving, hoping the road would come out somewhere. And—Willie, have you ever seen a horse in a cowboy movie just run away like crazy after somebody'd shot the cowboy and he fell off?"

Shields nodded. "Sure."

"Well, it was just like that. Here was this poor horse—it was Buck, of course—galloping right across the road in front of me, with nobody on him. I almost hit him, just like you almost hit that other horse. Of course I slowed down, and somebody in the back seat said not to pay any attention to the horse. Well, I'm telling you, I just about jumped out of my skin! I slammed on the brakes, and she bumped her nose on the back of the front seat. I think that's where most of the blood comes from."

Shields asked, "Who was she?"

"The French girl from the camp, Lucie something. She *had* to get to town, she *had* to meet somebody. And so she'd hidden in the back of our car—how do you like that? Well, I told her to

97

forget it, I was going to turn around and take her back the first chance I got."

Shields nodded approvingly, wondering whether he could have been so stern.

"But I couldn't. There's just this narrow dirt road, with no place to turn, so I had to keep driving. I knew I'd come out on the highway, and then I'd be able to turn around and go back without getting stuck. The shoulders were pure mud; I sank in up to my ankles, practically, when I got out."

"Why did you get out?" he asked.

"That's what I'm trying to tell you. Pretty soon I saw a man lying beside the road. She didn't want me to stop, but how could I drive past somebody who needed help? I stopped and got out, and it was Wrangler, the cowboy from the camp. I think he must have fallen off his horse. He was unconscious, and he was bleeding a little."

"So you put him in the back seat. I suppose I would have, too."

"That's right, I did. I tried to bandage him first, but my handkerchief wouldn't reach around his head. Women used to tear off the bottoms of their petticoats—I've seen it on TV. They must've been cotton, but my slip's nylon. It wouldn't tear, and it wouldn't have sopped up much blood anyway. So we laid him on the back seat, and I showed Lucie how to hold my handkerchief to his head. After that I drove as fast as I could. Did you know there's a hospital here, Willie?"

"So I understand—one ambulance."

"But I'll bet you haven't been in it. It's just a little place, smaller than our fire station. We came up to it like a hot-rod, Willie. You should've seen us! When I got out, there was blood all over in back; it was just terrible. I yelled when I saw it, and some people came out and got him; he looked awful, too—he was so white. After that I found a phone and called you here."

"Thank you," Shields said.

"So that's my story—captured at gunpoint, escaped, and a

daring rescue of a wounded cowboy. On TV that would be a whole season. You said that Bob—is that the man who was with you in the museum? That he was at Meadow Grass. How'd he get there?"

Shields shrugged; he had been considering what was left of the double-cooked pork, but had wisely decided he was too full for another bite. "All I can do is guess. I called the motel, and the old woman there said she thought you and Merc might have gone down to that camp; so I called the camp and talked to Sissy Stevenson. I gave her my name, and she wanted to know whether I knew Bob—they'd found one of my cards in his wallet. She told me that some girl was missing, and the counselor had gone out to look for her and come across Bob, lost and just about exhausted. I wanted to talk to him, but he was asleep and she didn't want to wake him. Then I asked to talk to the counselor, but she'd gone out to search some more."

Ann's eyes shone. "This's *strange*, isn't it, Willie?"

"Not really half as strange as seeing the castle. Somebody kidnapped Bob. God knows why, but they did. I think he must've gotten away from them. Not as easily as you escaped—"

"I was only teasing about that. Go on."

"I don't think there's much more to go on about. Bob ran away. In that rain they probably couldn't see him when he was twenty feet off, and it would tend to muffle any noise he made—breaking sticks, or anything like that. My guess is that he kept running till he dropped, and then this counselor . . ."

"Lisa Solomon," Ann supplied.

"Right, Lisa Solomon. He probably lay there till she found him. Anyway, Miss Solomon had Sissy call the hospital, but they wouldn't send their ambulance. They told her there was only one and it was at some accident; they said that if Bob wasn't hurt, she should just let him rest until morning. So the girls helped him undress and got him into bed, and as soon as he was asleep they went through his pockets to see who he was."

Phyllis Sun laid their bill on the table; it was in a brass tray with two fortune cookies. "Hwan's gone home. Or at least, he's gone."

Ann said, "I'm sorry to hear that."

"Maybe it's for the best—he'll feel better in the morning, I'm sure. Did you enjoy your meal? Would you like to take the leftovers with you?"

Shields said, "It was wonderful. Thank you."

Ann added, "And I'd love to take the rest home, especially the duck." There were two spoonsful of duck left. "But where we're staying, we wouldn't have anyplace to put it."

When Miss Sun had gone, she said, "Willie, we're supposed to leave now. They want to close."

"I know." He had already taken out his wallet. Should you tip a waiter who ran away before the meal was finished? Shields decided you should not. "I've still got the Cherokee I told you about. I want you to drive our car over to the agency and park in back. The mechanics will be in Monday, and they can clean up the rear seat. I'll pick you up in the Cherokee and drop you at the motel."

"You will *not*! I'm going with you."

"To the camp? You must be tired."

"I can hardly keep my eyes open; but I know those people at the camp now, so I can vouch for you. How would they know that you're not one of the gang that kidnapped this salesman to start with? Besides, you'll need somebody to look after him while you drive.

"Now," Ann continued, having settled the matter, "aren't we going to read our fortune cookies?" She took one and snapped it open. "Listen to this, Willie: 'You will save a king.' You've got to admit that's class! What's yours?"

He broke the brittle cookie and pulled out the slip of paper it contained. "'Be careful near the water.'"

14

HOUSEGUESTS

THE TELEPHONE rang as Sally shut the bedroom door. She picked it up, recalling that Tom had ordered it installed so that the third shift supervisor could wake him when there was trouble at the plant. "Hello?"

"It's me, Sally."

She sat down on the bed. "Hi, Mom."

"Kate and I have been conferring about you." Kate was her sister. "And we thought it might be nice if you came over here to sleep."

"I have to stay here, Mom—Seth's not home yet. What would be nice would be if Dad could come over and stay with me." She waited, tense and expectant.

"I'm afraid he can't do that, Sally. I could come."

A weight settled upon her heart; she had thought she could not feel worse, yet she did. "He isn't with you, is he? They haven't found him."

"I'm sure it's just some mixup, Sally. I didn't know you knew about it."

"There was a deputy here. He asked about Dad." It struck her that the deputy had never really finished talking with her, that she had not told him about her father's friends; she added, "He's coming back, I think. Have you called the hospital?"

"I just did, again. They still don't have him, but there's been a terrible accident out on the highway, and they thought he might've been in that. They say the ambulance should be getting in with some of those people soon. I don't see how he could be one of them, though."

"I don't either," Sally agreed. "Will you phone as soon as he gets home?"

"You're sure you don't want to come over?"

"Maybe I will, when Seth brings back the car." She thought of asking Kate to come, but that would leave Mom home alone and worrying. Besides, little Judy would be sleeping now, and Kate wouldn't come without Judy.

"I'll call just as soon as I can, Sally. But for now we'd better hang up. He might be trying to call me."

"Good night, Mom. Don't worry about Dad—he's all right." Sally remembered an expression he sometimes used. "He's an old cat that always lands on its feet." Cat—tomcat. Only Tom had not landed on his feet this time.

"Good-bye, Sally."

She hung up, staring at the bedroom door. It had moved— or at least had appeared to move—a trifle when her mother had said good-bye. Without turning the white china knob, she tugged it; the door was still latched. Like every other interior door in the house, it could at least in theory be locked with an old-fashioned square-warded key, although it had not been locked since Seth was a toddler. Tom kept a skeleton key in his desk that fit all the doors.

The house seemed very quiet tonight with Seth and Tom gone. They had often been off fishing, or Seth at school while Tom was at the plant; but this seemed different.

She went into Tom's study, a room only slightly larger than her pantry. There were inventories, still, in the basket on his desk, flimsy pink sheets weighed down with a bright casting; she would have to take them to the plant on Monday. Something there might be important, information that the new manager would need.

The skeleton key was not in the flat drawer, where she had

expected to find it. She pulled out the drawer labeled *Files*, finding (as she had known she would) several steel files—flat, triangular, round, and half round. Tom's little joke. The next drawer had a shallow tray in front; the key lay in it with a few yellow pencils and a ball-point pen. She picked it up and was about to shut the drawer when her glance was caught by the dusky gleam of blued steel: Tom's pistol.

Hesitantly, she took it out, reassured by its weight in her hand. It was only a twenty-two, but it had a long, heavy barrel and a big adjustable sight. It looked dangerous, Sally thought, as of course it was. Her finger well away from the trigger, as her father had taught her, she pulled back the slide and looked into the chamber and at the clip. Both were empty—but what if Kate brought little Judy over, and Judy got into Tom's desk? If she found Tom's pistol, wasn't there a chance she'd find the box of cartridges as well? Judy was too young, perhaps, to load the pistol. But in a year? Two years?

Sally reached under the tray that had held the key and took out the small, heavy box.

The slide had stayed back; there was a catch that kept it there, she remembered. She looked for it and found it, but did not push it down to free the slide. Not yet.

A rough button on one side of the handle—the grip—held the clip in place. She pressed it, and the clip slid out into her hand; she pushed shiny brass cartridges from the box into the clip—one, two, three, four, five, six, seven, eight. Tom had always shoved the clip back with the heel of his hand; Sally did the same. When she pressed down the little catch, the slide sprang forward, shouldering a cartridge from the clip into the chamber. Carefully and very firmly, she pushed up the safety so that the pistol would not fire.

With the blue cartridge box and the key in one hand and the pistol in the other, she started back toward the bedroom.

At the end of the hall, the wide front door seemed somehow menacing; she felt that the doorbell would ring before she left the hall, rung by something horrible.

And because she did, she did not leave it at all, going to the door instead, peering out through the thick glass panes and at last opening it and stepping out onto the long porch. Would the neighbors call the sheriff if they saw her come out onto her porch with the pistol in her hand? It wasn't very likely, Sally decided, nor were they very likely to see her at this hour. But if they did and they called the sheriff, so much the better—she would have someone there.

Fee's car—or had Fee come in a car? Fee's car was gone if such a car had ever existed. The rain had stopped at last, and for a moment at least an orange harvest moon bathed the lawn in mysterious light through a break in the clouds.

Slowly, she went down the porch steps. It seemed a fearful thing to do, to go around the house with a gun in her hand; she told herself firmly that there was nothing there, and that once she had made a circuit of the whole house she would no longer be frightened. She would be able to weep for Tom again, and worry about Seth and her father, because she would no longer have to worry about herself.

A wide strip of grass barred the big oaks and maples from her carefully-tended borders. She trod it slowly, cautiously, grateful for the moonlight when it came and sorry when it left. The annuals were brave still, though they would be dead so soon. The perennials were losing their leaves. The hybrid teas would have to be covered next month; she would try to get Seth to do it, or do it herself.

As she remembered the tall white Styrofoam rose cones in the cellar, she realized she was not going to sell the house, that she would never deposit Fee's check. Never! There would be some life insurance. They had saved some money for Seth's education, and she was still an attractive woman—or so Tom had always said. She knew it to be true. Let Seth get a football scholarship. She might (she would) find another man, a man who would take care of her and their home, and be a father to Seth. Just as there were so many lonely women, surely there were many lonely men in the world, many of them good men.

Her index finger had curled around the trigger in a frenzy of determination; if it had not been for the safety, the pistol would have fired. She smiled at herself and relaxed—plenty of time for all this in the morning. No, plenty of time when poor Tom had been decently laid to rest.

In the back yard, Rexy's dog house stood in a little island of tall grass, the grass left after Seth had ridden the mower as close as he could. Seth was supposed to trim that with the Weed Eater, though he seldom did. She remembered that the deputy had wanted her to get another dog and she had promised to consider it. Another dog seemed like a good idea, now that she had quite definitely decided to keep the house. The dog house ought to be cleaned out first, she thought—cleaned out and sprayed to kill fleas. Was Rexy's old bedding still in there?

Automatically she bent to look, and Rexy stuck his head out of the little door and licked her face.

Sally yipped and dropped everything—the skeleton key, the little box of cartridges, and the pistol.

Rexy said *"Woof!"* in a happy sort of way and danced around her in the dark.

"My God," Sally said. And then, "Oh, my God! Rexy is it really you?"

His answer was to jump up (something Seth had been trying to train him not to do), punching her in the stomach with his big front paws, and lick her face again.

"But you got run over—that's what Tom said. You were run over, and Tom and Seth buried you in the woodlot." She ruffled his ears, and he licked her hand.

Was it possible? Really possible? Suppose there had been another dog, a dog who looked a great deal like Rexy. *That* was certainly possible: half German shepherd and half Irish setter, Rexy had been born two blocks over, one of a sizable litter. So suppose that dog—the one who just looked like Rexy, probably a littermate—had been run over and mangled terribly. And suppose that on *that same day* Rexy himself had run away or been stolen.

It could have happened just like that, Sally told herself. In fact, it *must* have happened about like that.

But now Rexy was back, having found his way home or perhaps having escaped from some ghastly laboratory, and no doubt he was hungry and thirsty. Sally squatted, ran her fingers through the grass near her feet (getting one of her ears thoroughly kissed), and found the pistol, but neither the key nor the cartridge box. Rexy could have scattered them with his paws, and no doubt had.

"Come on, Rexy," she said. "We'll fix you a snack and get the flashlight." Wouldn't Seth be surprised!

Her hand was on the knob before she recalled that the back door was locked, the key in her brown purse in the bedroom. Out of habit, she twisted the knob anyway; it turned easily, and the door swung back.

When she switched on the lights, her kitchen appeared naked and innocent. Rexy sniffed in all the corners, emitting muffled snorts of pleasure, happy to be home; if he caught the scents of Fee or the deputy, or even old Mrs. Cosgriff, he gave no sign of it. The putrid stench that had drifted through the hole in the window had dissipated.

Sally glanced at that window and saw that it was open. Not merely broken, but wide open; somebody had (presumably) reached through the broken pane, turned the simple catch, and lifted the sash.

"We'd better phone the sheriff, Rexy," she said. But she knew the sheriff's deputy would find nothing, as he had found nothing before. He had searched the house, with Fee in it and searching too—by his own account at least—without finding Fee. She lowered and locked the empty sash, though she told herself that it would not keep even a child out.

Rexy's old dog food had been distributed among various dog-owning friends. Sally decided that Cheerios and milk would make a satisfactory supper for a previously lost dog, and prepared a bowlful for him that he accepted eagerly.

There was a three-cell flashlight beneath the sink, kept in

good working order in anticipation of the inevitable winter ice-storm and power outage. She carried it into the back yard and found the skeleton key and the little box of cartridges without much difficulty.

As she stepped onto the back porch, the kitchen door swung toward her, softly and slowly, as though it had been caught by a vagrant breeze she could not feel. Quickly she put the key and the little box of cartridges on the old table beside the door. Her hand reached for the knob; but the door closed, with a click of the latch, as she touched it.

Frantically she rattled the knob, but it was useless. The door was locked.

"This is silly," Sally said under her breath. "It's really completely silly. Take what you want and get out." It was not until she felt her own hot tears on her cheeks that she realized she was crying.

She gathered up the things again—the cartridge box in one hand, the skeleton key and flashlight in the other—and finished her circuit of the house. The front door stood wide open, just as she had left it. The lights in her living room still burned. She went inside, blew her nose on a tissue, and shut and locked the front door behind her.

Rexy was no longer in the kitchen; she whistled and called, but he did not come. Tom's pistol lay on the drainboard where she had left it. The blue plastic cereal bowl from which Rexy had eaten had been licked clean. She washed it and put it away, returned the flashlight to its place under the sink, and put the little box of twenty-twos on a high shelf.

With the skeleton key in one hand and Tom's pistol in the other, she returned to the bedroom. The lights were out; she could not recall whether she had turned them off herself. With her left hand, the one that grasped the skeleton key, she groped the wall for the switch.

Something lay in the bed, in Tom's place.

15

LUCIE

SOMEONE WAS sitting on the passenger's side in the front seat
of the Buick.

Ann had parked up the street; Shields had left the Cherokee
in the little lot behind the restaurant. They had parted at the
entrance, Shields saying, "Meet you at the dealership, in back.
Don't forget." And Ann, "I bet I beat you."

As she had walked back to the car, she had tried to tug her
girdle down without making a spectacle of it. She had eaten too
much orange duck—*entirely* too much orange duck, as she had
told herself. She would sleep like a log now for ten or twelve
hours, provided Willie and Mercedes let her, and wake up a
good three pounds heavier. After all her tugging, the girdle still
cut her tummy, and she had ruefully admitted to herself that
these days there was entirely too much tummy there to cut. She
had burped and muttered, "Damn!"

Then she saw her.

Ann opened the door, and Lucie said, *"Bon soir."*

"I thought it was you." With some slight difficulty, Ann slid
behind the wheel. "Didn't I lock the car?"

"No, madame." Lucie looked demure. "And so I have
chosen to protect it for you."

"Where'd you go, anyway?"

"From that hospital? To speak to my friend, but of course—it

108

was for it that I came into this village. First, I thanked you for your so-gracious help, though you did not perhaps hear. You were then so very much concerned for our injured Wrangler, *non?* I could no longer be of help to you; men from the hospital had come for him."

"You said something," Ann fumbled in her purse for her car keys, "that I meant to tell Willie a minute ago. But I forgot. They were laying him on the stretcher, and you said, *'Pullalue.'* It sounded insulting. Is it French?"

"It is no insult, madame. It is the wailing for the dead. You were at that time busy with concern."

"Well, I took a semester of French," Ann declared, "and it didn't sound like French to me."

"It is merely the custom of *Normandie*, that is true. But I am a French person, madame. French is that tongue from which we French persons speak, *mais non?*"

"Well, anyway, Wrangler wasn't dead, thank God. They have him in intensive care."

"*Hélas!* One cannot be correct always. You have not begun the engine, madam."

"No." Ann shook her head. "Not until you've told me what you want."

"Certainly it is plain—to be driven once more to *la* Meadow Grass. Or if that may not be, that you will provide me a place in which to sleep this night."

Ann pumped the accelerator and twisted the key. "Well, as it happens, Willie and I are going to Meadow Grass. There's no reason you shouldn't ride along."

Lucie's mouth formed a momentary little *O* that Ann regarded with some satisfaction.

Boomer shied at a big clump of brush, and Lisa pointed her flashlight at it; Boomer was not much given to shying as a rule. There was nothing there—or anyway there appeared to be nothing there.

The rain had started again, and a cold drip from the brim of her hat was nicely positioned to dribble into the neck of her raincoat whenever she looked down. She whispered, "All right, boy, let's go on," and nudged Boomer with her heels. The lanky gelding moved off at a quick trot that would rapidly become his jumping canter if she permitted.

A siren wailed from the direction of the main gate. There had been sirens there, coming and going, almost ever since Lisa had gone out this time—a wreck on the interstate, or perhaps on the old state highway. For the twentieth time it struck her that Lucie or Wrangler—or both—might be there and hurt. Nineteen times she had pushed the thought aside; this time she slackened reins and let Boomer have his head.

Shields was waiting when Ann pulled up; he grinned at her and said, "I thought you were going to beat me."

"I had complications, Willie, so it doesn't count. This is Lucie, the girl from the camp I was telling you about. Lucie, this is my husband, Will Shields."

Lucie had gotten out of the Buick as Ann spoke. She said, *"Comment allez-vous?"* and held out a hand as though she expected it to be kissed.

Shields obliged, taking it briefly in his own and brushing the cool backs of her fingers with his lips. "I'm afraid that I don't speak French," he said, "or any other language except for English."

"But that is sufficient. I comprehend English when it is spoken slowly and loudly—does not everyone?"

"I've heard otherwise. You're going back to the camp with us?"

"If you will be so kind. This thing—this old truck. This is yours now?"

Ann told her, "It belongs to the dealership. We own the dealership, don't we, Willie?"

"The bank lets us say so." Shields opened the rear door for Lucie, then the door in front for Ann.

"But this is *très comique!* Do you not know whose this is?"

Shields shook his head and walked around to get in on the driver's side.

"It is that woman's! She would drive this here to gain the supplies, but she was made to sell it because of a trouble about the payment of me."

Ann asked, "What woman?" craning her neck to look back.

"Mademoiselle Solomon, that Jewess. She loves this, though always it was Wrangler who draws away the soiled oil. Now it is gone—now it comes back!"

Lucie laughed, and it seemed to Shields as they pulled out onto the street that he had caught a note in her laughter that he had encountered earlier that evening—something frightening, with the soul of a lonely wind.

"Do not expect her to be gracious," Lucie added.

Ann said, "I'm sure she'll understand. Did she get a good price for it, Willie?"

He shrugged. "Offhand, I wouldn't know—I didn't make the deal." He chuckled. "I certainly hope not."

"Isn't it a good car?"

"It runs fine, but it's got seventy thousand on the clock."

"You always say that doesn't matter," Ann pointed out.

"That's what I say when I'm trying to sell them," Shields told her, "not when I'm buying them." He stopped for a light. "Where did you find Lucie again?"

"She was waiting for me at the car." It seemed best to Ann not to mention that she had forgotten to lock the doors. "And naturally I told her we'd give her a lift back. Lisa's probably worried to death about her."

Shields nodded as they pulled away from the intersection. "We should have phoned."

"Well, we had a lot of things to talk about. Besides, it's their business to keep track of these kids, not ours." Over her shoulder Ann added, "Isn't that right, Lucie?"

There was no response from the back seat.

Shields glanced at the rear-view mirror. "I think she must be lying down. She's probably tired."

"*She's* tired? What about me? Willie, I could just drop. Would you mind very much if I laid my head on you for a little nappy?"

"Of course not," he said.

The streetlights and the traffic signals were already well behind them. They were passing dark houses with bright windows now, living rooms in which men, women, and children sat reading in front of a television set or discussing the weather.

"Make yourself comfortable," he whispered, knowing that Ann was already almost asleep, perhaps truly sleeping. As gently as he could, he put his arm around her shoulders. The Cherokee was in third; he might not need to shift for some time, perhaps not until they reached this camp, whatever it was.

He found he had forgotten its name, but he felt certain Ann had said you got on the interstate and took the exit for Sixty-eight. Probably there would be a sign; Ann had said it was the main gate, the one that wasn't locked, the one she had gone out with the injured whoosis bleeding all over the back of their new car.

Not really new, Shields reminded himself—nearly two years old at this point. He ought to trade it in. He should drive a brand-new car all the time from here on, the newest model, top of the line—and not a GM either, though he had sold Buicks and Cadillacs for just about fourteen years.

Ann snored softly, and he wanted to hug her. He imagined the two of them in bed, Ann warm and soft, full of spicy-sweet duck. Sex was always best when Ann had eaten a big dinner and was ready for sleep, impossible when she was dieting.

You couldn't have everything, Shields told himself.

A white sign shone briefly in his headlights, informing him that he was on Sixty-eight already. Had he turned off onto the interstate automatically and exited it the same way? Or had he reached Sixty-eight by another route? That seemed more likely. Sixty-eight, he knew, was around Castleview someplace.

though it did not go through the town itself, or perhaps merely grazed it now that Castleview had grown a trifle.

He found he liked Castleview still, despite everything that had happened in the museum. That had not been the town's fault, he felt certain, had not been local people. He should take Ann there to see the big calliope that had started to play while he was looking for Bob, to see the old kitchen and the carvings she had been so interested in.

And he would, he decided, when they had found out what had happened to Bob, when this was all over—would most of all just because he was a little afraid to, and he should not be afraid. What had the biggest carving been? The sword in the stone, of course—the sword Arthur had drawn when no one else could, the sword that had made Arthur King of Britain.

Something nagged him about that. There was—surely there was—some connection he was not making.

"Let's see," he muttered. "It was a sword stuck completely through an anvil (which is pretty silly, on the face of it), and down into the boulder the anvil stood on. This whole affair had fallen from the sky, so it was a sign of some sort from God."

Ann stirred at the sound of his voice, and he fell silent.

The carved oak in the museum had been virtually black. Had the sword itself actually been black? There was no mention of that in Malory, or anyway none that Shields could remember. The anvil would have been black, though; anvils always were.

And the stone had probably been black, too, he thought; the stone had fallen from Heaven, so it had pretty obviously been a meteorite. In fact, the whole legend was clearly the gussied-up history of a king in the Dark Ages who had gotten his throne by learning to extract meteoritic iron, from which weapons could be forged. Thus Arthur had in a very real sense drawn a sword from a stone that had fallen from the heavens. And further-more, he'd drawn it through an anvil. Metallurgists still talk of drawing the temper of steel; drawing the temper makes steel tough instead of brittle.

But why should all that have fascinated the old doctor so? He'd been a physician, not a blacksmith or a mining man, though there were worked-out mines hereabout—lead mines, mostly. His name, Dunstan, that was it! He had been Dr. Dunstan, or so Bob had said, and Dunstan was *dun-stone*, dark stone or black stone, as those things had been said in Scotland and in the borderlands along the northern edge of England. King Arthur had fathered at least one Scottish son, by Queen Margawse. Quite possibly there had been others. If the old doctor's first name had been James, he might have imagined himself Prince James of the Dun Stone, or whatever.

Shields chuckled softly, recalling how he had romanticized his own name as a boy. After a minute or two, he began to sing under his breath.

> *'Twas just about a year ago,*
> *I went to see the Queen;*
> *She decked me out in medals,*
> *An' the trimmin's, they was green.*
> *She decked me out in medals,*
> *But they was made of tin.*
> *"Be off wit ya, ya rascal,*
> *Yer the mayor of Magheralin."*

Flashing lights glittered ahead, and there was the wail of a siren, coming fast. He pulled onto the shoulder and stopped.

Ann lifted her head. "Are we there, Willie?"

"No. Emergency vehicle."

It was a big white ambulance, rocking as it rushed toward them, the driver hunched over the wheel.

"Okay, it's past," Shields told Ann. He put the Cherokee in four-wheel drive, glad to have it, and pulled back onto the road.

Ann inquired, "How's Lucie?" without taking her head from his shoulder.

"Don't know—sound asleep, I guess. I haven't heard a peep out of her."

A pickup went past them in the wake of the ambulance, its driver shaking his head and jerking his thumb over his shoulder.

"Was he saying we can't get through, Willie?"

"I think so. An accident has the road blocked, but they'll have tow trucks out pretty soon."

He could see it already. There were two firetrucks there, three police cars, and a girl on a horse.

16

DR. VON MADADH

SALLY'S FIRST, wild thought was that it was Tom lying in his old place—that the call from the sheriff's office had been a prank or an absurd mistake. It seemed so natural, so inevitable, that it should be a mistake.

The doorbell rang, and the telephone. Sally ignored them both, and they fell into step, the longer, exasperated peals of the chimes stepping on the regular mechanical clamorings of the telephone like the notes of an all-percussion band in some sad institution for the severely retarded.

But the figure that lay upon its side in their bed was too small to be Tom. Those were not Tom's broad shoulders, surely, and that black hair was not brushed with gray. "Mr. Fee," Sally said. "Mr. Fee, that's my bed. You can't sleep there."

There was no response.

She walked around the bed and for a moment (though it was only a moment) she again thought the sleeper Tom. No, Tom lay in the mortuary, his body displayed on some hideous metal table while cheerful little Richard J. Fouque gummed down his eyelids and wired his jaw shut.

"Mr. Fee!" She tapped Fee's shoulder with the barrel of the pistol.

He opened both eyes, closing them again at once.

"Mr. Fee, get up!"

Without opening his eyes a second time, he said, "No!" loudly and firmly.

Sally jerked back the sheet and blankets, aware that the doorbell was still ringing though the telephone had stopped. Fee was naked and extremely hairy. She said, "I'll call the sheriff."

"Go 'head."

"Get out of my house!" Without Sally's wishing any such thing, her voice had risen to a wail.

"My house," Fee announced. He sat up, swinging his feet out of the bed, and belched.

"It isn't! I'm not going to sell it."

"Took m'money." Fee belched again and fell backward, so that he lay crosswise on the bed, his head on the other side, his feet not quite touching the floor.

"I've got to see who's at the door. Get out of my bed! I don't want to find you here when I come back."

She straightened up and realized that the pealing of the chimes had been stilled for some time; she crossed to the window and drew back the drapes. By angling her head, she could almost see the front door. The porch light was on, as she had left it. There was no one on the porch, nobody at the door.

"'m drunk," announced Fee.

Sally turned back and found him sitting up again.

"Li'l too much. Whole bottle. Weak head. Celebrate the deal." He covered his mouth with one hand and looked surprised.

"You can't be drunk! I just saw you five—fifteen minutes ago."

"Gonna—sick . . ." Fee moaned and fell sidewise.

She ran into the bathroom. The tin wastebasket there held only a few crumpled tissues. She dumped them out and filled it at the bath tap, inspired by the memory of her mother's throwing water on a drunken caller thirty years before. The wastebasket sloshing, she hurried back into the bedroom.

Fee lay again as she had see him first, his back to her, the blankets drawn up about his thin shoulders.

"All right!" She hurled the water toward him.

Behind her, a curious female voice asked, "Why did you do that?"

Turning around, Sally found a teenage girl staring at her; the girl wore jeans, a red flannel shirt, and a dark zip jacket, and looked as though she might be one of Seth's classmates.

"Who are you?" Sally asked.

"Lucie." The girl extended a small, neat hand with a junk-jewelry ring. "You're Mrs. Howard?" Sally nodded; she glanced back at Fee, but Fee had never moved. She accepted the girl's hand. "How are you, Lucie?"

"I'm swell, Mrs. Howard. I hope you don't mind me barging in like this. I was ringing the bell when I heard your voice in here. It sounded like you were in trouble, so I tried your door and it wasn't locked. Why'd you throw that water on the bed?"

Sally gestured toward Fee. "Because I want him out of it. Because I won't take no for an answer."

The girl stared for a moment, then pulled down the spread. As she did, Fee vanished; what had appeared to be Fee was only a pillow without a pillowcase and a wadded-up blanket, both soaked now.

"I'll take them off for you," the girl said helpfully. "Where would you like them?"

"There was a man in—" The words seemed helpless, useless. Sally tried to recast them to make them sound sensible. "A man came into my house this evening," she said, "and he won't leave. I thought it was him, there. He did that, fixed up the blanket like that to fool me."

The girl murmured, "Maybe you ought to sit down."

"Maybe I should. I'm terribly tired, and I'm going to have to sleep in a damp bed tonight, I suppose."

Sally let the girl lead her into her own living room. Her favorite chair (in which she had so often sat to talk with Tom, or read and watch TV) was full of peace.

"I could bring you a Coke or something," the girl offered. "Or tea—I can fix tea if you'll tell me where the things are."

"You don't know?"

The girl shook her head. "I'm afraid I don't."

"That's a relief," Sally said. "Such a wonderful, blessed relief. No, no tea. If you'd like a Coke, there's some in the refrigerator. Down the hall, and it's the second door on your right."

"Thanks," the girl said. "I'll get some—that salty stuff makes you thirsty. Sure you don't want any?"

Sally shook her head and watched the girl's departing back. I'll never see her again, she thought. Or I will, but she won't leave, ever. She'll have to marry Seth. Or if she won't, I'll tell everybody they're married.

For a few minutes she had nearly forgotten Seth. Thinking of him worried her; she put her head in her hands. After a long time, the girl said, "I brought a little glass in case you want some. I'll just drink out of the can, okay? Wouldn't you like a little?"

It seemed to Sally that whole years had passed since anyone had spoken to her with kindess; she nodded, not because she was thirsty, but because it was so much more pleasant not to refuse an act of charity.

Very carefully, the girl decanted cola into one of Sally's little juice glasses. "It's nice and cold," she said. "Thanks for not being mad because I came in."

"That's all right, it's only that I've had— My husband passed away today. Maybe you knew."

The girl nodded. "I heard about it."

"And then this evening it's simply been a madhouse. I had a gun, even. Did you see it?"

The girl shook her head. "When I came in, you just had the wastebasket full of water."

"That's right. I think I left the gun in the bathroom, on the toilet, with the key. I put them down so I could empty the Kleenex out of the wastebasket."

"It might be better to leave it there awhile," the girl suggested.

"I suppose so. And our dog came back. Did I tell you?"

The girl shook her head.

"He was run over last year, only he wasn't, really, because he was back in his dog house tonight. Seth built that dog house for him. I brought him in with me—he's housebroken, and the deputy said it would be better if I had a dog. I fed him, too." Sally sipped her Coke; it was cold and tasted good. "Then he ran off—exploring the house, I suppose. I've been thinking. I don't think he'd bite that man, but he might, really. Once he bit a boy who was fighting with Seth." She fell silent listening for the sound of dog claws on the floor upstairs. Silence brooded over the house.

"Rexy!" she called. "Here, Rexy!"

The girl touched her arm. "I wouldn't do that if I were you, Mrs. Howard."

"Call the dog? Why not?"

The girl shrugged. "You never know what may come when you call, especially on a night like this. I did it once."

"Oh, that's silly! Seth used to call him all the time. You're a friend of Seth's, aren't you? Are you in his class?"

The girl shook her head again. "Is Seth your son?"

"That's right. He's a senior this year."

"No, madame. I go to the camp here. But rather, the camp it is now over, but I do not go away."

Sally found a small smile tugging at her lips. "I've heard there were a lot of foreign girls there. You don't know Seth?"

"*Mais oui*, madame. *Mais non*, that I do not. *Est charmant?* I am so sorry."

"Then why are you here?"

"A certain one whom I know, he has given to me the address, thus I seek for him here." The girl raised her voice slightly. "The one whom I thought dead is not so, and I must inform him of this. Also that I tried very hard, very many times filling my mouth, spitting out when I could no longer drink. Of the Master of the Hunt, I have no further news."

Sally could only goggle at her.

"My friend, he has said he comes here tonight to buy this house from you. Has he done thus? He is here now, I think."

"Fee. You're a friend of Fee's."

"We are close, madame, let us put it so—in friendship most warm."

Sally was running down the hall and into the bathroom before she herself realized that she had sprung from her chair. Tom's pistol and the skeleton key lay on the flush tank where she had left them. She snatched up the pistol and pulled the slide back far enough to make certain there was a cartridge in the chamber, then went back into the living room, deadly calm now, pausing in the hall to whistle for Rexy.

She had not expected to find the girl; but she was in her chair still, still nursing the red can of Coca-Cola. "You act foolishly, madame. I have told you this, but the whistling is especially bad."

"Don't worry about the dog," Sally snapped. "Worry about the gun."

"For myself, madame, neither. For you, both."

"Won't you please stop talking like that? It was funny at first, but it's getting to be a trial."

"I speak as well as I know your language. Would you prefer my French? I fear you would not comprehend."

"Miss—" Sally had forgotten the girl's name, although she remembered that the girl had given it. "Get out, please. Leave this house. Mr. Fee's not here."

"Yet I must locate him, madame."

Sally discovered that her thumb was on the safety catch. "Rexy!" She whistled again.

"Please, madame. That is so evil, most especially when by a woman."

To annoy her, Sally whistled a third time, and the doorbell rang.

"I will answer it for you, madame. Possibly I will be able to send it away."

"I can answer my own door, thank you."

"It would be better that you put away your pistol."

"Maybe it would," Sally said grimly, "and maybe it wouldn't. I think I'll keep it and see what happens." Fear twisted at her stomach, tying three swallows of cobbler into frozen knots. She felt certain that if she were to lay aside the pistol, her hand would shake so badly it would go off.

The chimes sounded again, two short, polite peals.

Her thumb caressed the safety; it was still engaged. Quite deliberately, Sally put her finger on the trigger. It was Fee— who else could it be? Fee trying to find this girl. She would press down the safety catch, and shoot him through the heart as she opened the door. When somebody came, she would swear it had been an accident. She had grown up here, he was a stranger, they would surely believe her.

Or rather, they would acquit her whether they believed her or not. Tom had died today. Just today. Seth had—but where was Seth? What was the matter with Seth? Was this Seth? Had he lost his key?

"It is wise, what you do, madame. Do not answer, I beg."

The chimes sounded again, three short peals. "I m going to the bedroom for a moment. Don't answer that door."

"I will not, madame."

It wasn't Fee. Sally could see him standing on the porch, a man a great deal taller than Fee, with a curly beard. He was knocking now, having concluded, perhaps, that the bell was out of order.

She returned to the living room and opened the door. "I'm sorry I kept you waiting. I've been having a little trouble."

"So I understand, Mrs. Howard."

The stranger bowed, a slight inclination. His beard was bleached mahogany, Sally decided; a sort of light bronze.

"That's why I've come. Allow me to present myself, Mrs. Howard. I'm Dr. von Madadh, and I'm here as a researcher for the Daoine Institute. But are," he scraped his shoes on the mat, "my feet too muddy? There's been so much rain this week— not very good for tracking, I'm afraid." He offered Sally a large business card of the off-white shade called bone.

The girl grasped her elbow. "Madame, I beg you!"

"Not at all," Sally said, still thinking of her visitor's concern for her carpet. "No, really, Doctor. Please come in."

17

THE HAUNTED CAR

As SHIELDS had assumed, the accident blocked the road. At least three vehicles had been involved, he decided: a rusted-out Ford, a van, and a farm truck. The truck had apparently been carrying cattle—crestfallen black steers appeared from time to time in the headlights of the ISP cars and firetrucks, only to be shooed away by state troopers. One of the steers was hobbling on three legs.

"Willie, it's her!"

"It's who?" he asked.

"Lisa, the girl from the camp. The counselor. That's her, on that horse. I wonder what she's doing here."

"Rubber-necking, I suppose."

"Well, I ought to say hello to her. My shoes got all muddy getting Wrangler into the car anyway." Ann was opening her door as she spoke. She got out and waved. *"Yoo-hoo!* Lisa!"

Lisa looked toward her, waved, and neck-reined Boomer, who came trotting over. His mistress leaned from the saddle. "Mrs. Schindler? Is that you?"

"Yes, and I've got news for you. Willie, aren't you going to come out and say hello?"

Lisa dismounted and offered her hand. "Lisa Solomon, Mr. Schindler. Pleased to meet you."

"Will Shields," Shields muttered.

"Lisa, we just took Wrangler to the hospital. Not Willie and I—"

"To the hospital, Mrs. Schindler?"

Shields could not see her well in the glare and darkness of the accident scene, but he thought she looked very small to ride such a big horse. As she voiced her question she became smaller still, or so it appeared.

"He was lying alongside the road—just lying there. We saw his horse running away, then I saw him in my lights. I couldn't tell what had happened to him, but he bled *horribly*. We put him in back and brought him to the Trauma Center, and they put him right into intensive care. The doctor said he just about bled to death and it was a damned good thing I drove so fast. Willie taught me. Willie wanted to be a race driver once. Actually, he *was*, he raced his stock car and won some money that way, but when Mercedes was born he decided it was too dangerous and sold it."

Lisa whispered, "He's—Wrangler's—still alive?"

"Oh, yes. I'm sure—" Ann paused and gulped. "Lisa, he's going to be fine. They'll give him blood and everything."

"I have to see him—I've got to!" Suddenly, Boomer's reins were on the ground, and Lisa was in Ann's arms.

"She does, Willie. Can't we drive her to the hospital?"

Shields nodded. "We may be going there anyway after we get Bob."

"I mean right now. There's all this mess, these cars and so on, and we can't get through. But we could turn around and go back like those other people."

"I'm afraid not," Shields said.

"Will-ie!"

He shook his head. "I understand why she's concerned, and if I were in her shoes I'd be worried too. But Wrangler's in a hospital under treatment. Bob's our employee." Shields paused. "And he's my friend. I don't know how badly he may be hurt, and there's no doctor with him—a couple of teenagers are trying to take care of him. I shouldn't have waited to eat;

but because I was hungry and tired, and worried about you and Mercedes, I did. I'm not going back now."

Lisa had lifted her head from Ann's shoulder. "This is my car. You've got my old Cherokee." Her voice quavered, and her eyes shone with tears.

"That's what Lucie said," Ann told her gently. "Willie took it—we own the dealership."

"Lucie? Have you seen Lucie?"

Shields said, "She's in back—asleep, I think." He opened the rear door to show her, but the back seat was empty. So was the cargo area.

Ann stood on tiptoe to peer over his shoulder. "Lucie's gone. She must have gotten out to look."

Lisa said, "But she was with you? She was all right?"

"Certainly she's all right. She helped me with Wrangler. Lisa, isn't there any way we can get to Meadow Grass? That's where Willie's precious Bob is. Sissy told us."

"Is Bob that man I found? Mrs. Schindler, I don't want to go back to the lodge—not even if we find Lucie. I have to see Wrangler."

Shields nodded. "Of course you do, and you will. And we haven't even thanked you yet for taking care of Bob. But what about your horse?"

For a moment Lisa stared. "Boomer?" She pulled herself together with a visible effort. "You're right—I can't leave Boomer here."

"Then ride him back," Shields told her. "We'll meet you there, pick up Bob, and go to the hospital."

Ann said, "Except that we still can't get through this God-damned accident, Willie."

Lisa touched her shoulder. "Listen to me, both of you—you don't have to. See our fence? I jumped it on Boomer, but it's easy to take down the rails. You can put the car in four-wheel and drive through, then follow the fence to our private road."

Shields helped her lift out the white rails and lay them to one side, while Ann turned the Cherokee and eased it through the half-flooded ditch; they were taking away the last rail when a state trooper directed his light toward them. "Afraid I can't allow you to do this, folks. This is private property."

Lisa told him, "It's *my* property, officer, and I'm letting them go through."

"That's good of you, ma'am. But we ought to have a couple of hooks here before much longer."

Ann gave the Cherokee more gas, and it heaved itself out of the ditch as though playing tank. "We can't wait," Shields told the trooper, and climbed in beside her.

"Is that your horse, too, ma'am?"

The Cherokee rolled through the break they had made in the fence, swung to the right, and drove away at what Lisa estimated was a sensible ten miles an hour. She felt a bitter pride: it was still a wonderful car. "Yes, he's mine. Please don't shine your light in his face—you might spook him. I've got him tied to the fence."

"Don't worry, ma'am." Rather to her surprise, the trooper switched his flashlight off.

"Would you help me put these back up now? There's a horse loose, and I wouldn't want him to get out onto the road."

"Sure will. This's that camp, isn't it? Sweetmeadow?"

"Meadow Grass. Yes, it is." Lisa had taken one end of one of the white rails. "Was it a bad accident?"

He took the other, and together they set it back in place. "Real bad. Little boy killed in that van, ol' Chick Dickenson in his truck."

They replaced another rail.

"We got them in body bags now. Then there was four injured that went in the ambulance—four's all it holds. There was six people from Minnesota in the van."

"I see." Lisa bent to pick up another rail.

"And we've got three more that's not hurt so bad waiting up there with the paramedic for the ambulance to get back. Want to hear something funny?"

"Go ahead," Lisa said as they worked the rail into place, "what is it?"

"I was going up this road on patrol when that old Ford went by me like a bat out of hell, so I radioed. You know where the Turner place is?"

"Certainly I do. They're our neighbors."

"Well, I pulled in there to turn around, and that's when I heard them hit, a mile, maybe a mile and a half, down the road. It couldn't have been more than two, three minutes before I got there. One more rail, ma'am."

Stooping for it, Lisa nodded.

"And I'd a' swore that ol' car was full of people—couple in front and a couple more in back anyway. But I was the first on the scene, and there was only two. Couple of teenagers."

Lisa nodded, wiping her hands on her jeans. She found that she was sweating, despite the cool autumn night.

"The boy was in front, and the girl in the back seat. You ever hear of a couple of kids riding like that?"

Mercedes lay on a blanket on the ground; someone had spread another blanket and an orange plastic sheet over her. It seemed probable that there was another plastic sheet under her, beneath the first blanket. Dimly, Mercedes wondered whether doctors and nurses did not have some other name for the sheets, some special medical name like drop cloths.

Her head hurt and her arm hurt. There was a bandage on her head, she knew, another holding something cold and stiff against her arm. She thought they gave you something to stop the pain, but no one had given her anything, or she could not remember it. She had never used dope. Just say no. She wondered if she had told the doctor no. No, I don't want any, just go away. Take me home.

The blonde lay upon her back on the ground beside her, but if Mercedes had ever known her name it was gone now. Yet it was nice to have company, somebody she knew. She had no blanket, no sheet, Mercedes decided. Just lying on the wet grass smiling at her. The blonde was a great deal smaller than she was. Petite, Mercedes thought, really petite. "Am I going to die?" she asked the blonde.

"No. Would you like me to sing to you?"

Mercedes said yes, and the blonde sang, still lying on her back. Mercedes could not understand the words, but all seemed to rhyme, each word sister to the rest. The tune was something that should not have been a tune at all, chords she could never, nobody could ever, finger on a guitar. It was as if there were another universe of "other" music shimmering invisibly among the notes she knew. For as long as the song lasted, she could hear that other music in her head—then it was gone.

"I can't do that," she said humbly when the song was over. "I sing a little, but there aren't any strings there, and those keys aren't on our piano."

The blonde laughed.

Everything jumps, Mercedes thought, and that's the wrong way. Harmonicas, organs . . .

Pictures drifted behind her eyes: somebody with a polished black beard blowing a horn that really was a horn, the horn of a sheep or goat; a boy on a lonely Florida beach blowing a winding shell. The shell was broken at the tip and had lost its color—she had not been interested. While the boy had bathed it in the breakers, dipping it into the Atlantic and revolving it between his palms to get out the sand, she had left him. When she had gone a long way down the beach, she had heard the shell calling behind her, filled with a horrible, forever-unsatisfied longing for something that was not woman, the bugling of a beast whose mates all were dead, whose consorts do not yet exist.

She had not gone back.

"Perhaps someday you will hear them," the blonde said, "our horns blowing." It sounded important, but the thought dwindled and vanished; thoughts were a sleek train to Chicago that roared past her, never stopping beside her platform because she had no platform and the windows of all the cars were dark.

A woman in a white jacket bending over her. "The ambulance is here. Think you can walk?"

"I think so," Mercedes said. "Can my friend come, too?"

"He's already gone," the woman told her. "He went in the first load."

She helped Mercedes up. The blonde draped Mercedes's good arm over her shoulders, and they helped her into the ambulance.

There were narrow cots on each side in back, one above the other. The woman in the white jacket and the blonde put her in one of the lower ones, cramped and very firm, only a few inches off the floor. The woman in the white jacket laid her bandaged arm beside her and warned her not to move it, then covered her with a blue blanket and tucked her in.

"You're doing just fine," she said. "You're going to be okay." For the first time, or thus it seemed to Mercedes, she noticed the blonde. "You'll have to leave now," she told her. "This will be going back in a minute or so. Don't worry, we'll take good care of her."

"All right." The blonde nodded.

The man in the cot above Mercedes groaned; for a moment she thought he might be Seth, but his hand hung over the edge of his cot where she could see it, and it was not Seth's—somebody from the van, she decided. She hoped he would not bleed on her.

A man in a white jacket like the woman's stooped to ask if she was all right. She said she was.

"You don't have too much pain?"

The ambulance was moving, slowly and smoothly, then faster and faster. The siren wailed.

Somewhat to her own surprise she said, "No, I'm in pretty good shape. Where's Seth?"

But the man in the white jacket had turned away.

The blonde said, "He and Jim have gone already. They're at the hospital."

18

WRANGLER'S HAT

AFTER FIVE minutes, they swung onto a gravel road. "I'll show you where we found Wrangler," Ann promised.

Shields scratched his chin, peering through the Cherokee's window into the night. "I'd a lot rather know where that girl found Bob. I wish I'd asked her."

Ann glanced across at him. "What for, Willie? Besides you can ask him yourself when we get to the camp. Sissy didn't say he was unconscious or anything, did she?"

"No, just confused. They put him to bed—he was sleeping when I called." Shields hesitated. "You're right, maybe he'll be able to tell us where that girl found him. But she knows this place; I doubt that Bob does."

"Then you can ask her as soon as she gets to the camp. She waited to put the fence back—I saw her in the mirror—but once she has it done, she should get there on her horse about as fast as we can drive it."

Shields nodded. "And I will."

"You're worried about something, aren't you, Willie? I can always tell."

"Suppose the people who took Bob want him back? They must have grabbed him for a reason, and they can't have had him for much more than a couple of hours, so I doubt that they got what they wanted. How do we know they've given up?"

Ann laid her hand on his. "Be reasonable, Willie. How do you know that anybody took him? If you ask me, he just ran off. Probably he remembered something he had to do."

"And ended up way out here in the rain?"

"I know!" Ann snapped her fingers. "Didn't you say he was old? How old, Willie?"

"Over sixty-five; I don't remember exactly, but it's in his employment record. Remember the woman in that house we looked at today?"

"Mrs. Howard? Sure."

"She's Bob's daughter, I think the older one. She's got a son Merc's age, so Bob's no spring chicken."

"Exactly." Ann was triumphant. "So he had a stroke—not a big stroke that leaves you paralyzed or blind, but a little one. People who have strokes forget, and get confused. You said that Sissy said he was confused, Willie."

Shields nodded again.

"Well, there you are. No, here *we* are." Ann touched the brakes. "Wrangler was lying right around here someplace. Right along here. What are you muttering about?"

"Bob's stroke—the one that made him go down the back stair while I was coming up the front stair, and play 'Valse Triste' on the calliope in the carriage house."

"But don't you see, Willie—"

"What I see is that there's something going on around this place, this summer camp. It's where that girl found Bob. It's where somebody knocked this cowboy of yours on the head—"

"Wait a minute! If you can interrupt me, I can interrupt you. Wrangler probably fell off his horse, and right up here's the place. See that little tree close to the road? I remember it."

"Stop," Shields told her. "I want to get out and have a look."

"At where we found him? All right. But, Willie, you never want to see anything I want to show you."

"Ads in the paper, you mean. I want to see this."

They halted, and Shields got out. "Where was he, exactly?"

"About halfway under the little tree, on the other side. Should I come along and show you?"

Shields shook his head. "See if you can aim your lights at it."

For a minute or more he circled the tree, keeping his back to the headlights and stooping to study the sodden ground. When he had returned to his place beside Ann, he asked, "Was it still raining when you found him?"

"Only a little bit. It had nearly—blood! That's what you were looking for, wasn't it, Willie?" Abruptly, Ann opened her door and climbed out. "Wrangler bled just terribly all over our back seat, but there wasn't really much blood when we picked him up—I remember I was pretty proud of myself for noticing that he was bleeding at all. And I gave that kid my good hankie to hold against the place. Didn't you find any blood?"

"Not a drop. I'm not saying there isn't any, but if there is, there isn't much."

"Maybe this is the wrong place. You know, I was going the other way when I saw him. This could be the wrong tree."

"I don't think so." Shields held up a wide-brimmed, low-crowned hat. "Is this his?"

"I guess so. It looks like his."

He switched on the dome light. "There are initials on the band. They look as though they were printed with one of those waterproof laundry markers: AD. Are those his?"

"I don't know—everybody called him Wrangler. But, Willie, I think there's something else missing, besides the blood."

Shields tossed the hat into the cargo compartment of the Cherokee. "What's that?"

"His gun. Don't you remember, I told you he had a gun? He pointed it at me! It was a rifle, the kind that looks like a BB gun, with a thing underneath you pull down? If he fell off his horse, it would have to be here someplace, Willie, like the hat, because we didn't take it." Ann paused, thinking. "And his gun should be easier to find. It was bigger, and kind of shiny."

Shields had moved behind the Cherokee's wheel. "It's not there."

"Are you certain, Willie? We could look around some more."

"Not completely; I suppose I could have missed it, but I don't think I did. I would probably have tripped over it or stepped on it, if nothing else. Anyway, if it's here we won't find it at night without better lights."

Ann seated herself on the passenger's side. "He must've had it, Willie. He was going to ride around the camp again—that's what they told me. And I don't believe he'd have gone without his gun."

As the Cherokee picked up speed, Shields said, "In cowboy movies they have holsters for their rifles on their saddles—long straight leather affairs like the top of a boot. Wrangler didn't have one of those?"

"Not that I remember. When I stopped at the back gate and he came riding up, he had the gun in his hand. He kept it when he got off his horse."

Ann fell silent, but Shields said nothing.

"Willie, wouldn't that holster thing be on the right? So that the cowboy could pull out his rifle with his right hand?"

"I suppose so. Why?"

"Because I saw Buck when he ran in front of the car. You know, before we found Wrangler lying beside the little tree back there? Buck was Wrangler's horse, and I don't remember seeing the gun, or a holster thing either."

They drove across the rain-born stream Ann had forded with Lucie, traced the road down the same narrow valley, and at last climbed a hill from which they could see the lodge and the barn.

Ann pointed. "The lights are still on, that's good. I was afraid they'd be in bed—though I don't suppose they'd go to bed early with their counselor away, now that I come to think about it. Look, Willie. There's one of the girls."

She was walking, running in fact, back from the barn to the lodge. Someone inside opened the front door before she reached it, and stepped out as Boomer cantered into the bright lit area around the barn.

"Lisa beat us," Ann announced. "I guess because we stopped at the tree."

Shields nodded. "And she cut across country. Isn't that Bob—the one who just came out?"

"I wouldn't know Bob if he bit me, Willie."

"I think it is. That's a man with gray hair, right?"

"Light-colored, anyhow. Willie, they're having an argument or something. Lisa's got her face in her hands."

Lucie presented her hand to von Madadh, who bowed over it. *"Enchanté, mademoiselle."*

"Vous avez bon mine, Docteur. But I was departing. If you will permit . . . ?"

He smiled. *"Eh, oui, le train pour Paris.* Go, child, by all means."

Lucie turned at the door. "Be careful, Mrs. Howard."

Sally said, "Good-bye."

As the door closed behind Lucie, von Madadh smiled again. There was a warmth in his smile that made Sally Howard like him at once. "A charming girl. I take it you don't know her well?"

"No, and she's not French, not really. She was as American as you and I are when she came, then after a while she put on an accent. Won't you sit down, Doctor?"

"On the sofa? You don't object? No, of course she's not French. Her pronunciation's fairly good, but she wouldn't take in a real Frenchman for a moment." He chuckled. "Did you see her blush when I asked if she was catching the train to Paris?"

Sally realized that she was still holding Tom's pistol, and laid it on the coffee table. "I didn't notice." Her shoulders drooped; it seemed to take too much effort to square them again. "I'm just so tired, doctor. There've been all sorts of people here—so many I've lost count."

"And there was trouble. So you said a moment ago, and you have that." Von Madadh gestured toward the pistol. "I confess I don't like them; they're far too noisy. If you use it, please

135

make very sure you're shooting at what you think you are and not at me."

Sally shivered, realized she was still holding von Madadh's card, and laid it beside the pistol.

"Fatigued though you are, Mrs. Howard, can you spare me ten minutes? It will take no longer than that to tell you who I am and what I want."

Sally nodded, smiling. "Do you know, Doctor, I feel better just having you in the house. I don't think I'd get much rest if you left, anyway."

"Excellent." Von Madadh stroked his red-gold beard. "I'm glad you feel like that, Mrs. Howard—very glad. I'm going to make a little proposal to you in a moment, but first you should know who I am. Are you familiar with the work of our institute?"

Sally shook her head.

"Our province is the investigation of folklore in process." He paused as though waiting for her to object. "Suppose, simply as an example, that we receive reports of a dragon; this dragon, we shall say, lives someplace in Africa, where he feasts on the princesses of a local tribe. We'd try to get our agent to the spot before the dragon used his napkin, so to speak." His warm smile appeared again.

She could not help smiling in return. "I don't imagine you do a lot of traveling."

"More than you might think. Our records at the institute list dozens of virgins devoured by dragons since nineteen forty-five; most were in Asia, actually. Unfortunately, none of them has fallen to me. I have my practice to attend to; I can assist the institute—I'm a volunteer—only during vacations. I allow myself one month a year."

Sally said, "You've come about the giant, or whatever it was."

"Precisely. You saw him yourself, Mrs. Howard?"

"Only for a minute. No, it wasn't really that long. For a second or two. But I couldn't see him very well at all—it was too dark. Just a sort of outline in the dark. Do you know what I mean, doctor?"

"Perfectly," von Madadh said. "Did he have a horse?"

"A horse?" Sally stared at him. "Why no. But he did have—I heard—"

Von Madadh waved a hand negligently. "Please excuse that. I've learned not to lead my patients, but it seems I've still to learn not to lead my witnesses. It was merely that some reports we've received describe him as a rider. Now I'll hold my peace, and about time too, and let you describe exactly what it was you saw tonight."

"Well, now," Sally said slowly, "the man who called, he was from some paper in Chicago, had a name for it. A . . . a sasquatch, was that what he said? I'm not sure I know what it means."

"A sasquatch? This is very interesting. Please go on."

"It was a great big thing, that's all. Like a man, but it must have been almost twice as tall. Its eyes were red. They glowed, you know how an animal's do? And it smelled horrible, like something dead."

Von Madadh nodded encouragingly. "Please continue."

"That was all. I saw it, and then it was gone. The deputy shot at it—three times, I think. I suppose it must've been him who called the newspaper, or at least somebody in the sheriff's office."

The telephone rang.

19

The Number You Have Reached

LISA WAS still weeping when Shields and Ann pulled up. Shields shouted, "Bob! Hey, Bob!" and waved as he threw open the door of the Cherokee.

Roberts hurried across the muddy stableyard to shake hands. "By gosh, Mr. Shields, it's good to see you again!"

He was still too old to be selling cars and his teeth were still false, but Shields found he was delighted to see Roberts, too. As he asked, "Are you all right, Bob?" he could not keep from grinning.

"I'm right as rain, Mr. Shields. Never felt better. Oh, a little tired, but I'm okay."

Ann had thrown her arms around Lisa Solomon. "Don't cry. Please don't cry."

"Now Sissy's gone."

Tall and swarthy, the girl who had run from the barn looked from the two men to the two women. Lifting her hands to heaven, she uttered a prayer no one but herself understood. Something like a hornet (though much swifter) flew across the stableyard, followed instantly by a flat *crack*, the sound of a two-by-four breaking. The tall girl dropped her arms and looked stunned; a dark blotch appeared on her faded denim jacket, and spread.

Perhaps no one but Shields saw it. He lunged for her and caught her as she fell.

The hornet flew again. A second two-by-four snapped, and the windshield of the Cherokee exploded into frosty shards.

"Get down!" Shields yelled.

Ann and Lisa froze. Crouching, moving surprisingly fast, Roberts grabbed each by an arm and started for the lodge.

"Can you walk?" Shields asked the tall girl.

She tried to reply; but blood bubbled at her lips, drowning her words.

He got his arms beneath her and lifted, finding her flaccid body astonishingly light. Trying to bend, struggling to run, he scuttled after Roberts and the women.

Then the doorway was before him, and he had nearly cracked the tall girl's head against the frame. At the last second, he turned sidewise and stumbled through. Roberts slammed the door behind him, and twisted the handle of a brass-plated night bolt.

They propped her up on the couch and staunched the bleeding with towels while Lisa tried to telephone the hospital. After a dozen rings, she hung up.

Ann asked, "Don't they have an emergency number here? At home it's nine eleven."

"Not in Castleview," Lisa muttered. "It's too small."

"Ours doesn't work very well," Ann told her, "but at least we've got one." She was studying the wounded girl.

Her bloodless cheeks seemed gray—a dingy gray like the sky at the end of a bad day, Ann thought. Roberts had cut the denim jacket and torn away the faded work shirt beneath it; the lacy top of a brassiere, scarlet now with blood, showed above the towels. Dimly, Ann felt that the brassiere should have been discarded, too; but that the humiliation of naked breasts might in some way kill the wounded girl—though she would die anyway. A small gold crucifix lay upon her throat, a premature memorial.

Roberts asked, "How is she?"

"Breathing a little easier, I think," Ann told him.

"That's because we stopped the wound from sucking. Bullet nicked her right lung."

Her wheezing exhalations measured out each silence like the laggard ticking of a grandfather clock.

Ann knelt beside the couch. "Shouldn't she be down more? Flatter?"

Roberts shook his head. "She'd drown in her own blood."

"Is she going to die?"

"She's young. I think she'll make it."

Catching the lie in his voice, Ann said, "Can't you get the hospital, Lisa?"

"I've dialed twice. Nobody answers."

She was shaky, Ann thought, too shaky. She said, "Let me try. You read out the number for me."

Gratefully, Lisa surrendered the telephone. "It's three nine one. All the Castleview numbers are three nine one."

Ann discovered that her own hands shook as she pressed the buttons. She tried to count the chirpings from the earpiece.

"Nine nine nine eight. Got it? Three nine one, nine nine nine eight."

Ann wanted to shout shut up, be quiet, you're confusing me. She bit down on her tongue instead, punching numbers valiantly.

Somewhere a telephone rang. Would they answer? Recalling how Wrangler had bled all over the back of the Buick—Another ring, and still no answer.

"Here," Lisa whispered. She held out the white pages of a slender directory. "Do you want to look at it?"

"I've already entered the number."

Another ring.

"If you have to do it again. Maybe it would be better if you could see it. Three nine one, nine nine eight."

"That's not enough—"

An answer in the middle of the ring: "Howard residence."

"What? What did you say?"

"I said that this is the home of the Howard family. I'm Dr. von Madadh—Mrs. Howard's engaged at the moment. For whom were you calling?"

Ann swallowed hard to keep herself from shouting. "You're a doctor? A real medical doctor? We've called and called, but the hospital doesn't answer, then I got you. Doctor, a woman's been shot. We're trying to give her first aid. What should we do?"

"You say there's been an accidental shooting? Where is the wound?"

Lisa was beside Ann now, leaning close to hear. Ann said, "In her chest, just underneath her right breast. There's a man here, doctor, who was in the Second World War—he was on Anzio Beachhead, he says, whatever that was. He says the bullet hit her in the back and went through. What should we do?"

The calm voice at the other end of the wire murmured, "It might be better if you told me first what you've already done."

"She's lying on the couch, propped up. The man says you've got to keep their heads up—he says the bullet went through her lung. We've got lots of towels around her. They're all bloody, but I don't think she's bleeding much any more—except sometimes there's blood in her mouth. She coughs up blood."

"Touch her face. How does it feel?"

"I wiped it a minute ago, doctor. She's perspiring, but her skin's terribly cold."

Shields came in and went to the couch to look at the wounded girl.

"Is she covered?"

"You mean with a sheet?" Ann thought of the grim canvases used to shroud corpses in a morgue.

"Covered with blankets—with anything."

"No, but it's warm in here."

"Cover her, with blankets or coats or whatever you have. Your patient's in shock. You're in a home?"

141

"In a camp," Ann told him. "We're in the lodge at a camp."
Lisa was leaning closer than ever. Behind her, Ann could hea
Shields and Roberts conferring in low tones. She said, "Mead
ow Grass—it's a summer camp for girls."

"If there's an electric blanket, use it. Turn it to High. Sh
must be kept warm. Other than that, I can't help you. You nee
a surgeon, blood transfusions, and oxygen. You said you'd bee
calling the hospital. I suppose someone must have made th
wrong connection at their switchboard, because the hospita
just called us. Mrs. Howard's son's been in an accident; we'r
going there now. Anyway, try them again and keep trying—tr
anyplace that might send an ambulance."

"Don't you know?" Ann asked.

"I'm from out of town. Keep your patient warm, and get he
to a hospital as quickly as you can. I'll tell them about this whe
I get there." He hung up.

Ann passed the handset to Lisa, then snatched it back. "G
get the blankets, you know where they are and I don't. He sai
to cover her up, keep her warm, understand? Oodles o
blankets. Willie, how does it look?"

Shields shrugged. "I've checked all the doors and windows
can find. Most were locked already, but we can't do more tha
patrol this place—it's too big. If the sniper wants to get in, he
going to get in."

"It might have been an accident, Willie. Have you thought o
that? It might have been somebody shooting at a rabbit or a ti
can or something."

"It might have been," Shields admitted. "I don't believe
was."

"Well, I was talking to this *doctor*—" Ann pushed buttons o
the handset. "And *he* said it might have been an accident."

"You got the hospital?"

"No, I got a wrong number, but it was a doctor. He said w
have to get her to the hospital right away, and to cover her u
and keep her warm. Lisa's getting blankets. He said he'd te
the hospital where we are, too." (There was only silence in th

earpiece.) "This time it didn't go through," Ann muttered. "Go away, Willie, you're distracting me."

He had already turned back to Roberts and the dying girl. "What do you think, Bob? Is he out there?"

Roberts shrugged.

"Why her?"

"Why not? Truly, Mr. Shields, I don't believe it makes any difference to them."

"You think it was the people who got you? So do I. Who were they, Bob?"

The old man shrugged. "Be darned if I know, really. Some were kids, or anyhow they looked like kids. But . . ."

"But what?"

"They weren't all of them kids. But they were always sort of messing around, messing with this and that, and showing each other things. Know what I mean?"

"Certainly," Shields told him.

"So if they had a gun and saw somebody standing out there, they might try a couple of shots. Or not."

Ann was only half listening, the majority of her attention on the slow buzzings in the earpiece; now they were interrupted by a hushed voice: "Fouque's Mortuary."

"I'm sorry, I must have—no, wait! Do you have ambulance service? Sometimes you do, I know, around Chicago. Do you? Please!"

"Not any more, ma'am. The insurance got to be too much."

"Could you—a woman's dying. Could you call the hospital for me? I think there's something wrong with this phone."

Lisa returned with an armload of blankets.

"No, ma'am. You'll have to call them yourself, ma'am. The number's three nine one, ninety-nine ninety-eight. Did you say the lady's dying?"

"Yes!"

"All right, when she's dead you have to get your doctor to sign the certificate, and then we'll come and get her. We'll be glad to."

Gene Wolfe

Ann hung up. Three nine one . . .

"It's those damned lights on the barn," Shields said. He might have been addressing the whole room or talking to himself. "Miss Solomon, where's the switch to turn them off?"

She was spreading a gaudy Indian blanket over the wounded girl. "In the tack room, but he'll be able to see you even if you go around back. There are lights all around the barn."

"Maybe not," Shields said. "There's a rear entrance to the barn?"

She nodded. "It's padlocked, but I have a key."

Ann slammed down the handset, picking it up again at once. "Willie, you're not going to go out there and get shot!"

He grinned at her. "I certainly hope not."

"Hello," a distant voice said in the earpiece. "Hello? Hello?"

"I'm here! Is this the hospital?"

Speaking mostly to Roberts and Lisa, Shields said, "He may be gone, whoever he was. If he's not, our big problem is those lights."

"No," replied an elderly voice. "Heavens no, I'm not the hospital, dear. Did they find you already? This is Emily."

"If I can switch them off, I'll pull the car up as close to the door as I can," Shields continued, "with the headlights off, of course. If he doesn't start shooting, we can lay the girl on the back seat and make a run for the hospital."

Ann pressed her hand against her ear. "Excuse me—they're talking in here, and I couldn't hear you. Who did you say you were?"

"Emily, dear. From the Red Stove Inn—you got my receipt for pear jelly?"

"Oh, yes. Yes, of course."

"I called there because your husband got me to read him the number of it. And I knew your voice right off. Only I didn't recollect him phoning till Alfred reminded me. Are you quieted down, dear? You sounded kind of upset there for a minute."

"Yes, I am," Ann lied. "I'm fine."

"All right. I'm awfully glad I'm not the first one to give you the bad news. I only called you because the hospital's been calling us about your daughter, trying to find you. I'm awfully sorry, dear, honestly I am."

Ann looked around wildly for Shields, but he was gone. So was Lisa.

20
HIDE AND SEEK

SALLY INSISTED on paying when the cab let them out in front of the hospital. Von Madadh shrugged and acquiesced, scrutinizing with equal curiosity the modest brick building and the dimly lit street. "Rain has cleansed the air," he muttered. "Old smells are gone, and none but the new remain: your perfume, that dirty car, which has left its traces on our clothing; and these trees, weary for their winter sleep."

Sally told him, "I have to see if Seth's—if he's not hurt too much." She had already turned away from the cab driver and was hurrying up the steps to the hospital.

"I did not intend to distract you," von Madadh apologized, "and I'm as anxious about your son as you are yourself. But the physician who becomes emotionally involved—" he pulled open the hospital's heavy glass door for her, "—does a disservice to his patient."

The gray-haired woman at the reception desk proffered an official smile. "Can I help you?"

"I'm Seth Howard's mother." Sally gasped for breath. "And I came just as fast as I could—we had to call a taxi. Somebody phoned, and said. . . ." She found she could not complete what she had begun; no words came.

"Oh, yes. Mrs. Howard." The receptionist looked properly concerned, as she had no doubt looked concerned many hundreds of times before. "That was me. At night, we're supposed to. The paramedics go through their pockets and purses, you see, and if there's any identification—sometimes there isn't—they bring it in here to me, with the money and the other things."

"I want to see him."

"Of course you do. I'll have to call the Trauma Center and have them send somebody to take you back there. It's what we used to call our Emergency Ward." The receptionist smiled and shook her head. "Makes us seem more up-to-date in Castleview to call it the Trauma Center, I suppose. Besides, most folks don't know what it means. I think they think that helps."

She had pushed numbers on her switchboard while she talked. Now she spoke into the tiny microphone held before her lips by a wire brace. "Trauma Center? Mrs. Howard's here, can I send her back?"

She listened, then nodded. "Mrs. Howard, they'd like you to wait just a minute. It shouldn't be long. They have injured coming in right now, so they're rather busy."

Sally gripped the edge of the desk. "Can't you tell me how he is?"

"Oh, he's fine. He's been hurt, of course, but they don't think he's in any danger."

Sally said, "He was playing football—it's his senior year. He's on the first team."

The receptionist shook her head. "He should have been more careful about his driving. Of course it might not have been his fault. When one of them is a teen-age boy, you always think he caused the accident, but that's not always true."

Chimes sounded softly. The receptionist pushed a button, listened for a moment, and shrugged. "It's been doing that all night," she said. "The phone rings, but when I answer there's nobody there. I suppose it's a problem with the wires. Won't you sit down? Those chairs are very comfortable, and there are magazines and things. It shouldn't be long."

Sally looked around. "Where's the doctor?"

"The one treating your son? That's Dr. de Falla. He's still in the Trauma Center."

"Dr. von Madadh," Sally said. "He came in with me."

Lisa caught up with Shields as he was about to slip out the rear door of the lodge. "Mr. Schindler! Wait, won't you? For just a moment, please."

He unbolted the door. "My name's Shields, actually."

"I wanted to remind you about Sissy. Do you remember her? Your wife met her."

He nodded. "I talked to her when I called here. To some foreign girl, and then to Sissy. I suppose the foreign girl . . ." He jerked his head toward the lounge.

Lisa told him, "We have two, poor Sancha and Lucie. Lucie disappeared first—or anyway I thought she'd disappeared. She'd hidden in your wife's car. Then Wrangler didn't come back, and didn't come back, and finally I went looking for him and Lucie, and found Mr. Roberts. I left him with Sissy and Sancha when I went out again, and Sissy went to check on the horses; she was like that."

Shields nodded—encouragingly, he hoped.

"And she never came back. That's what Mr. Roberts and poor Sancha told me just before Sancha was shot. So if you're going into the barn, if you should find her . . ."

Shields nodded again. "I'll keep my eyes open."

"And Boomer. I forgot all about poor Boomer. He's still out there, if they haven't killed him."

"I'll keep an eye out for Boomer too," Shields promised.

"You've got the key. Do you have a flashlight? It will be pitch dark in the barn, even with the lights on outside—they're on a different switch."

"No, I'm afraid ours got left in the Buick."

"I'll get you one, if you'll just wait. Will you wait?"

He said, "All right," and watched as she hurried off. The truth was that he did not want to wait. If he was going to get hot, he wanted to get it over with, to take the bullet before his nerve failed. He told himself that as soon as Lisa handed him the flashlight he would turn without a word, open the door, and go out—describing to himself exactly how he would move, how he would shut the door behind him.

No, it might be best to turn off the lights in here first, so they would not see him when he went out. Whoever they were.

He pondered that for a moment or two. Then Lisa was back, a long black flashlight in one hand and a big butcher knife in the other. "I thought you might need this, too," she said. "We don't have another gun; Wrangler's was the only one. He used to get a deer every so often."

"That's all right," Shields told her.

"Only during deer season, of course, and he kept it locked up when he wasn't using it. Don't you want the knife?"

Shields was examining the flashlight; he switched it on and off, and thumped the larger end against his palm. "Thanks, but I don't think so. I don't have a sheath for it, and it would be pretty awkward if I had to hold it all the time."

"You could stick it through your belt."

He shook his head. "This is the kind of flash the police use, bigger and heavier than a nightstick. Besides, you or Bob may need the knife yourself while I'm gone."

He had found the light switch when he had toured the lodge inspecting doors and windows; now he flicked it off. "So they won't see me going out," he explained. "You can turn them back on when you hear the door close."

Then there was nothing left but to open the door and step outside. He did so, braced for the shot.

It did not come, and he shut the door behind him as quietly as he could.

The lights inside flashed on at once, illuminating a window six feet to the right of the door. Lisa had been afraid, then—a good deal more frightened than she had appeared. Shields was frightened, too; Sancha's blood had washed away the bravado he might otherwise have felt. Crouching instinctively, he

jogged off into the gloom, wishing he were not quite so tall, and
very much for a familiarity with the ground that he did not in
fact possess. It would be madness, he knew, to use Lisa's
flashlight out here.

He used it just the same, not as a blind man does his
cane—though long, it was not long enough for that—but
extending it above shoulder level to feel his way. Soon he found
himself in what seemed a grove of young trees, each an inch or
two through the trunk. Their bare limbs spattered him with
water and twice slapped him in the face; but there was ample
room between them, and the ground was reasonably, blessedly
level.

A twig snapped under his right foot. He started, thinking for
a second that it had been the snick of a rifle bolt.

Despite the darkness (and it was still very dark, the moon and
stars masked with cloud) his eyes began to adjust. The tree
trunks became visible, narrow bands of blacker darkness
against the night. He had been angling left ever since he had
fled the lights of the lodge; the barn was in sight now
remote-seeming in its circle of electric glare. Walking parallel
to it until he was well behind it, he swung sharply left again to
approach it from behind. He glanced at the luminous dial of his
watch; the trip had occupied about ten minutes. Not bad, he
thought, for an amateur.

Ahead, from the direction of the barn, faint and yet quite
distinct, he heard the mournful clanking of a chain.

Judy's mom braked in Aunt Sally's driveway, and Judy
opened the door and bounced out. Only recently had Judy
been permitted to stay up this late. It was still a thrill, unfamiliar
enough to be exciting. "I'll do it!" She clattered up the porch
steps far in advance of her mom and rang Aunt Sally's doorbell.

The slow, sad chiming from Aunt Sally's house reminded
Judy that her uncle was dead, though that seemed a long, sad
time ago and Judy did not like to think about anything being
dead. "It's all dark," she called to her mom.

Coming up the steps, her mom said, "She's probably gone to bed. Grandpa said he called but nobody answered."

"But we have to wake her up." Judy was afraid they would have to go home.

"She'll want to know that he's all right. She's got enough trouble without worrying about your grandpa."

There were soft footsteps inside the house, though no light showed through the glass in the front door.

"Somebody's coming!"

Judy's mom nodded. "Maybe she's having a problem with the electricity, a blown fuse or something."

The door was opened by a big man with a thin, black beard. He did not speak, and after a few seconds Judy's mom said, "I'm Sally's sister Kate. Is she home?"

The man answered, though he seemed to be addressing Judy. "Not at the moment. I expect her very soon. Won't you please come in?"

He opened the door wide, and Judy walked slowly into her aunt's dark hall.

Judy's mom asked, "May I turn on the lights?"

"Yes, of course. I have just awakened; I have been looking for the controls, but I fear I am not adept at it. Per'aps you know where they are?"

Judy whispered, "Mommy, I'm scared," but so softly that her mom did not hear it.

Then some lights came on and Judy felt better—although it seemed to her that they should have been brighter, Aunt Sally's lights coming on all of a sudden like that after the dark. But the man looked a lot smaller in the light, which Judy considered a great improvement.

Judy's mom was looking at him, too. "Did you say you just woke up? Have you been sleeping here?"

He nodded. "We concluded a business transaction and had a few drinks on it—or at least I did. I was extremely fatigued; I have been traveling a good deal. I ought to have known better than to drink on an empty stomach. Would you care for

anything, by the way?" He opened the living room door and
motioned them in.

Judy's mother shook her head and switched on the chande-
lier.

"Anyway I nodded off, and when I woke the lights were out. I
suppose your sister thought it would be best to let me sleep
which was kind of her."

The man had been standing with his back to the door; Judy's
mom did not hear the faint squeak as the key turned in the lock
but Judy did, and the rusty snick of the bolt.

Judy's mom said, "And you have no idea where she's gone?"

"Not the slightest, actually. I can only tell you that she did
not mention an errand during our discussion. Since she left me
here, I assume she will return shortly."

"I noticed that the Oldsmobile was gone as I drove up, but I
didn't think Sally would go out. I thought Seth probably took
it."

The man nodded. "He did, as a matter of fact. Mrs. Howard
expressed some anxiety about him while we spoke. For myself,"
he touched his chest, "I can say only that I felt her concern a bit
premature; I doubt that there is any need for you and this
enchanting child to share it. Tell me, does your daughter come
here often? It must be a wonderful place for a little girl to play
hide-and-seek, this big old house of mine." As he spoke, he
advanced to the center of the room. Judy edged toward the
dining-room door.

"Of yours?" Judy's mom sounded surprised.

"Yes. I have purchased it. Mrs. Howard and I concluded the
arrangement tonight."

Judy's mom pursed her lips. "Tom didn't want to sell it, not
really. I could tell."

The man nodded again. "Only too true. When I approached
him, he confided that he had decided to retain it, commuting to
his new position. He assured me that he could make the trip in
less than an hour. Thus when I heard that he had passed away
I contacted your sister."

"I see. That was quick."

"We wanted this house very badly, and neither your sister nor I saw any reason to delay. Per'aps I should also tell you that she will continue in residence here, as my tenant."

"Really?" Judy's mother bent to pick up the card lying on the coffee table. "Is this yours? Are you Dr. Rex von . . . ?"

She looked up as she spoke, and discovered that both Judy and the new owner were gone.

21

IN THE TRAP

SALLY PICKED up an old issue of *Newsweek*, put it down again, and remembered that she had done the very same thing at least twice before. This won't do, she told herself. Seth isn't dying. If he were, they certainly wouldn't make me wait like this. They'd have somebody get me right away, because they'd know I'd sue—I'll sue the britches off them, if Seth dies with me sitting out here. (Oh, please, dear God, don't let my son die!) There are plenty of lawyers in this town.

That reminded her of Fee, with his lawyer-like briefcase. Had he taken it when he disappeared, or was it still leaning against the coffee table? There might be something in there that could be turned against him. Yes, there might! She would blackmail him if she had to, tell the FBI, do whatever she had to do to get Fee out of her house.

The gray-haired receptionist said, "Pardon me?"

Sally looked up. "I didn't say anything."

"Oh. Sorry."

The switchboard chimed, and the receptionist turned away to answer it. "Yes, doctor." Head cocked, she listened for what seemed at least a minute to Sally. "It was a wrong number, you say? I'll call them. I know the place."

There was an airplane on the cover of *Newsweek*. The main article was about air travel or about bombing, Sally could not be sure which—no, it was about both, about terrorists who put bombs on airplanes. Because of all those bombs that have been dropped out of airplanes, she thought. It comes right back to you. Everything comes back to you in the end.

An oriental came into the reception room and stood quietly beside the desk, a small neat man Sally recalled having seen—without really noticing—before; there was something bothersome about him now, she thought.

The receptionist pushed buttons and turned to the oriental. "Yes, sir. What can I do for you?"

He handed her a note. She glanced at it and said, "I'm sorry, but he's still in the Trauma Center. He should be out soon. Would you like to take a seat?"

He went to the plastic chair farthest from Sally's and sat down. Soon she saw him fish out a battered pack of Camels and a folder of matches; the yellow flame trembled when he held it to his cigarette.

They're supposed to be so calm, she thought, but they're human after all when somebody they love is hurt. Of course I should have known.

When he replaced the Camels, she glimpsed something that seemed made of smooth brown wood and steel. It looked, Sally thought, exactly like the handle of a big kitchen knife.

Mercedes lay upon a narrow cot in the Trauma Center. They had given her a drug, she was sure; she felt vague and strange, as if she were awake, yet dreaming. It seemed that she recalled the feeling, now, from the months in the womb—that she had felt thus before she was born, hearing as though through wool remote sounds, seeing everything her mother had without understanding anything, from a strange perspective. And that only now could she remember this, when such a seeing time had come once more; that she would forget everything as soon as she was well, if she was ever well.

The blond woman was no longer with her, yet Mercedes could see her from where she lay, crouched by the man who was getting so much blood. She was whispering to him; and though her words were never clear, it seemed to Mercedes that they were taunts at times, and at others words of love. The tall thin man paced up and down, looking angry and dead.

Seth bent over her cot, leaning on the arm of a big man with a red-gold beard. "So how are you feeling?" Seth asked. Half his face was swathed in bandages.

"Spaced out."

"I can't hear you. Louder—okay?"

"Spacy. How about you?"

"I can't gripe. I went through the windshield, that's what somebody said. They say I got a concussion, and I guess my face is cut up pretty bad." He grinned, a lopsided grin that broke her heart. "I won't rate with you girls any more, but I'm still alive. I'm glad you're not marked."

Oh, Seth.

She sat up, though it seemed someone had taped a block of concrete to her head. "They can fix things. There are doctors who specialize in that, I'm pretty sure."

The bearded man nodded. "I'm one of them."

"And he can be fixed, can't he?"

"He certainly can." The bearded man patted Seth lightly on the shoulder. "But your mother's waiting for you. Wouldn't you like to see her? She's very worried."

Seth said, "Sure, if they'll let me out of here. Mercedes, I'm truly, truly sorry I got you into this. That's all I wanted to say."

She smiled as nicely as she could. Her face felt numb; she suspected she was smiling like a drunk. "Sorry you took me out to look for the castle? Next time I'll take you, okay?"

"Okay!" He grinned again, touched her arm. "Hey, that's a date."

And then they were gone, and the doctor, in his white coat, was walking out of the Trauma Center with a paramedic who wore a white jacket and white trousers.

Almost immediately (or so it seemed to Mercedes) Seth came

back and stood in the doorway looking around. She waved to him, but he paid no more attention to her than to anyone else. After a moment, his right hand slipped into his blue and green letter jacket, as if to make certain that something there had not been lost. He did it without unzipping the jacket, and as Mercedes lay down again she thought about what a swell trick it was. She would have to get him to teach her.

The noise was coming from the barn—Shields had thought so before, and now he felt sure of it. Furthermore, the rear doors Lisa had mentioned were no longer locked; there would be no need for the key in his pocket. One wide door stood a quarter open already. Torn free of the wood, the hasp and padlock lay on the ground in front of it.

Logic told Shields that it was in the brightly illuminated circle around the barn that danger lay. Fear warned him of the darkness in the barn. He thumbed the sliding switch of the big flashlight and dashed toward the open door.

It seemed to take an eternity to cross the strip of yellow light. He was not out of breath, his sprint had been too short for that; but it felt as though he ran, not in air, but through a clear jelly that slowed every movement of his legs to a clumsy absurdity— jelly that soon would harden altogether, leaving him suspended in the light like a spider cast in Lucite. Pear jelly. Ann had mentioned it, and he had only one pair of legs. Perhaps that was the problem. A target should have more legs.

If he was a target, he was surely a target for beginners, meant more to give them confidence than to test their freshman skills.

Then it was over and the dark opening rose narrow and high before him. He darted through, lost his balance and went flying as he tripped over something or somebody just beyond the light.

A boxer's fist, the barn floor knocked the wind out of him and sent the flashlight spinning away. For a minute or more he sprawled, gasping for breath. When he rose, cautiously and even fearfully, still breathing noisily though he struggled not to, he found that the quarter-open door had swung shut. He assured himself that he had bumped it as he dove inside.

The interior of the barn was as dark as any pit except for a single bale of straw, radiant to no purpose in the beam of his fallen flashlight. He could hear the horses stir and snort in their stalls, and the hard thudding of their iron-shod hoofs on the boards. The air was heavy with their odor, but reeking too with the stench of carrion.

The chain clinked as it had before. A pencil-line of light showed that it was between him and the rear doors.

As silently as he could, he made his way down the barn to the flashlight, knowing that as soon as it moved, whoever (or whatever, he thought) was in the barn with him would know that he held it. Stealthily he closed his hand on the long, heavy, black tube—then swung the beam around as quickly as he could.

The mild eyes of horses shone in the light as they watched him over the tops of their stall doors; at the other end of the barn, near the doors that opened toward the lodge, one whinnied. Something misshappen, small and dark, crouched before the door through which he had come.

His hand shaking uncontrollably, he directed the beam toward it again, and this time held it there. For an instant he seemed to see a half-human figure; there was a fleeting impression of gleaming teeth, surmounted by a swarm of fireflies. In a moment he realized that it was only a very soiled child, a boy of about nine.

"Well, well," Shields said. "What are *you* doing here?"

"Please, mister. Please!"

Shields stepped over to the boy, reflecting that it was no wonder those eyes had sparkled in the flashlight beam—they were full of tears. "I don't think you belong in here, sonny. Are you staying at this camp? Nobody's mentioned you."

The boy shook his head, pointing in the general direction of a pile of loose hay in the corner. "Over there a ways."

"And what seems to be the matter?"

"I'm caught!" Sobbing, the boy indicated his foot. Steel jaws—smooth, not toothed like the jaws of the traps Shields had seen in cartoons—gripped the boy's ankle; a chain as massive as a tow ended at a big staple in the floor.

"Get me loose, mister, please. Please!" The boy's grimy hand clasped Shields's wrist with infantile weakness. "I'll do anything you want me to, and I swear I'll never, ever come here any more. Oh, please!"

"I'll try," Shields promised. He bent to examine the trap, shining his light on its simple, well-greased mechanism. As he studied its jaws, trigger plate, and bow springs, it seemed that something stirred, something as large as a horse that was not a horse, unless there was a horse loose in the dark barn, a horse out of its stall. Vaguely, he remembered Lisa's Boomer; Boomer had not been stalled or even hitched to a post, and had bolted at the first shot.

Straightening up, Shields swept the entire length of the barn with his flashlight beam, but saw nothing.

Could Lisa's horse have gotten into the barn? Of course he could have; one door had been ajar. In fact, it seemed likely enough that he *would* return to the barn, a place he must surely associate with food and shelter. But it was utterly impossible for there to be a horse in the barn that could not be seen.

"Can't you make it let go?" the boy whimpered.

"I think so. It looks like all you have to do is stand on the springs. Put it flat on the floor so I can get my weight on them and bend them down."

The boy looked at him helplessly.

"Here." Shields positioned the trap. "Now hold it like that for a minute."

He put the instep of his shoe on one spring and leaned on it. The spring bent gratifyingly, and there was a sharp click as the trigger mechanism caught it.

"That's one. Now we'll do the other the same way, then you should be loose. Pull your foot straight out, without touching that flat plate."

The boy sniffled, wiping his nose on one bare forearm. "All right."

The second spring bent as easily as the first, and the jaws parted. Gingerly, the boy drew his foot free; when it was clear of the trap, he spat on his hands and rubbed his ankle. Shields stooped to look at the bruise.

"Don't burn me with your light, mister, please."

"It's not hot, sonny." Shields put his hand over the lens to demonstrate.

There was a dry rustling behind him, and he started to turn around. Arms thicker than human thighs seized him, crushing him against the hairy chest of something that towered above him; the carrion stench was suffocating, as if the creature were rotting.

His left arm was pinned to his side; but his right, with the flashlight, was still free. He swung the flashlight at the unseen head above him like a club, and it hit with a solid thud, the note of a dull axe in a hard knot. The mighty arms did not loose at all, crushing him, bending him back.

He struck again with desperate strength, and the flashlight went out. His spine was bowing backward; instinctively, he had raised his feet, but the slight relief it had given was already gone. Ribs and straining vertebrae creaked like rusty hinges. Somehow he managed a last, despairing yell, the agonized protest of a dying animal.

An answering roar sounded outside, louder than the hunting cry of a pride of lions. The wide doors at the end of the barn burst inward.

22

THE ASSASSIN

THE OTHER door went to the big dining room. Judy had opened it softly and darted through to where the thick carpet let her move quietly, knowing that the man would have to go around the long table while she ducked under and scooted to the other side where the door to the kitchen was—you could go through the kitchen to the back door, and onto Aunt Sally's back porch, and then you'd be safe, you could run down the street and he'd never catch you.

But she heard the squeak of the hinge as she went under the table. Fingers brushed her skirt as she jumped up, so he'd gone underneath too, but he should have left the door open so there'd be light for him to see her.

The kitchen door was no good now, he'd guess that was where she was going, so Judy dodged to one side, around the chairs and the big table until she knew somehow that he was waiting at the kitchen door, then she got under the table again and ran through the hall door instead, knowing that he was right behind her and she had only fooled him for not even a minute. His flying feet made less noise than hers in the hall.

The kitchen door swung both ways—you just had to push it. Judy remembered, pushed, ducked into the kitchen, and flattened herself against the wall.

He came after her, a silent whirlwind that sped to the back

door to catch her before she got out, as she had known he would. In a wink she was in the hall again, hearing Mom's slow step in the living room and knowing that running to her would only bring more trouble. (Judy had made Daddy leave, she knew she had.)

The back stairway door was almost across from the kitchen door. She flew through it and up the long straight stair; the twisty steps were at the other end, with the front door at the bottom. But he was at the bottom of the twisty steps too, and coming fast on feet lighter even than hers. She ran up instead, feeling frightened and heavy and clumsy, as she had when she had found the baby bird.

For a second she paused to listen in the little tower room. The window where you could look out at the woods ought to have been full of black night sky, but was golden with candlelight. Another tower stood there like a tall man waiting, so near that its little balcony almost touched the windowsill. Judy opened the window though it was stiff with paint, climbed across, and slammed it shut behind her.

I'm seeing double, Mercedes thought. Seth was standing by the door in his green and blue letter jacket, hesitating (so it appeared) as the blonde. . . .

Ms. Morgan. Mercedes nudged herself. Viviane Morgan. . .

And the tall thin dead-looking Jim. . . .

And now Ms. Morgan herself had left the man who was getting so much blood—so God-damned much blood. Would he get AIDS, and would she?

Ms. Morgan was talking to Seth.

But Seth had come through the door with his blue and green jacket hanging all to pieces, Seth on the arm of an orderly or a paramedic or whatever the hell. And Seth hardly looked a Seth, or Jim, or Ms. Morgan.

And now Seth was going back to bed, and Seth was going over to the bed of the man getting blood, and Mercedes sat up and put her legs over the side of her bed and stood up.

The Trauma Center rocked and rolled. She was on a ship, a boat, a roll. Never take brownies from a stranger.

"Seth?" She waved her good arm. "Hey, Seth?"

One Seth looked but one did not, and the man who had been getting so much blood sat up looking as woozy as she felt and said, "Sissy? That you, Sissy? What'n Blazes you doin' away out here, girl?"

Ms. Morgan screamed, "Strike! *Strike!*"

And suddenly this Seth had a thin and gleaming knife. He raised it to stab the man, and somebody shouted. Mercedes was holding his wrist with her good hand before she realized that the shout had been hers. This Seth—it was exactly like waking up from a dream, or at least so she told herself afterward. The man with the knife was not Seth, and Seth was holding back his arm too. The man with the knife was Chinese, older than Seth, and shorter. And the Chinese with the knife was wearing a white waiter's coat, not a green and blue letter jacket; there was no way she could have mistaken him for Seth.

Yet she had.

He tried to push her down, and she hit him on the side of the head with the plastic splint on her broken arm. It hurt in a vague, far-off way that was almost pleasurable. She hit him again.

Seth had one arm around his neck. He and Seth fell to the floor together, and the knife went skittering toward a startled nurse. Mercedes chased it and picked it up.

The nurse said, "What in the world . . . ?"

"It's a boning knife," Mercedes explained. "My mother has one. Mother's is a little nicer, though. My mother has every kitchen gadget there is, even a fish poacher and a big expresso machine. She calls it *la batterie de cuisine*. It's for taking the bones out of capons—stuff like that." Mercedes discovered that she was giggling and tried to stop. "I mean the knife is, not the expresso poacher." She collapsed in helpless laughter.

It seemed like a long time later when the deputy came and got her. They had given her a private room, and he knocked on the doorframe to wake her up. "Mercedes? That's your name? I always thought it was just a car."

"Yeah," she told him. "So'd I. The hell with it."

He had a wheelchair. "You feel up to talking a little with the sheriff?"

A nurse—not the same nurse—peeked in through the doorway. "Let me help you."

Mercedes told them she could walk, but they insisted that she sit in the wheelchair. The deputy, who had a thin mustache and was as tall as her father and a great deal heavier, held it for her while the nurse helped her into it and tucked a blanket around her legs. "You've had quite a shock," the nurse clucked. "What if you were to faint? These floors are *hard*."

"She ain't going to faint," the deputy said. "I hear she's a scrapper." When they were out in the hall on their way to the elevator, he added, "You saved his bacon for that young fellow from Arizona—that's what he says. A lady from the newspaper came to talk to you and take your picture, but they wouldn't let her. She'll be back tomorrow."

Mercedes's head hurt; shutting her eyes seemed only to make it worse. "What time is it, please?"

"'Bout tenish. That arm hurt you much?"

It had not, until he reminded her of it.

The elevator doors slid open before he pushed the button, and a woman and the big doctor with the red-gold beard stepped out.

Mercedes exclaimed, "Mrs. Howard! Hi, Mrs. Howard—I mean good evening."

Sally smiled wearily. "Oh, hello. You're a friend of Seth's, aren't you?"

Mercedes nodded. "He's okay, too. He's cut up a little, but he'll be all right. Are you going to see him?"

The bearded doctor asked, "You don't happen to know whether he's awake? We wouldn't want to wake him up."

Mercedes shook her head. "I remember you. You're the plastic surgeon."

Sally said, "I suppose I'm being a nuisance. I've seen him once already—Dr. von Madadh was kind enough to bring him out to me for a moment when he was still in the Trauma Center. But he wanted to leave us alone for a while, and they didn't like that. An intern saw Seth and made him go back, but now it's all right. They said I could go up and see him."

The deputy rumbled, "Guess you've had kind of a troublesome night, haven't you, ma'am?"

"Oh, it's you. I'm sorry I forgot—so much has happened."

The chair rolled into the elevator and the doors closed. "Smells funny in here," the deputy said.

"Why does the sheriff want to see me?"

"I guess he'll tell you."

The elevator slid silently to a stop. "You were at Mrs. Howard's tonight." Mercedes had nearly said *Seth's mother's*.

"Two-three hours ago."

"Was something the matter there?"

The deputy hesitated. Mercedes could not see his face as he wheeled her along the corridor, but she knew he was mulling over the advisability of telling her about it. At last he said, "Her pa's lost—his name's Leonard Robert Roberts, but everybody calls him Bob. Don't suppose you know him?"

"Sure I do," Mercedes said. "He works for my parents."

They stopped abruptly. "You're Mr. Shields's daughter? The one that has the cars now?"

"Yes, sir," Mercedes said, trying to sound like a girl who never got into trouble.

There was another pause. "I believe you'd better tell me just exactly what your name is."

"Mercedes Schindler-Shields." She struggled to keep from lapsing into singsong. "Schindler's my mother's name, and she wouldn't give it up. Shields is my dad's name, and he wouldn't give *that* up. So she's Mrs. Schindler, and he's Mr. Shields, and I'm Mercedes Schindler-Shields."

"Ah," the deputy said. "The sheriff gave me your name, but

Gene Wolfe

I thought it was all one word—Shindlersheelds. I don't suppose you know where Bob Roberts has got to?"

Mercedes shook her head. "I didn't even know he was gone."

"He was with your pa when he disappeared."

"You're kidding!"

"Nope. There's a couple of officers that think your pa had something to do with it, too. But I don't." After a moment the wheelchair glided forward again.

The sheriff did not look at all as Mercedes had expected. He was certainly no bigger than average, and might have been a bit smaller. His wavy black hair and smooth face made him seem not much older than Seth. "Well, hello there," he said. "How are you feeling?"

"Okay," she told him; but the deputy was already whispering in his ear, and she heard the name *Shields*. "I'm his daughter," she said. "You can ask me about Mr. Roberts if you want to, but I don't know anything about it. This guy told me while we were coming down here."

The sheriff smiled—he had good teeth—and glanced at the deputy, and the deputy went out and closed the door behind him. The sheriff said, "Would you tell me about the last time you saw your father? That would be earlier this evening, I imagine?"

"That's right. We went to look at another house. My folks want to buy a house here."

The sheriff nodded encouragingly.

"Then we went back to the motel. We're staying at the Red Stove Inn for now."

The sheriff nodded again.

"Then Dad wanted to go out to the dealership and check on things there. Mom and I didn't want to go, so he went alone."

"About what time would that have been?"

"Maybe five or five-thirty. It was pretty dark, but it gets dark early now, and it was raining."

"And you haven't seen him since?"

"No, sir."

"All right." The sheriff straightened up as though their interview were over, although Mercedes felt certain it was not. "I wanted to tell you, you're one brave little girl, smacking that Chinaman the way you did. You hit him with that cast on your arm, is that right?"

She shook her head. "I didn't have it then; they had my arm in a long plastic thing, taped down. They hadn't set the bone."

"I see." The sheriff leaned back and made a little steeple with his fingers. It made him look older.

I was right, Mercedes thought. *This isn't nearly over. No way.*

"Now just exactly when did you first see the Chinaman?"

Mercedes bit her lip. "I think it was when he first came into the Trauma Center."

"Good. Good. Was he alone?"

"Yes, sir."

"And what did he do after he came in?"

Mercedes said, "He just stood there awhile, looking around. I don't think he had expected so many people."

"And then?"

"Ms. Morgan came over and talked to him. She was telling him to go ahead, I think."

"Who's Ms. Morgan?"

Mercedes shrugged; it hurt, and she resolved not to do it again. "The woman who was sitting in back with me when we had the accident. She wasn't hurt, but I guess they brought her in anyway to check her out."

The sheriff nodded slowly, scratched his nose, and picked up a sheet of paper. "Describe her, please."

"She's shorter than I am, and—about a size eight. She's blond and really cute. She has long—"

The door opened, and the plastic surgeon looked in. "I'm sorry," he said. "Seth Howard's not here?"

23

THE TOWER BY THE SEA

THE DOUBLE doors at the far end of the barn seemed to explode, smashed inward by sound and blinding light. Bigger and faster than any charger, light roared down the broad aisle between the stalls. For an instant the blare of a discordant trumpet rose above the roar, shriller and shriller until it was higher than the scream of brakes.

Shields flew, the barn floor dizzy overhead.

He had been asleep and wished to sleep again, but he could not. Everything hurt—or if there was anything that did not, he was unconscious of it, could not discover it; there was too much pain for him to explore it all, too much for him to do anything but try to push it away.

The floor was bounding and jolting beneath him, every jar a separate and distinct agony. A chill wind whistled unceasingly, a wind wet with rain.

"How you feeling, son?"

Shields wanted to spit; he swallowed instead. He had never swallowed anything like that before, and decided it had probably been clotted blood. "Bob?"

"It's me all right, Mr. Shields." Roberts was sitting very close, with his legs crossed and his head bent. "How are you? Think anything's broken?"

"How the hell should I know?"

"I ran my hands all over you and couldn't find anything, but I couldn't be sure. I didn't want to flex everything to see. Don't sit up—roof's pretty low."

"We're in a truck, aren't we?"

From somewhere Ann called, "Willie, is that you? Are you all right?"

"No!"

"That's my Willie."

Roberts told him, "We're in the back of that old Cherokee you took off the lot, Mr. Shields."

Lisa Solomon's voice: "My old car. I had to sell it."

"It's yours again," Shields told her. "I just gave it back to you."

"*Willie!*"

"Ann, shut the hell up." He resolved to be quiet himself; but as soon as he fell silent, pain rushed upon him. He turned and thrashed, vainly seeking a position that hurt less than the previous one.

"Lie still, son. That don't do no good."

"What makes it so windy in here?"

Lisa said, "That maniac smashed the windshield the second time he shot."

Roberts was tucking a blanket around Shields, who had not been aware of it until now. "How's Sancha?"

"About the same," Lisa told him. "Once in awhile she says something, but it's in Portuguese."

"Sancha's on the back seat," Roberts explained to Shields. "Lisa's taking care of her. We put her in there first, and we didn't want to move her again."

"Bob, what happened to the ape?"

Ann called, "What'd you say, Willie?"

"The ape—I was wrestling with an ape." Painfully, Shields lifted himself on one elbow, impelled by an invalid's weak anger in the face of contradiction. "And don't tell me I wasn't, Ann. I was."

She called triumphantly, "See! I told you."

Roberts whispered, "She said she ran over a gorilla. Lisa and me were still ducked down, so we didn't see it. I figured she'd hit one of those horses. I don't know what Lisa thought."

"It was going to kill me," Shields said. "It was trying to break my back." He remembered how near he had come to death and shook with a chill against which the blanket could do nothing.

". . . and so you could see Sancha was going to die." Roberts was advancing some argument whose opening phases Shields had not heard. "So I said the heck with this, give me the keys and I'll put her in the car, and if he gets me he gets me. But your wife said you had the keys and if she'd had them she would've gone already. Then Lisa said there was another set, up in Wrangler's room. So we did it, and she got in back with Sancha. I was up front with your wife."

Ann called, "She was *dying*, Willie. The lights hadn't gone off, and we didn't know *where* you were. Besides, Emily called— So Lisa gave me Wrangler's keys and Bob carried Sancha."

"Anyhow," Roberts continued, "your wife started her up, and we were about to pull out when we heard something—"

"I heard *you*, Willie. You yelled just like you do when you have nightmares. I'd know that yell anywhere, because it always wakes me up."

Shields muttered, "I think I must have been dreaming about this. You saved my life." But he spoke too softly for her to hear him.

Roberts said, "She just spun this clunker around and went bang through those doors. I never seen anything like it outside of a movie."

"And there was this tall ape, Willie, right in my lights. I knew he must have been after you, so I went for him. At the last minute I got chicken and put on the brakes, but we still hit him pretty hard. Where were you?"

"I'll tell you later. Did you see a little boy?"

"A kid?" Ann asked. "No, I certainly didn't, just the ape or gorilla or whatever it was, and it was dead, I think. Where it came from, I can't imagine, unless it escaped from some zoo. Calamity Annie meets King Kong! Was it really chasing a kid, too, Willie?"

Ann braked for the main gate, and Lisa sprang out to open it. For a moment the domelight flooded the inside of the old Cherokee with weak illumination. In it, Roberts caught Shields's eye. Shields said, "No, Ann, I don't think it really was."

There was an old rug on the wall behind the candlesticks. Judy hid in back of that for what seemed like a long while, but when she came out it was still dark, and all the candles were still burning.

At least they looked like candles when she looked right at them, tall candles with wax the color of skin, some thick, some thinner, and some very thin, all of them tall; but if she looked at something else—at the floor or the old rug with its bounding lions and sad unicorns—they were not candles at all, but ladies crowned with fire, ladies who stood and burned as quietly as if they were thinking, with eyes and faces shut like little stores that have turned against you, locking up their doors while their lights are still on inside and the people who seemed so friendly walk around moving things and pretending not to see you. Judy spit on two fingers and tried to pinch out one of the candles. Fire rose around her wet fingers, hotter and madder than ever, and she snatched them away.

She had heard nothing and no one while she hid in back of the rug; it had seemed to her that she had this whole place to herself. She knew that the man with the terrible hands had not followed her because she would have heard him. Quiet though he was, he was not that quiet. Now she listened again, and again heard only stillness; and yet it did not seem the stillness of mere emptiness. It was, she told herself, just like the whole place were full of people with bees on them, people not moving at all. Standing or sitting absolutely still was a thing that Judy could not do, although she often tried. Even when she had hidden behind the rug, she had moved, even though she had been so quiet—swaying from side to side without moving her feet, and pushing back her hair with one hand and then the other.

She chewed a lock of hair ruminatively while listening to the bees. Would the people talk if she told them she knew? She doubted it—not coming out would make her feel silly, and they *wanted* her to feel silly. Or at least she hoped it was no worse than that.

The door by which she had come into the tower stood open. Night breezes crept through like the smallest children and tried to wake the candles by touching their hair. The tower room of Aunt Sally's house was gone; Judy should have been able to see Aunt Sally's through the doorway, but the stars were there, far and cold and bright, like the lights of Davenport when Mom had gone away with Judy in the back pretending to sleep but really peeking out through the wide back window and watching lights get smaller and smaller as they grumbled across the river and purred up into the hills.

She went out onto the balcony and looked around.

The tower—this tower—was higher than she had thought; she could see a long way. Aunt Sally's house was there, but it was far away and getting farther and farther all the time, floating off like the bright toy boat she used to sail on the lake in the park. Between Aunt Sally's tower and this one were black waves, more waves and more water than Judy had ever seen.

The air had a new smell. Inside, even the little breezes had been scented by the candles, as warm and bright as so many waxy flowers. The new smell was not a sweet one but sharp and stinging, like Daddy's aftershave. Judy spit out the hair and patted her mouth. This was not a good smell, but she liked it; lately she had noticed that she liked bad smells, sometimes.

But Aunt Sally's house was floating away with Mom inside; Judy would have to go downstairs and find somebody with a boat. She returned to the room where the candles burned, eyes leaking tears.

It felt hot and stuffy inside the tower now, and the candle ladies were just candles, because Judy was watching them. The other door was made of wide boards and looked thick and heavy. It had no knob, only an iron bar from which a string hung. The bar lay in a bent one fastened to the doorframe. Judy tried to lift the first bar, but both were old; they had rusted together like glue. The big hinges were rusty too, rotting into a rough powder that blackened her thumb and stained her fingers orange, green, crimson, and violet.

Judy did not like to knock on doors (it hurt her knuckles) so she kicked it instead. Her kicks made an empty booming noise like men emptying garbage cans in the next block. At the sound, all of the people she could not hear stirred without making any noise, though the bees did not seem to care. The stirring made her stop kicking.

She examined the door to the balcony. It was smaller, and its latch and hinges were hardly rusted; she could move it with a touch. The wind ran through the doorway and ruffled all the candle flames. Judy discovered that when its hands were in the fire she could see them, fingers and thumbs, and that it had a great many more hands than she, enough to touch all the flames at once.

She went out onto the balcony again and leaned across the railing to watch Aunt Sally's house. The railing was stone and came almost up to her armpits, but it felt old and shaky, as if nothing was holding its stones together except the ivy. Once, ever so softly, she heard two stones grate, one sliding on the other. She stood up straight and just rested her hands on the stones after that.

All of Aunt Sally's lights were on, all her windows bright and yellow, like the eyes and noses and mouths of a whole family of jack-o'-lanterns. Judy pictured her mom running from room to room in that big house, switching on the lights and calling her. Her mom had even gone up into the high old attic, where Judy was not allowed because she would get dirty—all the little windows that pulled the roof around their heads were yellow, too. And it seemed to Judy that they and all the rest became brighter as they floated away. Pretty soon Mom would ask somebody to help, Judy decided, but no nice policeman would ever find her up here. Nobody would ever find her to take her home.

There was a loud click behind her.

The door of the room filled with candles had swung shut. A moment passed before Judy pushed on it, but if she had pushed at once she would still have been too late. She might as well have matched her small strength against the great, dark stones of the tower.

When it was quite clear that the door would not budge, she stopped, gasped for breath, and dried her eyes on the hem of her skirt. There was a hole not much bigger than her finger in the door where a doorknob should have been. When she put her eye to it, she could peer into the room beyond, bathed in golden light as before; and in fact she could see the tall candle ladies even when she looked right at them: so many smooth-faced ladies, all ivory and white. Their big dark eyes were open wide and moved, looking now at Judy's own as it peeped at them through the hole, now at one another, now at something moving, that Judy could not see.

Effort had left her warm, but the wind from the sea chilled her quickly. Soon, she thought, she would be very cold. In a long time it would be morning; the sun would come, and then—perhaps—people on the ground could see her when she waved from this high porch. They would (maybe) climb the stairs and open the door in the room where the candle ladies burned.

Or at least they would, Judy thought, if it weren't that the latch was latched on the inside. They would have to break down the door, probably; and meanwhile she would starve if the cold wind had not frozen her first. She did not know how long it took somebody to starve, but she suspected it was not very long.

She went back to the stone railing. Aunt Sally's house had drifted out of sight; there was nothing left but the sea, tossing andkerchiefs in the starlight. She stood on tiptoes and leaned over, looking way down. It was so far to the bottom that she ould not tell how far it was, but not straight up-and-down like he wall of a house. It sloped instead, exactly like the side of a teep hill covered with ivy. That would be thickest at the ottom, she decided—or if it was not thick, then at least there vould have to be a lot of big branches like a tree's. Judy had climbed big trees before.

Far below, an owl fluttered slowly against the leaves like a moth. There were little day-birds hiding there, and she heard heir soft, clear voices: *"Look out!" "Don't go!" "Look out!" "Don't fly!" "Look out!"*

The wind stirred the ivy as she scrambled over the railing, but there were a million places to put her feet and jillions of handholds, although some tore loose when she put her weight on them. She laughed a little bit—just to herself—thinking about how scared she had been.

24

TOM'S TARGET PISTOL

"No," THE sheriff said, "I've finished with the Howard boy.

"He's not up in his room, either." The plastic surgeon gnawed his lip.

"I'm sure you'll find he's around here someplace, Mr.—"

"Doctor," the plastic surgeon corrected him absently. "Dr von Madadh." He snapped his fingers. "I think I've got it."

"Might be in X-ray," the sheriff suggested helpfully.

"And you're the girl who assisted him." Von Madad stepped into the room. "You were wonderfully brave, I'v heard." With grace surprising in so large a man, he crouche beside Mercedes's wheelchair so that their eyes met at a leve

He's like a tame lion, Mercedes thought. And indeed ther was something leonine about his sleek, wavy, red-gold hair an full, curling beard.

The sheriff said, "She didn't just assist—she was the mai one. She yelled at the Chinaman, and that's what made hi stop. That's when her boyfriend—that's the Howard boy, th one you're looking for—got hold of him. Then she hit hi with the plastic dingus they had her arm in. That took the figh out of him, and her boyfriend threw him down."

"Wonderful!" von Madadh exclaimed. For a moment h stared into Mercedes's face, and she could almost hear the clic of the shutter.

He rose as gracefully as he had crouched, and brushed the fingers of her good hand with cool lips. "What's your name, my child?"

"Mercedes Schindler-Shields."

"The merciful one. What a lovely name! What a noble name! But what is mercy toward *this* is so often cruelty toward *that*. How well we physicians know it! You saved a life—yet wasn't it at some cost to an unfortunate Chinese?"

Mercedes shook her head. "I didn't think of that then, but it wasn't. If I hadn't stopped him, he'd have been a murderer, and he might have been electrocuted. He couldn't have escaped with so many people around."

Von Madadh nodded and smiled. "Well reasoned, although one can never be certain. I thank you both." He smiled again, and was gone, leaving them alone in the little conference room.

"Not from around here," the sheriff said. "Nice fellow, though. I guess he's just come to work here."

Mercedes nodded cautiously. "I suppose."

"You were about to tell me about this blonde." The sheriff glanced at his notes. "Ms. Morgan—you say you and she were in the back?"

Mercedes nodded.

"And Seth Howard was driving?"

"No. Jim was driving. I heard his last name, but I don't remember it now. It was his car, I think."

The sheriff leaned forward in his chair and scratched his nose. "And what did *he* look like, this Jim?"

Mercedes reflected. "Tall. Probably six four or six five. Seth's pretty tall, and he was a lot taller. Real skinny. You could see the cords in his neck, you know? All the parts. His cheeks pulled in—that might have been because there were teeth gone in back. He needed a shave."

The sheriff had scribbled once or twice while she spoke (he was probably writing his mother, Mercedes told herself); now he asked, "How was he dressed?"

"Old felt hat, leather bomber jacket, jeans like everybody wears, and I didn't notice what kind of shoes. I think he had on a plaid flannel shirt under his jacket."

"And he was out with this Morgan woman? Seemed to be?"

"That's what he said. When he came up to our car, he said his was broken down and he and his date were stuck out there, or something like that. Some girls have funny tastes."

"Uh huh. This was a different car, the one this Jim came up to, your car."

"Seth's mother's car; that was what he told me." After a moment Mercedes added, "I'm sure it was true—there isn't any reason it shouldn't be."

"Where'd all this happen?"

"I don't know the name of it, but it's up on a hill, pretty close to here. There's places to park about a dozen cars, and a stone wall. Seth said we might be able to see the castle from there, but we didn't."

The sheriff nodded. "That's the scenic view on Baker's Knob. It's a lover's lane—I have a man check it a couple of times every night."

Mercedes said, "Well, there wasn't anybody up there when we were."

"I can't keep somebody up there all the time. I don't have that kind of manpower. If you two gave this Jim a lift, why was he driving? Are you telling me Seth Howard let a stranger drive his mother's car?"

"That wasn't Seth's car—his mother's." Mercedes paused. "This gets pretty complicated."

"I'll listen."

"Well, Seth had Jim get in our car, and we drove down the hill to his car. But his girlfriend—Ms. Morgan—wasn't there. We thought she'd started to walk home."

The sheriff nodded again, pencil poised.

"So we went down the road a little farther, maybe a quarter mile, and we found her. But then Seth's car wouldn't start. So

Jim walked back up to his car, and this time his car worked, and he said he'd give us a ride back to town."

"His car wouldn't run," the sheriff said slowly, "but then it would."

"Yes, sir."

"So all four of you got in that one—you and this Morgan woman in back, Seth Howard and Jim in front, with Jim driving."

"That's right, sir. That's exactly how it was."

"You went down Baker's Knob Road to the state highway—"

"No, sir," Mercedes interrupted. "We took a shortcut, a dirt road."

"From Baker's Knob onto the highway?"

"Yes, sir."

The sheriff stared at her, tapping the table with the end of his pencil. At last he dropped the pencil, folded his hands, and said, "About how far down does this shortcut turn off?"

"If you mean in elevation, like maybe four hundred feet."

He shook his head. "How far down the road."

"Half a mile. Maybe a little more."

"Does it turn off to the right or the left?"

"To the left, sir."

The sheriff sighed. "Miss Schindler, I've—"

"Schindler-Shields, sir."

"Right, thank you. I was going to say, Mercedes, that I've been sheriff of Castle County for almost five years. I'm in my second term now."

"Good for you, sir."

For a moment he regarded her narrowly. "Before that, I was a state trooper for eight years, and for most of that time I was assigned to the Castleview Barracks, ten miles outside of town. I know the roads around here like the back of my hand. I know Baker's Knob Road like my wife's face."

I'm really in deep shit now, Mercedes thought.

"So let me tell you a couple of things. In the first place,

nobody except you and Seth Howard claims to have seen either the blond woman or the tall man. The officers who were at the scene say there wasn't anybody there like that, and the people here at the hospital say there wasn't anybody like that brought into the Trauma Center. Understand?"

"But—"

"And there's no dirt road from Baker's Knob Road to the highway—not a one, anywhere. And if you were to drive up to the scenic view on Baker's Knob and turn around, and then go down half a mile and turn left, you'd be headed straight down a slope so steep it's almost a cliff. You couldn't stop and you couldn't steer, and the first time you hit a rock, you'd start rolling. If you were lucky as hell, you might get caught in the trees. If you weren't—"

The door opened, and a woman's voice asked, "May I come in, Sheriff? A few pictures for the *View*?"

As though a switch had been thrown, the sheriff smiled. "Of course, of course. Come right in."

It was Viviane Morgan.

"There's been no answer to the page," the receptionist told Sally Howard.

"You remember Dr. von Madadh, don't you? He was sitting right here beside me. A tall man, very nicely dressed, with a reddish beard. You saw him."

The receptionist nodded. "I saw him, but I don't know where he is, and he doesn't answer his page."

"He went to look for my son," Sally told her.

The receptionist said nothing.

"Now I can't find Seth either. How could they lose him like that?"

"This is a hospital," the receptionist told her, "not a prison."

Sally stared at her.

"You son was ambulatory. I know, because Dr. von Madadh brought him out here. They hadn't taken his clothing yet and given him a gown. And then he was angry because Dr. de Falla made him go back. So quite possibly . . ." She let the sentence lapse. After a few seconds she added, "Your Dr. von Madadh is *not* accredited to this hospital. I checked."

"You think that Dr. von Madadh took him home."

The receptionist turned back to her switchboard, although the telephone had not chimed and there were no blinking lights. "It would appear to be a possibility," she said frostily, "since they're both gone."

Sally shrugged, sagging shoulders telling her how tired she was, how very tired. "Would you call me a taxi?"

The receptionist pretended not to hear, and when a minute or more had passed, Sally turned wearily and went out through the heavy glass hospital doors, into the wet, windy night. Most houses here were already dark.

There was no chance of hailing a passing taxi in Castleview this late, she knew—no chance at all. Even during the day, you seldom saw a taxi unless somebody had telephoned for one.

She tried to estimate the distance from the hospital to her house; fourteen blocks, she thought, or perhaps sixteen. At any rate she could walk it. She would not beg that woman for a taxi, no, never. And perhaps she would see somebody she knew, perhaps somebody she knew might offer her a ride. Or if someplace open had a telephone, she could call. Then Kate would come and pick her up. Kate liked to watch TV late; she wouldn't have gone to bed yet.

The rain had ended; but the sidewalk was still dotted with puddles, and icy water dripped from the leafless trees. An old Cherokee Chief skidded dangerously, swinging wide for the abrupt turn into the hospital lot. It seemed to have no windshield at all, so that for an instant Sally saw clearly the drawn face of the woman at the wheel. It was vaguely, naggingly familiar; but Sally did not permit it to nag very long; she was much too tired.

Was this really the day Tom had died? The same day? That did not seem possible, was not possible. It seemed to her that it had been only a year or so ago that they had met in American

History. Lost in a waking dream, she recalled how Tom's smile had lit up his eyes.

Judy was gone. As Kate spooned powdered coffee into one of Sally's cups, she thought about that in the same way she thought about Stan. It hadn't worked out, she and Stan. They had never quite fitted, and now Stan—now Stan's daughter— was gone. Kate really and sincerely hoped that the two of them would be happier out of her life than they had ever been in it, and it was nice to be able to start fresh.

Damned nice.

She should report it to the police, she knew, so that they could laugh at her, that being the key duty, the main point of police. Here was Sally's avocado-green phone, right here on the wall, so why not?

She added boiling water from Sally's teakettle and stirred. Sally had gotten a good man who was crazy about her, or anyway had been while he was alive. Sally liked—loved her kid, even if she understood him no better than she herself had understood Judy. No, worse—much, much worse, because Sally didn't really understand Seth at all; because Seth was a boy, would be a grown man the next time you looked, and who the hell understood *them*?

Kate went to the refrigerator and found a carton of half-and half. When she had been a little kid herself, Mom and Dad had poured thick, yellow, country cream into their coffee; now you couldn't do it, because it made you die too soon. The CIA had a plan for spiking every samovar in Moscow with thick cream, or if it didn't it should. So now Dad had gray hair and false teeth, and he was still working; he had even gotten loose from whoever the hell had stolen him. (Who would want to steal Dad?) And Mom bitched about her feet hurting, when she had walked to town only three times today.

I'm blasted, Kate thought. I haven't had a thing to drink, but I'm blasted anyway because I got blasted when Stanley split and went to bed with that salesman, and now Judy's gone and 'm thinking drunk again. So I may as well have one—it isn't oing to make any difference.

She carried her coffee into the living room and got a fifth of Vild Turkey out of Tom's liquor cabinet; two fingers of Wild urkey improved the instant coffee beyond belief. Tom's target istol lay on the coffee table. She set down her empty cup and ngered the long, black barrel.

Back in the kitchen, there was a sticker on the wall beside the hone that gave the sheriff's number. That was convenient— ou never knew when you might have your kid stolen. Kate vedged the handset between her shoulder and her ear, leaving er a free hand with which to dial.

There was only a single ring before an authoritarian female oice said, "Sheriff Ahern's All-Night Help Line."

"My name's Kate Roberts."

"And what can we do for you, Miz Roberts?"

"I'm at my sister's house. Sally Howard's. I'm afraid I can't emember the address. The big old house on Pine Street?"

"What seems to be the trouble, Miz Roberts?"

"My little girl's gone—her name's Judy. Well, it's really udith Youngberg. She's seven years old, and she has on a pink lress, her good one. And white stockings and maryjanes, ecause Tom's dead."

"Your little girl's run away?"

"No. I mean, yes. She ran away from this man, I think. I ooked down for just a moment, and I heard them running, or hen I looked up, and when I looked they were gone." Like a hostly echo, Kate heard running feet beyond Sally's broken vindow—no, hooves, galloping hooves. Riders crossing the eld behind the house.

"Have you been drinking?"

"Oh, God," Kate said. "Oh God!" How could she make them elieve that this was real, that she was serious? She knew and hrust the knowledge from her.

"Who was the man?"

"I don't know. He told me his name, I think, but I can't

remember. He said he'd bought it." *One swift motion—put the gun to her head and pull the trigger.*

"He bought his name?"

"Bought this house. Listen, please, she's only seven—"

"Then your sister doesn't live there any more."

Very calmly, Kate said, "Please listen, and remember this: tell Stan I was serious, understand? Find Stan, and tell him I was completely serious." Her finger tightened on the trigger.

It moved not a hair. She had expected a very loud bang—a report. You were entitled to a full report before the silence, but there was nothing.

"Who's Stan? Is Stan your sister's husband?"

The safety, of course. There was a switch-thing on these, and unless it was on they wouldn't fire. Kate found the safety and pushed it down with the mouthpiece of the telephone. In her mouth, that was the way.

"Three eleven North Pine? Is that where you're calling from?"

It seemed that there was a safety on her index finger, too; it would not move. The drumming hooves grew louder—big horses, Morgans with ground-devouring legs, real rattlers.

Grandfather had always loved horses. "Why'd you call him a rattler, Grandpa?" "'Cause that's what he is, Katie. See, soon as our folks had gone off somewhere, me an' Jeff would fetch out Cannoneer—that was my pa's Morgan. 'Hold him, Ed,' Jeff'd say, 'Hold him good, till I got him in the traces.' Cannoneer'd toss his head—lifted me clean off my feet one time—but I'd hold on till Jeff had him hitched to the good buggy, an' a good hold on the reins. Then I'd let go, and he'd rear, so I just had time to jump on. Didn't have to crack the whip or nothin' for *him*. No, sir! Off we'd go, knowin' we was goin' to get warmed good for it. Down the hill and over the bridge! Crackin'? Why you never seen the like, Katie! There'd be ol' George Johnson with a load of apples, but he'd not catch sight of us for our dust. The new buggy'd sound like she was about to come apart, and then Jeff, he'd say, 'He's a rattler, ain't he, Ed?' But I wouldn't answer a thing, just hold on with both hands, 'cause he was, for certain sure."

"Hello? Are you still there, Miz Roberts? Hello?"

"Yes," Kate whispered. "Yes, I'm still here." Perhaps she could press the trigger with the thumb of her other hand.

"If you're in somebody else's home—"

The hoofbeats stopped, and Kate glanced at the shattered window. There was nothing, not even a pane of glass, between her and the big—the enormous—man peering in. His face was bearded; above the black hairs his skin was a pale green. His eyes met hers, and at the shock her hand tightened convulsively.

There was no report, no loud noise, only the feeling that she had been struck a terrible blow.

25

ROSARY CHEESECAKE

A WOMAN who looked Italian was saying the rosary. Ann decided it was a swell idea—she could use a big string of worry beads herself, and the prayers. She could use the prayers most of all, and so could her baby, who "just" had a broken arm, they said. (She was talking to the sheriff, okay, but what the hell did they find to talk about? "Lemme tell ya, Miss, I got me a heck of a video tape fer tomorrer night. *True Grit.* Yep, th' Duke hisself.")

So could the dying girl, Ann thought, the Brazilian girl. Sancha, that was her name.

And so could Lisa Solomon; perhaps Lisa most of all. She was sitting quietly on the other side of Bob, but her face was awful, just terrible. The Italian woman completed her rosary and kissed its silver crucifix. Could you use your knuckles?

A cup and a quarter of cookie crumbs.

A quarter cup of white sugar—castor sugar, they call that in England, God knows why.

And a quarter cup melted butter and two and a half *pounds* Philadelphia cream cheese. Because a sugar bowl was a castor, that was why. Sugar-bowl sugar.

Lisa said, "When she dies, will they even tell us?" It was said softly, almost in a whisper, but Ann heard her.

So had Bob; he said, "We'll keep checking." And then, "You mustn't worry."

It was when people told you not to worry that you worried, Ann reflected. More sugar, a scant two cups. That's to go in the filling—the other's for the crust. (The other hand now.) Three tablespoons of white King Arthur flour. Grate the rind of a big lemon.

The Italian woman had begun again; her voice floated softly across the room: *"Holy Mary, Mother of God, pray for us sinners, now and at the hour . . ."*

Then grate half an orange rind the same way. You'll need five large eggs—my mother always thought the brown ones worked best. (Back to the first hand.)

The gray-haired woman at the reception desk said, "This is the hospital, can I speak to Mrs. Howard? What? Why officer—"

And besides those, two egg *yolks*. You have to throw away the whites, or find something else to do with them.

Boomer had a grievance. In fact he had several. There was the smell of blood, just to start with. Blood was bad, it meant bad trouble in the herd. It had sent him galloping off into the night—not that he minded night much—when he should have gotten his saddle off.

He had grazed for a while in the big unfenced meadow west of the lodge, although that was scarcely a grievance. He had pricked his ears at the strange stories the wind told, and had drunk from Indian Creek, all of which was well and even good. But now he was left standing in front of his own personal stall with nobody to unsaddle him and nobody to open the door. That was deeply and disturbingly wrong. Where was Lisa? Where was Wrangler? Where was Sissy? Where was Sancha? Where was—for that matter, though he himself had never liked her. . . .

These thoughts had hobbled through Boomer's slow, tenacious mind a score of times already when, at that exact moment, Lucie strode into the barn. "There you are, you big ox," Lucie said, "all ready to go. Fine with me—*tres bien, mon boeuf.*"

Boomer rolled his eyes and backed off, then made the error of trying to turn. As he swung around, Lucie caught him by the bridle.

He knew already that Lucie was not there to unsaddle him. There is a way a rider looks when she means to take your saddle off, a way when she is just making sure you have hay, a way for grooming, a way for a short ride, a way for jumping, and a way for a long ride. Lucie meant to ride far, and in a moment more she was in his saddle, reining his head hard to the right while bullying him with both her heels. He reflected with a certain satisfaction that Lucie's seat was not quite as good as Lisa's. There were limbs, there were trees—

"Okay, *charogne*, let's see some speed."

He went from a walk to a trot, from a trot to a canter, and from a canter to a gallop before they were out of the barn.

Less than five minutes after Mercedes was wheeled back into her hospital room, Dr. von Madadh entered it, quietly and almost furtively. "I take it that the sheriff has done his worst?"

"I sure hope so."

"As he did with poor Seth. There ought to be a law against policemen who browbeat patients—or rather, there ought to be a law punishing physicians who permit it. I would never allow one of my own to be harassed in the way that you and Seth have been tonight, believe me."

Mercedes sat up. "There was another couple in the car with us, and the sheriff kept going on about them. I guess I should say, about them not really being there and what'd they do, split right after the accident? They didn't, I saw them in the Trauma Center, and— Then he said the hospital didn't write them up."

Von Madadh sighed. "I suppose this is the moment, although I hate to give you a shock. First, let me say that his injuries are fairly minor. Is that understood, Mercedes? They are by no means severe."

"Seth? I thought he got cut up pretty bad."

"No, I wasn't referring to Seth, but to your father. Will Shields is your father?"

"Dad's been hurt? What happened? That's right, his name's Will."

"So I was informed," von Madadh said. "A young friend of mine—a very dear friend—spoke with your parents earlier today. And I must confess to eavesdropping a bit outside before I broke in upon your tête-à-tête with the sheriff. I had hoped to learn Seth's whereabouts without interrupting you."

Unconsciously, Mercedes touched her hair. "Well, did you? Where is he?"

Von Madadh sighed again. "We'll get to that in time; I'll track him down, you may be sure. But meanwhile, don't you want to see your father? He's had an accident, too; and I'm sure he would be here already, sick with worry for you, if he knew that you were here."

"Yes, of course I do."

"Good. You were in a wheelchair when you were interviewed by the sheriff; but from what I overheard about your battle with the unfortunate Hwan, you didn't really need it. Can you walk?"

"Sure." Mercedes swung her legs over the side of the bed. She was very tired—so tired it seemed she stood beside herself and watched her own body as she might have watched an actress.

Von Madadh appeared to sense it. A little sadly he said, "High adventure is best enjoyed at a distance, or so I've heard. Take my arm, please. I will be flattered."

Fee opened the door wide as Sally climbed the steps to the porch. "Ah, there you are! I was afraid something had happened to you. Your son is not badly hurt?"

Sally snapped, "What are you doing in my house? Get out!"

Fee closed the door softly behind her. As he had earlier, he conveyed an impression of deformity without actually showing a crooked back or a clubfoot. "Per'aps you forgot—this house is mine: I bought it from you tonight. You are welcome to stay on as my housekeeper, but you must not forget whose house it is you keep. You and I discussed this earlier, I thought, at some length."

"I'm going to call the sheriff," Sally told him. "I'll be God *damned* if I'll listen to this any more." Recalling that she still had Fee's check, she opened her purse and began to rummage through it.

"Please," Fee said. "Mrs. Howard—Sally. Do you mind if I call you Sally? Sally, there's something urgent we must settle immediately. Then I will telephone the sheriff for you, if you wish. What are your feelings toward your sister? Are you very fond of her? Or would you, per'aps, prefer that she intrude no more?" He waved a hand airily.

"Kate? Are you talking about Kate?"

Fee nodded, with a suppressed smile.

"I love my sister, if that's what you're asking. Not that it's any of your business. Has something happened to Kate too?"

"You would not prefer . . . ?"

"No! For God's sake what is it?"

"Per'aps it would be better if you sat. If you will just come into my living room. . . ."

"What is it!"

"Your sister has shot herself in the head. Intentionally, or so it would appear."

The old Victorian house spun as though it were the Gale's, flung aloft by the tornado that would carry Dorothy to Oz. The hall light winked and flickered, and Sally's purse was no longer in Sally's hands.

I'm not going to faint, she thought. Women don't really. Faint.

Fee fluttered like a rag in the wind, first present, then replaced by something else, then replaced by nothing at all, so that she stood—stumbled—all alone in the long, cold hall. A siren howled outside; it was still some distance away, but came perceptibly nearer before the hall light vanished.

Lisa was sitting with Mr. Roberts when Dr. de Falla came to speak to them. Rising, she asked, "Is Wrangler going to be all right?"

"Yes, I've got good news for you there. He lost a great deal of blood, but I think he's out of danger now."

"Thank God!"

Dr. de Falla glanced at the gray-haired receptionist, who ignored him studiously. "I'm not supposed to do this, but if you like I could take you up to see him, just for a few minutes. He's fully conscious—talking about going back to Meadow Grass, actually—and I think it might do him good."

Lisa nodded mutely, her eyes shining.

Mr. Roberts said, "Don't worry about me, Doc. I'll wait right here."

"Fine."

De Falla's voice sounded curiously flat; Lisa looked from one man to the other, and at last knew what de Falla had known before he came into the reception area, what Roberts had known as soon as he had seen de Falla. "She's dead, isn't she? She died here, so far from home."

Abruptly, Lisa's eyes filled with tears and Roberts's arms were around her. "There, there," Roberts said softly. "There, there, there."

De Falla told her, "The sheriff's going to want to talk to you afterward. I thought perhaps Bob here could be talking to him now. That should keep him off your back—and mine—for half an hour or so."

Lisa raised her head. "I've called Rio. Did anybody tell you? I talked to their chef; he speaks a little English. Her parents are in Europe, he doesn't know where. He said he'd tell them the next time they phoned, that he'd pray."

"You did all you could," de Falla told her.

"No." Lisa pulled a red bandana from her hip pocket, wiped her eyes, and blew her nose. "Now I'm going to have to call Rio again."

Ann shouldered the nurse aside for the third time. "Let's get this straight. If my daughter's in here, I'm going to see her. And if you have him grab me and toss me out," she jerked her head in the direction of the large attendant, "I'm going to sue this place for every dollar it's got. Now take those rules and do something obscene with them."

The attendant, who was black and well over six feet tall, tried to look serious and even frightening but signally failed.

"So where is she? Mercedes Schindler-Shields."

"Right down here," the nurse said, capitulating. "That room."

"My baby!" Ann rushed past her, stopped, and stared. The bed was empty, the bedclothes thrown back. A muddy smudge as big as a man's hand soiled the sheet where Mercedes should have lain.

Behind Ann, the nurse said, "She may still be talking with the sheriff. He's been questioning lots of people."

"That's a dog's footprint," Ann gasped. "Somebody brought a dog in here." Five whole eggs . . . two egg-yolks . . . one third cup whipping cream. . . .

26

FROM THE DAOINE INSTITUTE

"MERC!" NOT without pain, Shields sat up in his hospital bed. "Merc, what the hell are you doing here, and what happened to your arm?"

"Hi, Dad. I'm afraid it's broken; we were in an accident."

The big, blond man who had come in with Mercedes mumbled, "That, of course, is why your daughter is here in this hospital. But if you're asking why she's here, now—here in our room—it is because I brought her."

Mercedes nodded. "That's right, Dad. I didn't know you were in here any more than you knew I was. This is Dr. von Madadh."

Von Madadh bowed, his head inclined three degrees from the perpendicular. "And I'm here in pursuance of my volunteer work for the Daoine Institute, Mr. Shields. Although I'm an M.D., I'm not associated with this hospital; I practice at Ravenswood, in Chicago."

Shields said, "I see—or rather, I guess I don't. Merc, you said *we* were in an accident. You don't mean you and your mother, since she drove me here just a little while ago. Who were you with?"

"Seth Howard. Remember, Dad? That guy at the house we looked at. Only he wasn't—oh, it's all so complicated."

Von Madadh had found a white plastic chair on casters fo her. He pushed it into position and steadied it while she sa "Mr. Shields, what your daughter is trying to tell you is tha Seth Howard was not driving at the time of their accident; th police here insist that he was. In my view, they're mistaken."

Shields nodded. "If Merc says he wasn't, you're right. Wh was, Merc?"

"A man named Jim. There was a woman with him who sai her name was Viviane Morgan; she was in the back with me. Mercedes turned to von Madadh. "I didn't tell you that sh came in while I was talking to the sheriff, did I?"

Von Madadh shook his head.

"Well, she did. She said she was from a newspaper, and sh took our pictures. I kept waiting for her to say hello, but sh never even smiled."

Von Madadh nodded. "Has it occurred to you, Mercede that it may not actually have been the same woman?"

"It was her! I recognized her."

"Mr. Shields, do you mind if I smoke? Do you, Mercedes? She shook her head, and Shields said, "No, not at all."

From a gold-plated cigar case, von Madadh produced a lon dark cigar; he rolled it between his palms as he spoke. "Wh Mercedes has just told us carries me nicely to the work the Daoine Institute—the work that brought me here Castleview. From your expressions I judge that neither of yo are familiar with it."

Shields shook his head.

"I assumed you wouldn't be, which was why I wanted speak to you together. I'm a bore on the subject, but though must necessarily bore others from time to time, I much pref to bore myself as infrequently as I can." With surprisingly shar white teeth, he bit the tip from his cigar and spat.

"Let me begin with Michael Daoine, an Irish immigrant. I came to this country, a boy of seventeen, in the closing years the preceding century. Like so many of his countrymen, I entered one of the building trades—first carrying a hod, the aying brick, then subcontracting brick and stone construction, and at last becoming a full contractor. America was expanding rapidly in those days. There was a great deal of construction and thus a great deal of work for such contractors. Daoine was a good one, and he became rich."

Mercedes asked, "He founded your institute?"

"Correct. He was an intelligent man, you understand. When he came to America he could scarcely write his name, but he read widely, as so many poorly educated people in his day did; public libraries encouraged it, a thing that seems almost inconceivable now." Von Madadh clamped his extraordinary teeth on the cigar and produced a gold lighter. "Sure it won't bother either of you? Thank you."

Shields said, "I take it this has something to do with the photographer, Dr. von Madadh—the woman who was with Mercedes at the time of the accident."

"I think so. Probably with one and possibly with both. My first name's Rex, by the way, and it's a whole lot shorter."

"Call me Will," Shields told him; rather belatedly, the two shook hands.

"Have you ever heard of the Fairy Faith?"

Mercedes said, "There was a thing about it on TV—people in Ireland who still believe in leprechauns and banshees."

Von Madadh nodded. "It's found in many parts of the world; among Caucasians, belief is actually strongest in Iceland. It's weakest in the Western Hemisphere—in fact it can hardly be said to exist here at all. That was something Michael Daoine found puzzling. The Fairy Faith was widespread in western Ireland at the time he was growing up; his parents had been believers, and several relatives had actually had brushes with the fairies, or at least claimed to have had them. He studied the matter in his spare time, talked with his workmen—there were Swedes, Greeks, and Italians among them, as well as Irishmen and black Americans—and read a good deal of folklore and a great deal of history. As you might expect he came across quite a few oddities, such as the giants of Patagonia."

Von Madadh puffed his black cigar, staring not at them but out the dark window of the hospital room.

Shields cleared his throat. "Are you talking about man-like apes?"

Still watching the night, von Madadh grinned and shook his head. "No, not at all. Those are so common there's no need to go afield for them. Mercedes, can you name the first man to circumnavigate the earth?"

"Was it Magellan?"

"Correct. He was a Portuguese explorer, and what he and his bold crew accomplished in the Sixteenth Century was every bit as brilliant and every bit as important as all the triumphs of all the cosmonauts and astronauts in our own. The record of their voyage was compiled by an Italian named Antonio Pigafetta; he survived it, as Magellan himself did not. As far as we are able to judge, he was a thoroughly reliable officer. Certainly the rest of the crew seemed to think so; and if ever a group of men had passed through fire, it was that crew."

Mercedes asked, "Did he say he'd seen giants?"

"Yes, he did. Oh, not giants as lofty as church steeples, such as one finds in children's books—it's easy enough to show that those could not exist. What Pigafetta actually wrote was, 'This man was so tall our heads scarcely came to his waist; his voice was like the bellowing of a bull.'

"In other words, Pigafetta didn't merely *see* his giant—he stood beside him and talked to him. Now the distance from the ground to the waist of a normally-proportioned man is just about fifty-five percent of his height. Let's say that Pigafetta and the rest averaged five foot five—men were smaller four hundred years ago. That would make Magellan's giant slightly less than ten feet tall."

Von Madadh turned back toward them. "But we don't believe them, do we? Spics and wops." He drew deeply on his cigar and puffed pale, fragrant smoke, like an incense burner. "In fact, most of the safety and sanity of our safe and sane little world depends upon our disbelieving anyone who doesn't speak

English. Your name's Schindler-Shields, isn't it, Mercedes? That's what Seth told me."

Mercedes nodded. "Schindler for my mom."

"Then your ancestry is German and Irish; so is mine. Your forefathers spoke Gaelic or German, and are thus entitled to no credence." Von Madadh chuckled. "Besides—Pigafetta? Who'd believe somebody with a name like that! And it was four hundred years ago, so let's move up to the Eighteenth Century —George Washington's time. Everybody believed George, eh? A British warship, the *Dolphin*, dropped anchor at Patagonia. Her skipper was a Commodore Byron—that's a step above captain, notice; if the commodore was promoted again, he died an admiral.

"Commodore Byron was just under six feet. He could barely reach the tops of the natives' heads when standing on tiptoe. That makes them at least eight feet tall; and in fact a report by one of the *Dolphin*'s officers states, 'There was hardly a man there less than eight feet, most considerably more; the women, I believe, run from seven and a half to eight feet.' Science, to be sure, denies the existence of any such race."

Shields asked, "Does this have anything to do with Mercedes's accident?"

"Perhaps not," von Madadh admitted. "I can take it, then, that neither of you have seen any giants?"

Shields shook his head.

"We did, Dad!" Mercedes exclaimed. "Don't you remember the man on the horse? We just about hit him. I bet he was at least eight feet tall."

"But he was mounted?"

Shields said, "He was a big man, certainly, riding a very big horse; but I don't think he was eight feet tall or anything close to it. Six feet six, maybe. It was raining and getting dark, and we only got a glimpse of him."

Von Madadh puffed thoughtful smoke. "You didn't see his face?"

Shields shook his head; so did his daughter.

"How was he dressed?"

Shields shrugged. "I'd say he had on a long coat of some kind, probably a slicker or something like that. I remember it covered him to the ankles."

Von Madadh nodded. "Riding boots, I suppose?"

Mercedes closed her eyes to summon up the dark figure once more. "I don't think we could see them, because his feet were inside the whatchacallums—the stirrups."

"A stirrup doesn't really cover much of the rider's foot," von Madadh protested mildly. "They're just iron rings, shaped like the letter *D* lying on its face."

Mercedes shuddered and shook her head. "These weren't— or anyhow the one I could see wasn't. You know what it reminded me of? A wooden shoe! Grandmother had one she used to grow ferns in, remember, Dad? Only it was—I think it was metal."

Shields said, "How about leveling with us now, Rex? This is what you're looking for, isn't it? This giant, if he really is a giant. He's the reason that the Daoine Institute sent you up here from Chicago."

"That's right." Von Madadh tapped ash from his cigar. "I didn't realize I was quite so transparent; perhaps I should say I hadn't realized you were quite so percipient. I tried to lead you into it, as you obviously understand. I hope you understand also that I was doing it in a very good cause. One simply can't go up to strangers and say, 'Have you met many of the Fair Folk lately? Are you much troubled by trolls this fall? Is there a giant active hereabouts, sir? Madame? Are the jinn abroad?'"

Mercedes giggled.

"You see. Yet the answers are frequently yes, because such things are encountered far more often than you might imagine."

Shields said, "But still unrecognized by science? That's pretty hard to swallow."

"Indeed it is. And they mean to keep it so, for as long a

possible. Have you any notion how many species of animals there are on this planet?"

"No," Shields said. "Thousands, I suppose."

"You're being extremely conservative, believe me; there are literally millions; and yet—supposedly—only one has developed sufficient intelligence to make tools and use fire. Do you find that plausible? Honestly, now."

Shields shrugged. "It seems to me that if there were any others. . . ."

"They would be seen and reported? Yes, of course. And of course they have been, thousands upon thousands of times. The truly surprising thing is how frequently they're still reported, despite the torrents of ridicule directed at the witnesses. When I brought up giants, you mentioned man-like apes; and there have been tens of thousands of sightings of those hairy giants with protruding teeth—from every state in the Union except Hawaii, and every Canadian province except Nova Scotia. Witnesses in California call the thing they saw Big Foot. At the southern end of our own state it's the Big Muddy Monster. Here and over in Iowa, it's generally called Big Mo, presumably because many are seen along the Missouri River. Farther north it becomes the Minnesota Ice Giant. In the mountains of Tibet and Nepal it's a yeti or an abominable snowman. Over in Northwestern Europe it's a troll, and so on."

Mercedes had been staring at her father. "Just exactly what happened to you, Dad? Dr. von Madadh said you'd had an accident. I thought he meant in a car, like Seth and me."

Shields grinned at her. "I met a troll, Mercedes. Met—hell, I wrestled one. Your mother hit us both with an old Jeep Cherokee. The troll had its back to her, so she couldn't see me, or at least I hope she couldn't. Now if you tell them that here, I'll disown you. Rex, what about the couple that was in the car with Merc and the Howard boy? They weren't giants or trolls, from what I've heard, and they weren't kids, either. When are you going to talk about them?"

Mercedes tried to imagine her father wrestling a troll and failed; the twilit yet vivid memory of the mounted giant rose before her mind's eye in its place. It still seemed to her that his huge horse had too many legs.

27

SATURDAY

LIKE A giant in golden armor, a Canadian high had driven off the wet and stormy low that had dominated the north-central area for nearly a week. Crystalline and visible, it stood guard above it now, so that the new day was born in sunshine. Flecks of cotton cloud hurried across the blue toward the Great Lakes. It was a lovely morning, but colder than it looked.

Sally sat up in bed when she heard the whine of the vacuum cleaner. "Seth? Seth, is that you?" Then she remembered that Seth was in the hospital, Tom dead. Passionately she longed to sleep again.

It was Momma, of course. Only Momma would vacuum her rugs for her. Momma or Kate, and Kate—

That thought too had to be pushed to one side. Sally went into the bathroom, brushed her teeth, took a shower, washed her hair, and put it up. When she came out, the vacuum cleaner was silent, and the rich smell of frying ham filled the hall. She opened the kitchen door, and Dr. von Madadh waved a spatula and wished her a good morning.

"I'm so sorry, Doctor! I thought you—I must've overslept, and—"

He glanced at the clock in the console of the stove. "Ten till ten. That's not too late for somebody who was up half the night, I think. Whenever a patient heals too slowly, I ask how much sleep she's been getting. Nine hours plus does wonders for a post-operative patient, I assure you. I wish I could convince the hospital of that."

"And you were vacuuming, weren't you? That was wonderful of you."

Von Madadh shook his head. "Not wonderful at all, since my racket woke you. I didn't think it would, with the hall between us. At any rate, I called it quits when I heard the shower. To tell the truth, I'm ready for a few comestibles myself. You'll have some eggs, I assume? I've decided upon three—the laborer is worthy of his hire, as whoosis says. Scrambled? Sunny-side? Basted? We called that *blinded* in my youth, and I'm partial to those unseeing eggs even today—I don't feel so bad when I stick a sharp piece of toast into them."

Sally smiled, despite her best efforts. "Blinded will be fine. I'll set the table."

"The shirred is king of eggs, in my humble opinion, and I confess I'm an expert; but we really haven't the time for them." With one quick motion he cracked two eggs against the frying pan and opened them together. "Blind three for you?"

"Two," Sally told him. "You said we wouldn't have time. Did the hospital call?"

"About Seth? No, I—"

"Or about Kate."

Von Madadh shook his head. "They didn't call at all, about anybody. I merely meant that our ham would be overcooked if we took the time for shirred eggs. We shall enjoy shirred eggs à la von Madadh tomorrow morning. That is we will if . . ." He let the thought hang.

"Oh, you're perfectly welcome to stay here, Doctor. For as long as you want. I mean that."

"Thank you. I like it here, although I hope I won't have to impose on you for more than a few days. You're really very kind." He was ladling hot ham drippings onto the eggs with a cooking spoon.

"You're sure they didn't call?"

"The hospital? No. Someone did call, however, although I had hoped to postpone the news until you'd finished your coffee."

Sally had been setting a cup and saucer at his place; they rattled in her hand. "Who?"

"A funeral parlor. Fuchs? I believe that was it—*fox* in German. Ugly, sneaking, thieving little critters." He had left the stove to pour coffee into her cup. "Now sit down and drink this."

"What did they want?"

Von Madadh replaced the coffee pot on its burner. "Follow my prescription, please, and I'll tell you. You do know your father's safe, don't you? You recall that from last night?"

"Yes," she said. "That's right, he was missing, wasn't he? But he was here, later, after they . . ."

"After your sister was taken to the hospital," von Madadh prompted her.

"That's right, you came back. I was at the hospital, and the receptionist wouldn't call a taxi for me. I couldn't find you. Where were you?"

"With Seth, in a little break area he'd discovered. There was water for tea there and a pop machine. I suppose the place was really intended for nurses, but the deputies had been using it, which was how Seth knew about it. He wanted to go home, you see—just walk out of the hospital and come back here, and I had to talk him out of it. That took quite a time."

Sally nodded, mostly to herself. "I should have known it was something like that."

"When I got back to the lobby, the receptionist said you'd left. I felt like stretching my legs and was rather hoping to run into a friend I'd seen in town earlier, so I walked, too." With the dash of a card sharp, von Madadh dealt a smoking slice of ham to each of the plates Sally had taken from the cupboard, and added basted eggs.

It was nice, she reflected, to have a man in the house. It had been nice to have Tom. She had loved Tom and still did; but it was nice now to have this doctor, to have Rex. She attempted to picture herself living nearer Chicago, "where my husband's practice is." It wasn't terribly far, really. Three hours or less, if you drove fast.

Boomer was galloping no longer, had not galloped much in a long while; he trotted now except when there was a fallen tree to jump, and once Lucie had dismounted and led him for a mile or more.

A fresh wind stirred the hemlocks and sang among the naked branches of the oaks, chanting sometimes of bears, sometimes of wolves or rabbits, sometimes of other things that Boomer did not know; always he pricked his ears to listen, flaring his nostrils as his heart remembered the old, wild ways of the uplands, the gray dawns when stallion fought stallion with teeth and flashing hooves, and neither was ever stalled, nor knew the touch of man.

Bushes parted on his mounting side. A slender woman had separated them with thorn-torn hands; her cheeks bled, and her ragged dress was stiff with blood. "Please," she murmured. "Miss? Oh, Miss?"

Lucie clucked and dug his ribs with both heels.

"Judy? Have you seen Judy, my daughter? My little girl, Judy? Please, oh, please stop."

Boomer broke into a weary canter, iron-shod feet wounding the moss with every stride. The woman and her plaintive voice were left far behind, and with them the quick, muffled drumming of other hooves upon the moss—hoofbeats not his, tapping out a rhythm that reminded him of the barn, and long, easy rides with laughing girls.

"How are we this morning, Mr. Shields?"

Making a face, Shields sat up. A perky nurse's aide put a green tray across his lap, and he dumped the skimpy jigger of whitish powder into the noxious-looking coffee. "Starved," he told her. "Starved and in agony."

"You're one of the last ones getting breakfast. You were asleep when I came in at eight."

He nodded. "I drifted off around seven forty." The coffee was every bit as awful as it looked, and boiling hot. As it happened, he liked boiling-hot coffee. Score three points. "Am I getting out of this place today?"

"I expect you will, but I don't really know." The nurse's aide lowered her voice. "Mr. Shields, isn't Mercedes Schindler-Shields your daughter?"

"Sure." A tablespoon of hard scrambled eggs (they'd better never give Ann *that* one) a slice of white toast, and Corn Flakes and milk.

"Do you know what's happened to her?"

He looked up, startled. "What's happened to her? Run some tests, for God's sake! This is a hospital, isn't it? Do a CAT-scan. If you haven't got the equipment, send her somewhere that does."

The nurse's aide put a finger to her lips and looked about conspiratorially. "What I meant was what's become of her. She walked, sometime last night."

"Then she's with my wife, Ann Schindler. Ann's at the Red Stove Inn."

The nurse's aide brushed back her hair. "Not now she's not. She's in Dr. Bray's office. She came here to see you—visiting's at nine—and naturally Jan grabbed her right away. Jan's Dr. Bray's secretary." Her voice dropped to a whisper. "The Howard boy's gone, too. Everybody says they eloped."

"She's only sixteen, for Pete's sake!"

"*Shh!* You don't know?"

"Get out of here," Shields ordered her. "If you can't find her, I'll have to."

The nurse's aide left, looking offended; he picked up the telephone beside his bed and dialed the agency.

"View Motors. This is Bob Roberts."

It was astonishingly good to hear Roberts's voice. "Hello, Bob. Will Shields. How's it going?"

"Good morning, Mr. Shields! Not too bad. Remember the big blue Linc?"

"You sold it?" Even the coffee tasted better.

"They signed 'bout fifteen minutes ago. I had to give 'em a pretty good allowance, but I think it was justified. How are you feeling, Mr. Shields?"

"Not bad. I'm getting out of here as soon as I can get the paperwork done."

There was a pause, slight but significant. "Mr. Shields, you haven't heard anything about my daughter, have you?"

"Your daughter? Mrs. Howard?"

"No, my daughter Kate, Mr. Shields. Kate Roberts."

"I don't believe I've even heard her name before."

"Or Judy Youngberg? Judy's my granddaughter."

"No, I haven't," Shields told him. "What happened?"

"Kate and Judy went over to Sally's place last night, Mr. Shields. Mother—that's my wife—had been trying to call Sally to tell her I was back safe. Mother doesn't more than half believe me about all that happened, I'm afraid, but she's glad I'm back just the same. Anyhow Sally didn't answer, so Mother and Kate thought she was most likely asleep, with the bedroom phone pulled out. Mother wanted to stay home for when I got there, but she thought Sally ought to know. So Kate and Judy drove over."

Shields said, "Go on."

"Only Sally wasn't there—she'd gone to the hospital to see Seth. She must have left her door unlocked, because Kate went inside and she didn't have a key. Then there was some kind of accident."

"Is she badly hurt, Bob?"

"She's in a coma, there at the hospital, Mr. Shields, which is why I thought maybe you'd heard something I hadn't. Mother's there sitting with her."

"You didn't have to come to work today, Bob; you know that."

"Sure, I figured, but it's Saturday. Saturday's usually a real good day for us, and I knew you wouldn't be in. I couldn't leave Teddie here all by himself."

Shields reflected that there would be medical bills, in all probability. Bob's daughter might have insurance, but it didn't seem likely; in any case, insurance never paid the whole cost of treatment, no matter what they implied when you signed.

"What can I do for you, Mr. Shields?"

"To start with, make over the title of the Cherokee; we're selling it back to Miss Lisa Solomon for one dollar and other considerations. Mail it."

"That's already taken care of, Mr. Shields. I did it this morning before anybody came in."

"Good. Has she got the car yet?"

Shields could almost see Roberts shake his head. "No, not if you mean right this minute, Mr. Shields. I drove her back to Meadow Grass last night and dropped her off. She was worried on account of the horses—"

"That took some guts."

A slight hesitation. "They were gone, Mr. Shields. I felt it as soon as we got there; so did she, I think. I went through the barn with her—there's a couple horses missing—and through the lodge, too; but I knew there wasn't any use in it. If there had been, I'm not sure I'd have done it."

Shields said, "It took guts all the same."

"Anyhow, I drove her car back here. I said if you could give it to her, I could fix her windshield. Pay for it, that is."

"Bob—"

"That one's on me, Mr. Shields. I'll have the boys do it Monday, and I'll write you a check."

"Okay, Bob, if that's how you want it." Shields decided to try a shot in the dark himself. "Did you say your granddaughter was missing?"

"That's right. We're hoping she'll turn up soon."

"You were missing yourself yesterday, Bob."

"That's right, too, Mr. Shields."

"Do you think that what happened to you could have happened to her?"

In the same flat voice, Roberts answered, "I suppose that's possible."

"So do I. There are a couple of other people missing as well. Do you know about that? My daughter and your grandson."

For twenty seconds or so, Roberts did not speak. At last, when Shields was about to call his name, he said, "I see."

"Here at the hospital they think they've gone off together; I hope to God that's all it is. I want you to check with Mrs. Howard and see if she knows where they are. See her in person, understand?"

"Yes, sir."

"Let me know as soon as you find out anything. And there's a doctor here from Chicago, looking into the sort of thing that happened to you and me last night. He had a talk with Merc and me, and from several things he said I gathered that he'd talked to Seth earlier. His name's von Madadh. Let me know where he is, if you run into him."

As Shields hung up, the nurse's aide pushed a wheelchair into his room. "This is Mr. Shields," she announced. "Mr. Shields, this is Mr. Dunstan."

The deeply tanned young man in the wheelchair extended his hand. "You call me Wrangler," he said. "I'm just awfully proud to meet up with you."

28

FLYING ISLANDS OF THE NIGHT

JUDY AWAKENED on a gargoyle. He was a specially big one, nicer than most of them, having a cat's head and wide wings poised for flight. His wings had been the railings of a cozy little bed for her, and more than enough ivy grew between them to make a rough mattress.

More than once this gargoyle had made personal appearances in Judy's dreams, walking along his own back or balancing upon one of his own wingtips, and at last he had brought her a dead sparrow and lain down beside her, black and very soft, warm and comforting, smelling slightly of Hartz Three-in-One Flea Collar. And after what seemed a very long time, filled with that strange dream and many others, he sniffed her lips (being by then a bit peckish himself) to find out whether she had *entirely* finished his sparrow. His whiskers tickled; Judy sneezed and sat up. "Why, Kitty," she said, "it's really you."

G. Gordon Kitty blinked twice and nodded, his eyes blazing like emeralds.

Shield's telephone rang. "Excuse me," he said to Wrangler, "this might be news. Hello?"

"Mr. Shields. This's Lisa. I had to tell you—absolutely had to! You and your wife were so grand last night, but they won't

let patients take calls before nine, and then I tried to tel
Wrangler first and he wasn't there. I hope he's all right. I
hope—"

"He's fine," Shields told her. "He's right here in my room
talking to me."

"Oh! Oh, God! Wonderful! Could I? I mean—"

"Of course. Just a minute." Shields passed the handset to
Wrangler. "Lisa wants to speak to you."

Shields envied him. Had there ever been a time when Ann
had been so anxious to hear his voice? Yes, for a few months
before their wedding, and a few months after it. It had ended
when Ann found that she was carrying Merc, but he had hoped
for a year or three that a certain cadence of Ann's would
eventually return. He knew now that it never would.

"What! What's that you say?" Wrangler leaned forward, his
free hand clutching the arm of his wheelchair, his mouth
agape. "Lisa, honey . . . Lisa . . ."

Shields asked, "What is it?"

Wrangler glanced up. "She's alive!"

"Who is?"

Wrangler gestured for silence.

"Is it Merc?"

Wrangler paid no heed, listening intently. After a few
seconds he said, "Maybe somebody could come out for you. I'l
ask Mr. Shields here about that."

You'll play hell getting it, Shields thought grimly; then
chuckled inwardly at himself.

Wrangler hung up. "I told her I'd tell you what she was going
to tell you, and ask a favor for her and me."

"She wants a loaner," Shields said. People who left their car
to be repaired always wanted loaners, as if nobody could live for
more than half an hour without having an automobile available
at an instant's notice. In the case of Lisa Solomon, who lived at
least five miles outside Castleview, a loaner might even be
justified.

"You mean another car? Nope, that's not it. Miss Lisa can ride into town to see about me. We don't really need one 'cept for trailers and haulin' hay and so forth." Wrangler hesitated. "Sissy's gone. You know about that?"

Shields nodded.

"And now it seems like Lucie's gone, too. She ain't around, and Miss Lisa says her bed wasn't slept in."

Shields grunted. "There are an awful lot of missing people all of a sudden."

"That's a certain fact. Anyhow, Miss Lisa wondered if you might know of a lady that could stay with her till I get back."

Ann's voice boomed from the doorway. "He certainly does —I'll be delighted to. Willie, how are you, how are you feeling? I've been talking to the doctor in charge of this place, and he says you can go today. I told him I needed you to help me find Mercedes. How are you feeling, Wrangler? They got you, didn't they?"

Ann herself looked tired, Shields thought. Her eyes were red and puffy, and the lines about her mouth showed through her makeup. She was wearing her good red dress, however, and exuded energy and confidence as she strode into the room and sat down in the chair that Rex von Madadh had found for Merc.

Wrangler was grinning at her. "Real good to see you again, Miz Schindler. I owe you, ma'am, and I'm grateful."

"That's nice," Ann told him, "because I'm going to ask a favor of you in half a minute. A big favor."

"After all you done for me? And you're goin' to stay with Miss Lisa? I'll be proud."

"*You're* going to stay out at Meadow Grass with Lisa, too, Willie. So is Wrangler, just as quick as I can get him there."

"Ann, we can't—"

"Oh, yes, we can, Willie, till we find Mercedes. I've been thinking over this whole crazy business while I was talking to Dr. Bray. Where are they, these lousy people who shot that poor kid from Brazil, sicced their pet gorilla on you in that barn, and left Wrangler for dead, lying in the rain? Where are they coming from?"

Neither man answered her.

"Meadow Grass! The first time I went there, Wrangler stuck a gun in my face because they'd been having all sorts of trouble. Isn't that right, Wrangler? Besides, Willie, we saw the accident Mercedes got hurt in on the way to Meadow Grass. *We* were going to pick up that nice old salesman, remember? So where were *they* going, I ask you?"

Shields shook his head.

"Willie, we were so! You'd phoned Meadow Grass from the Chinese place and talked to Sissy, and—"

He interrupted. "You're wrong, Ann. I was thinking that way last night, I admit. But as far as you and I are concerned, this whole thing began when Bob and I went to the county museum; and that had nothing to do with Meadow Grass. Hell, I didn't even know the place existed. I'd seen the castle when we were looking at the Howard house, the same way lots of other people have seen it at one time or another, all over town; and when I got to the dealership, Bob told me they had some information on it there, which they did."

Ann sighed deeply, a martyr whose sufferings were picking up. "Willie, *please* don't be so dense. Whose car were you driving?"

He started to speak but fell silent, dumbfounded.

"It was Lisa's, of course, Willie. Her old Cherokee. They— whoever they are—saw her car parked at the museum and thought that Lisa or Wrangler was inside, or maybe both of them." Ann paused, staring hard at Wrangler. "If you ask me, it's Wrangler they're really interested in. You know, I'd never realized how much he looks like Bob Roberts."

Shields studied Wrangler for a moment, then shook his head. "I wouldn't have said so."

"That's because you never notice people unless you want to sell them cars, Willie. Bob must be forty years older, and I'd say an inch or two taller and a little bit heavier. But look at Wrangler's face, the eyes and nose particularly."

The subject of their scrutiny grinned, revealing teeth that were slightly uneven and tobacco-stained. "Reckon I'll have to meet up with Mr. Roberts. 'Cordin' to Miss Lisa, he's a mighty good man, only she never told me what a all-out *handsome* rascal he was. Miz Schindler, have you heard the good news? Miss Lisa told me about how you drove her and Sancha here."

Shields asked, "What good news? It seems to me we could use some."

Wrangler grinned still more; his face shone with pleasure. "Sancha's alive, that's what. Last night when Miss Lisa came to see me, she told me Sancha'd passed on, and—"

"But she hasn't?" Ann squealed. "That's marvelous!"

"Yes, ma'am. No, ma'am. That was what the doctors here told Miss Lisa, and it was what they thought themselves; they wasn't lyin' or nothin'. They'd gave her blood and so on, but her heart flat give out. Miss Lisa says they tried everythin' there is, but they couldn't get it goin' again. Then in the—this place where they keep the dead bodies, the whatchacallit—"

"The mortuary," Ann supplied.

"Yes, ma'am. One of the hands in there, he noticed Sancha breathin'—real late last night, this was—so he hollers for a doctor. They told Miss Lisa that don't happen one time in a million, but it happens now and then just the same, and Sancha was the lucky one. Her bein' so healthy didn't hurt none, I'd guess, and she always was real strong for a girl. Anyhow, she's still out, and the doctor told Miss Lisa she ought not to count on her pullin' through at all. But what you did, Miz Schindler, and you, Mr. Shields, wasn't wasted, and you ought to know it. She's gettin' oxygen, now, Miss Lisa said. I sure do hope she makes it. She's a real nice girl."

Boomer slowed at a freshet, hoping for a drink. Lucie had to fight him to make him follow the narrow track that wandered beside the wanton water instead. It was only then, while

Boomer backed and sidled, that she heard the hoofbeats behind them, the regular, ground-devouring gallop that stretches back to Arabia Deserta and can match a falcon mile for mile. Lucie wished for a weapon then, for it is never certain that riders are harmless in the country she and Boomer traveled.

She had none. She urged Boomer forward instead, trotting down a steep defile where the white water muted their pursuer's hoofbeats and small sly eyes peered from crevices between rocks.

A green twilight overlay the whole land, and though Lucie feigned to prefer it, she longed for sunshine and sharp shadows now, in place of this sickly light and the pale tendrils of fog that seemed to reach out for her. That fog, she knew, did not always leave living things quite as it had found them.

All the while the beating hooves behind her drummed louder; Lisa Solomon's hulking jumper slackened to an uneasy walk, his ears cocked rearward. Lucie damned him aloud, kicking him with her heels and wishing for a heavy quirt and Spanish spurs with rowels the size of shuriken, until he trotted once more.

He stumbled where the fading path circled a fallen hemlock. An hour before he would have sailed over it with hardly a break in stride, but his forelegs crossed at the turning of the path; he lurched sideways and forward, so that Lucie nearly fell. She screamed—as much in fear as in anger—and only afterward when Boomer had his feet beneath him once more, reflected that the rider behind her knew now that there was a woman ahead, if he had not known it before.

A long, level meadow went well enough. There was little hope of losing their pursuer while he remained in earshot, but Lucie turned Boomer from the path there, letting him trot across the lush grass and between mossy-trunked oaks that were at the memory of fog.

It's the country of the clouds, she thought. It seemed strange that she had not realized that sooner—never realized she rode

e flying islands of the night, with the day land ten thousand
et below her horse's belly. Would the sun rise at last?

Through the bare limbs of the oaks she glimpsed the
mmits of the tallest towers before the other rider overtook
r; and she recognized Buck, Wrangler's roping horse, before
e haggard girl astride him.

"Lucie! Lucie, *pode ajudar-me? Estou com fome, com sede,
nsando.* Wait, Lucie. I am so hungry." Sancha attempted to
ile, but it was the smile of a wolf, a sneer of gleaming teeth
d famished eyes.

29

THE CASTLE BY THE SEA

"WAS THERE a god for cooks, Willie? Or a saint?"

"Martha, I suppose," Shields said absently. "She's alw
shown with a ladle in her hand. I don't think there wa
god—more likely a goddess. Hestia was goddess of the hear
which was where they cooked in those days."

Then please, please both of you watch over my daughter, a
don't let anything really bad happen to her. Think of all I
done for you: all day, sometimes, in the kitchen. Remember
sauces and desserts.

Ann tried to imagine what Hestia looked like. Younger t
Martha, because if you were a goddess you could be as young
you wanted. Older than Martha, because Martha was N
Testament and Hestia went back a whole lot farther than th
Both bent over the stove, Martha skimming her soup a
Hestia tending the fire, adding wood from the old olive t
Lazarus had cut down the year before, the old apple. Feed
the harvesters.

A secretary or something walked quickly through the of
pretending not to see them.

Mix the crumbs with sugar and butter, and press the mixt
into a spring-form cake pan. Chill the whipping cream a
fruit.

"Mr. Shields?"

He nodded.

"Mr. Shields, we admitted you last night although you were without hospitalization insurance."

Ann said, "He was hurt. You couldn't have turned him away."

The secretary nodded primly. "This hospital operates at a loss because of such things; every year our deficit has to be made up by fund drives and grants from the state. If you could pay—now—we'd be most grateful."

Ann snapped, "You admitted our daughter, too. Where is she?"

"If she chose to leave, we could not have restrained her."

"Then if Willie wants to leave, you can't stop him either."

Shields said, "How much is it?"

The secretary smoothed her skirt before favoring him with a brief, frosty smile. "Under the circumstances, there will be no charge for the emergency treatment given your daughter."

"How much?"

"Three hundred and seventy-five dollars. The sheriff's looking for her, you know. And the Howard boy."

"We haven't got it," Shields said.

"Willie!"

Shields shook his head. "I'm not going to lie about this, Ann. There isn't that much in the account." He recalled that Roberts had sold the blue Lincoln, also that Roberts had given the buyer a big trade-in allowance; no doubt that allowance had covered the down payment—perhaps more than covered it.

To the secretary he said, "We've bought Castleview Motors. We only signed last week, and it took a big loan from the bank and just about every cent we had. If you'll give us a month, I should be able to pay you in full. We're selling our house in Arlington Heights, but we haven't got the money yet."

The secretary studied him, and he studied her in return, trying to decide whether she was as inhuman as she looked; he decided she was.

"From what you say you're operating on credit, Mr. Shields. If this hospital reports to the credit bureau that you wouldn't pay your bill, it will hurt your credit rating severely."

He nodded. "But if I write you a bad check, that will hurt it a lot more. I'm not going to do it."

Another pause. "Could you pay us one hundred dollars down? With a firm promise to pay the balance at the end of the month?"

"Yes," Shields said. "We could swing that."

"All right, then."

Sally knelt alone in the small room that the undertaker had called the chapel; von Madadh had slipped discreetly away. She looked up, studying the face of the man in the casket, then rose so that she could see it better. Tom's newest suit was freshly cleaned and eerily unwrinkled. His hands reposed at his sides.

He always had so many things in his pockets, Sally thought. Keys and his jackknife and that little steel ruler, his notebook and three or four pens. He always had something in his hands, a screwdriver or a cup of coffee or a fishing rod. This couldn't be Tom. If we are but mortal, Tom had been destroyed and was no more; if immortal, he was somewhere else. Those truths were clear to her now as they had never been before.

She touched the cold lips that had been his with hers, and turned away. Outside in the reception room, Dr. von Madadh was seated beside a small man wracked by silent sobs. The doctor rose when she came in. "Shall we go now, Sally?"

She nodded; and it was not until they were in the street, with von Madadh whistling a doleful waltz, that she realized that the small man had been Mr. Fee.

Judy had wanted to carry G. Gordon Kitty in one arm as she climbed down the ivy, but G. Gordon Kitty had raised strenuous objections to the proposal, and Judy had deferred to him. G. Gordon Kitty was inclined to scratch and bite when things were not going his way, and he had given unmistakable signs that he was fully prepared to do so in this instance. Now he climbed with her, sometimes behind her—when there was this or that in the ivy worthy of his investigation—sometimes before her, half falling and catching himself in the tangled stems.

Never wholly sheer, the tower wall sloped increasingly as they neared the ground, making their climb easier. Not so long ago the narrow little window had been far below and off to one side. A step down, a handhold and a second step, and Judy was right beside it. She leaned over to look in, and saw a big girl in jeans and an old king who stared into a smoldering fire.

Neither of them were paying any attention to her, so after a moment or two she said, "Hi?"

The big girl looked around, then came to the window and helped her in. "What in the world were you doing out there?"

"Getting down. I tore my dress."

The big girl examined it and shook her head. "It's ruined, sweetie. Don't you have any shoes?"

"They made it harder to climb," Judy explained, "so I let them drop down. I'll find them again when I get to the bottom." Belatedly she remembered her manners. "My name's Judy. What's yours?"

"Sissy," Sissy told her. "Sissy Stevenson. And this is King Geimhreadh."

Judy said, "I knew he was a king because of the crown. That's how you can tell them."

"I suppose. Do you know where we are?"

Judy shook her head.

Without looking up from the fire, the old king muttered, "This is the Isle of Glass, child."

Sissy asked, "Can you tell where that is, sir?"

"West of Ireland."

Judy said, "I studied about that in school—Dublin, and it's on the River Liffey."

"I'm afraid that isn't much help, sir. Everything's west of Ireland."

The old king answered nothing. Judy crossed the room to stand beside him, mostly because she was cold. "You're older than my grandpa is. A lot older."

The old king still did not speak, but very slowly laid his arm upon her shoulders, drawing her to him. He wore a long fur cloak, and Judy caught the edge of it with one hand (it was not as soft as she expected) and pulled it around her.

Sissy whispered, "He's got Alzheimer's, I think. Where do you live?"

"One eleven Chestnut Street."

"In Castleview?"

Judy nodded. "We used to live in Davenport, but we moved. We're staying with my grandpa and grandma now."

Sissy looked thoughtful. "How did you get here?"

"A bad man chased me, so I climbed out the window at Aunt Sally's."

"And you were here?"

"Uh huh." Judy pointed. "Only way, way upstairs, and the door was locked so I couldn't get out, so I climbed down outside on the bushes. Can you get down from here?"

"Yeah, sure." Sissy gestured toward a wide door. "That's how I came up. But King Geimhreadh's the only person I've been able to find here who'll talk to me."

Kitty leaped from the windowsill, clearing half the distance to the fire in a single bound. "My cat," Judy announced. As if to prove it, he rubbed her leg, purring loudly, his arched back higher than her knees.

"He's beautiful," Sissy said. "I love cats." She stroked his scarred black head.

"His name's G. Gordon Kitty, and he's half Siamese and half alley cat. The lady we got him from said that half Siamese cats are always black like that, except one kitten was gray."

The old king nodded. "At night all cats are gray." Kitty sprang into his lap and kneaded his chest. "That's a fine omen you bring us, friend: good planting, and a harvest. See, child, how he plants the corn."

Judy grinned. "Mom says he's a good-luck cat. Only when she's mad at him, she says a witch's cat. Is it always so cold in here?"

The old king shook his head and touched something at the edge of the fireplace; flames leaped into the chimney.

Skillfully, Judy ducked from beneath his cloak. "I better go home—my mom will get worried. Here, Kitty."

Sissy helped her open the heavy door. Judy had expected an inside stairway, probably one that turned around. Instead there was an open ramp, very steep, with ivy and briers growing from the crevices between its wide stones. "I must have been climbing down the other side," she said. "I didn't see this."

"It's the way I came up," Sissy repeated.

"How did *you* get here?"

Sissy sighed. "I'm staying at Meadow Grass. Do you know where that is?"

Judy shook her head.

"Outside Castleview a little way. It's a riding camp, and lots of girls get dumped there—this's my second year. Where's your dad?"

Judy shrugged, her eyes upon the sharply slanting surface. Some of the stones were glass, as the old king had said, and all of them were wet with fog and very slick; but she was afraid of stepping on the briers with her bare feet.

"Okay, suppose when you're a little older your mother gets a new boyfriend. She might send you to Meadow Grass, except she probably wouldn't if you were still living in Castleview because it's too close. But if you went back to Davenport, she might. Do you like horses?"

"I'm kind of scared of them," Judy admitted.

"Well, I think horses are about the greatest thing in the world, and Meadow Grass has lots of them, and some are really good. Mostly I ride Lady, but sometimes I ride Popsicle, and once Lisa let me ride Boomer—he's her prize jumper."

"I wish I had a pony right now," Judy told her. "I'd ride right down this old thing."

Faintly, as though far out over the sea on the other side of the tower, a gull mewed. Or perhaps a voice called.

Sissy grunted. "Yeah, that would be okay. Want to see if I can carry you?"

"Huh-uh. I'm scared you'd fall."

"So'm I. Well, anyway, they've been having lots of trouble at Meadow Grass; people riding horses at night and leaving gates open and so forth. I like Lisa and Wrangler—they're the ones that run it—so I tried to keep an eye out, but for a long time I couldn't spot anything. Pretty soon it got to be September, and all the girls went home except Lucie, Sancha, and me, and it got worse."

Judy looked sympathetic.

"Lisa was calling the sheriff or the state troopers almost every week, but nobody could catch them. Not even Wrangler, and he was only getting two or three hours sleep. So I figured that there had to be somebody— Did you hear something?"

"Over on the other side, I think. The side I was climbing down."

By now they were nearly at the bottom of the ramp, and the proximity of the courtyard urged them forward. After a few more steps, Judy ran, leaping the worst of the briers, and waited for Sissy at the bottom. The courtyard seemed deserted, though there was corroding machinery here and there, and in one of its myriad corners a cart with a missing wheel. Tower like, yet unlike, that from which they had come rose around them, their tops lost in the churning mist, some leaning so that it appeared they must fall. But no banners flew, and the only voices now were those of gulls.

When Sissy had joined her, Judy asked, "Did he mean these stones when he called this the Isle of Glass?"

"Maybe. You know how old people are."

Judy said, "Somebody must take care of him."

"I suppose, but I didn't see anybody. What happened to your cat?"

"He said he wanted to stay with the old king awhile."

They began to walk around the wide base of the tower, Judy stopping here and there to poke among the bedraggled weeds for her shoes. "You never did finish telling how you got here," she said.

"Well, I knew it couldn't be Wrangler or Lisa, because I could see they were both worried sick. And I knew it wasn't me. So it had to be Sancha or Lucie. This evening—I guess it was today—Lucie was supposed to be missing; but when I went out to see about Lady, I saw her down by the creek, talking to somebody I'd never seen before. When they split up, I followed him."

"We're not going to be able to go very much farther," Judy pointed out. "This tower grows into the big wall up there."

The call came again, only slightly louder than before.

"They're on the other side of the wall," Judy said.

Iron shoes rang on the cobbles. Both turned to look.

30

WILL

"NATURALLY YOU'RE wondering why we're here," von
Madadh began. "Why I've called this meeting and brough
Mrs. Howard with me."

They were sitting before a blazing fire in the big, field-stone
lodge at Meadow Grass: Will and Ann, Wrangler and Lisa, Bob
Roberts and his daughter, and von Madadh himself. Lucie'
funeral had been conducted that afternoon by the priest from
St. Stephen's; the fine weather of the weekend had vanished
with the shutting of Lucie's coffin. A cold and weary wind
moaned among the poplars and pines, tangling them as a sick
child tangles its blankets, shaken with chill after chill, a lonely
and abandoned child whimpering for the return of summer.

Ann glanced at Lisa. "I think I can guess."

Von Madadh nodded. "Then go ahead."

"It's about the missing kids. They're all kids now, though
that may be just coincidence. Willie and me for Mercedes, Lisa
and Wrangler for Sissy Stevenson, Mrs. Howard for Seth
Howard, and Bob for his little granddaughter. Willie told me
what you told him and Mercedes. You think you know who ha
them."

Von Madadh nodded again. "I do, and stealing children is ar
ancient tactic of theirs. I propose that we rescue these children
or at least that we try. I've spoken at length with Mrs. Howar

nd Mr. Roberts already, and I know they're anxious to
nake the attempt. What about the rest of you? Will? Mrs.
chindler?"

"I'll do whatever I have to, to get Mercedes back. So will
Villie."

Shields nodded, his eyes guarded.

"Very good. Wrangler? Ms. Solomon?"

Wrangler said, "We don't have a whole heap of money. Mr.
hields—"

Von Madadh raised a hand. "I don't believe any great sum
ill be required—perhaps none. But will you risk your person,
Vrangler? Will you risk your life?"

"Mine, sure. Not Miss Lisa's."

Lisa set her cup on the coffee table with an audible click.
You go to hell. Sissy's your responsibility and not mine? You go
traight to hell!"

Von Madadh motioned her to silence. "Then you're with us;
nat's well. I want you all, because I don't know exactly what
ill be involved. Not outright fighting, I trust. We may have to
egotiate, and certainly we will need all the cunning we can
uster, and all the courage. Those who have talents of any sort
ust be prepared to use them, because we cannot anticipate
hich will be useful."

Shields said, "Negotiation's all very well, and I usually enjoy
. So is cunning—but how are we going to get in contact with
em?"

"We're going to knock on their door, I hope," von Madadh
ld him. "Have I made it clear that I mean tonight? I do."

To the group Roberts said, "He knows where they are."

"I hope so, Bob. On Friday, Mercedes Schindler-Shields was
terviewed by Sheriff Ahern. I interrupted them, although
nly briefly, looking for Seth. Shortly afterward, when I spoke
ith Mercedes and Mr. Shields, I learned that mine had not
een the only interruption. A young woman had taken pictures
f Mercedes and the sheriff for the *Castle View*."

Von Madadh paused, extracting a cigar from his gold case as

he looked around the circle. "Mercedes stated emphaticall
that this woman was none other than Viviane Morgan, who ha
been in the car with her at the time of the accident. Mr. Shield
will confirm that I was somewhat skeptical."

Shields nodded.

"I had good reason to be. Every human being possesses th
ability to change his appearance to a surprising degree, as yo
must know. Not infrequently, women dye their hair; an
there's nothing to prevent a man from doing so if he choose
Men grow beards and mustaches." Von Madadh smiled as h
stroked his own. "The proof is before you. And these elementa
ry things I've just mentioned are only the beginning. There ar
wigs and toupees; many entertainers wear one or the othe
whenever they appear in public. Furthermore anyone who'
seen that classic of the stage *Peter Pan* has seen a boy personate
by a woman; it's how Peter is virtually always portrayed, an
invariably a sizable part of the audience leaves the theate
under the impression that it has in fact been entertained by
boy in his early teens."

Lisa said, "Go on."

"Those who have kidnapped Sissy and the rest are adept a
such disguises, if human testimony is to be believed. In our file
at the Daoine Institute we have hundreds of deposition
describing instances in which a supposed husband or wif
uncle, daughter, sister, or brother was revealed as an impostc
only by some uncharacteristic word or deed. A man return
early from a fair, giving some reason or perhaps refusing an
His wife and children suspect nothing until he eats wit
monstrous appetite, or is addressed by the cat. When the actu
husband and father returns, the impostor is nowhere to b
found." Von Madadh bit the tip from his cigar and spat it int
the fire, which crackled for an instant with blue flames.

Shields said, "Fairy stories."

"Yes, sir, although nineteen of twenty lack all the wonder w
associate with Charles Perrault and the Brothers Grimm. Her
are no princesses—the persons involved are nearly always poc

peasants. Here are no wishing rings or glass mountains, and no enchanted palaces. There has been an imposture—seemingly quite purposeless. It is over with now, and no evidence remains save for the sworn statements of the witnesses. Cynics are at pains to point out that each phenomenon is restricted to one cultural group—that Irish fairies are reported only from Ireland, for example. Peris and drujes appear soley in Iran; the *asë* are to be met with in Burma alone, and in all cases there seems to be some confusing connection between these things and the spirits of the dead. If somebody has the temerity to point out that the peoples instanced speak radically different languages, that is dismissed as irrelevant."

Ann asked, "What about this photographer Mercedes saw? Are you saying she was one of them?"

Von Madadh lit his cigar. "No. Mercedes said she was. I am saying that she was not. I found her and talked to her—and performed a certain simple test. She has lived here four years and is employed by the newspaper."

Shields asked, "Then what are you getting at, Rex?"

"I outlined to her some of the things Mercedes told you and me, and she vehemently denied ever having ridden in such a car. Moreover, she insisted that the route Mercedes claimed that car had followed was impossible. Her duties have required her to photograph several accidents in which cars left that road. You will recall that Mercedes said the sheriff was also skeptical."

Roberts said, "I used to hunt up there before the road was thought of. The doctor's told us about this turnoff that your daughter says they took, and if it's there I want to see it."

"So do I," Shields muttered.

Von Madadh puffed pungent smoke into the fireplace. "Good. Because that's where I propose we go tonight. There are seven of us—too many for a single car. Let's say that Mrs. Howard, her father, and I go in Mrs. Howard's Oldsmobile. That leaves Will and Mrs. Schindler in Ms. Solomon's car, with Ms. Solomon and Wrangler. Would that be satisfactory?"

Wrangler grunted. "You sure haven't told us a whole lo
about what you're plannin' to do."

Von Madadh grinned at him. "If I cannot locate that road
nothing."

"It's Boomer!"

Boomer nodded emphatically, nickered, and trotted over the
cobblestones to nuzzle Sissy.

Judy interpreted. "He says he's really glad to see you," and
Boomer nodded again.

"Yeah, I heard. I wish I had some sugar for you, good boy
I'm glad to see you, too."

"Maybe we could ride on him back home," Judy suggested
She remembered how Aunt Sally's house had floated away. "O
anyway maybe if we rode around we could find a boat."

"He's been ridden hard already. Here, feel him—he isn'
going to hurt you. That's sweat, and feel how hot he is. H
ought to be walked, and that saddle should come off." Siss
unbuckled Boomer's cinch as she spoke. "We'll walk him coo
then see if we can find him a drink. After that we might rid
him a little, maybe."

A new voice said, "Nice horse. Steeplechaser?"

Boomer reared, throwing saddle and blanket to the ground
his eyes rolling.

"Easy, *easy*!" Sissy grabbed for his bridle and got it. "It's just
man. He won't hurt you."

The man was lean and over six feet tall; he wore a swea
stained slouch hat and an even older brown-leather windbrea
er. There was something about him that frightened Judy wors
than Boomer's rearing. "I'll keep away from him," the ma
said, and took a step backward. He cleared his throat—
hoarse rattling. "Name's Jim Long. Long Jim, they call me.'

"Sissy Stevenson," Sissy said, "and this is Judy. I don't kno
her last name." She paused, glancing toward Judy; but Jud
only stared down at the damp cobbles and said nothing. "We'r

ost," Sissy concluded. "Do you know where Meadow Grass is
from here? Or Castleview?"

Long Jim nodded absently, still looking at Boomer.

"Where are they? We ought to take Boomer back, and we
want to go home ourselves."

"Dangerous out there. You oughta have a man with you."

"Then will you show us? Or anyway just tell us, and we'll risk
it."

Long Jim advanced slowly toward Boomer, his hands extended. The big horse waited, trembling, staring at him with
frightened eyes. "I might take you. I wouldn't let you go off
alone. You got a gun?"

Sissy shook her head.

"I do." Long Jim's hands touched Boomer, and Boomer was
no longer fearful. "That's right," Long Jim told him. "You
know what I am now, don't you, fella? Ain't goin' to hurt you
none."

Judy was still frightened, as Sissy saw; she found Long Jim
frightening herself, but kept her grip on Boomer's bridle. "He
says that you don't scare him any more. It's funny, but I could
understand him. It's as if he could talk."

"You can do that here," Long Jim told her. "You can do it
here, too, only not so many trouble. It's better here—easier. I
got a gun. Want me to show it to you?"

Sissy shook her head.

"Here 'tis." He pulled down the slider on his windbreaker
and drew a large automatic. "Colt forty-five, same as we had in
the Army. Wasn't my T/O & E weapon, but I took familiariza-
tion. Everybody had to."

When Sissy did not reply, he added, "I'm compelled."

"You're sick," she told him. "You ought to see a doctor."
The wind from the sea had chilled her; she shivered.

"I've seen some, and they ain't much. Walkin' down the road,
had a snoot-full, I guess. It don't do much for me any more."
He replaced the automatic, zipped his windbreaker, and picked

up Boomer's saddle and blanket. "We best put these back on him—don't want to carry 'em. Girls don't do much for me neither."

"Maybe if you felt better—"

"But they do somethin'. Morgan give me this gun. You know Morgan?"

Sissy shook her head. "Where's Judy?"

"The little girl? Gone off someplace. She's not comin' with us anyhow."

"Oh, my God!" Seth exclaimed.

Mercedes glanced up. "What is it?"

"It's that damn cat."

She rose and stepped to the tiny window cut into the rock. The sheer cliff beyond the stone sill dropped fifty feet or more to a boulder-strewn beach; a black cat was leaping from boulder to boulder just clear of the breakers, apparently in search of stranded fish. "Have you seen it before?" Mercedes asked.

"You bet I have. He's my cousin's, and the first time I tried to pick him up he ruined my lucky shirt."

"You can't possibly tell from here."

Seth pointed. "I'd know that dirty cat anywhere—see how he holds his head? That white patch on one side? He got hurt there, and the hair never grew back right."

"Maybe that's why he scratched you."

"What?" Seth glanced at her.

"Maybe you reminded him of the way he got hurt that time."

"He fights. He comes home all bloody, and little Judy has to clean him up before my grandmother will let him back in the house."

"You ought to find out what he's fighting before you blame him for that," Mercedes told him, "and why he's fighting them." She thrust one hand through the narrow space between the side of the window and its single bar. "Here, kitty, kitty, kitty!"

"It's just fighting with other tomcats," Seth assured her.

Besides, nobody but Judy would want a tomcat. They fight all the time, and they spray the furniture."

"Must leave him hard up for sparring partners," Mercedes remarked. "Here, kitty! Up here!"

Slowly, G. Gordon Kitty turned to face her and sat down on the boulder on which he had been standing. For a long time he stared up at their narrow window through slitted emerald eyes, absently washing one paw after the other.

31

RESCUE PARTY

"OH, IT is a grand old city," sang Shields,

> *"In the fine old country style.*
> *A credit to the County Down,*
> *The pride of the Emerald Isle.*
> *It has the finest harbor,*
> *For the bread carts to sail in.*
> *And if ever you sail to Ireland,*
> *You'll sail by Magheralin."*

"Willie, I do wish you'd stop that."

"'Tis the custom of the Irish," Shields told his wife, "to sing loudly before going into battle."

Wrangler twisted around in his seat to look at him. "You expecting a fight?"

Shields nodded.

Ann said, "Negotiate, Willie. You know, just like selling a car."

"To negotiate," Shields observed, "one must have something to offer in return. I have a new car, the customer has dollars. I'll undercut the sticker if he'll take the deluxe trim package with air conditioning, finance through us, and so forth. What exactly, are we going to offer the Deeny Shee?"

"Who in the world—?"

"The Fair Folk, Ann. The People of Peace. We've been sold a bill of goods."

The old Cherokee swung off onto the road leading to Baker's knob.

From the front seat Wrangler said, "Reckon we got the same idea—he's one himself. That what you've been thinkin'?"

Shields nodded. "One of whatever they really are. Or else he's working for them."

"Willie! That nice doctor?"

"The nice expert who showed up just when we needed such an expert? Yes. The nice doctor who told us that fairies can make themselves look like somebody we know but never bothered to make any of us prove we're who we say we are, and who's sending seven people off in a couple of cars to bring back four more. Can you imagine squeezing all eleven of us into these two cars, even if one's a child?" Shields recalled the huge and hairy creature he had wrestled in the barn and shuddered. "The nice doctor who's taken us off fairy hunting without weapons."

"Why'd you come, then?" Wrangler asked.

"Because the only way we've got any chance of getting Merc back is to walk into the trap and break out," Shields told him.

Wrangler nodded. "Makes sense."

"I sure as hell hope so."

"Only you're more'n a hair off about not havin' any guns." Wrangler's hand dipped into his denim jacket and emerged with a long-barreled revolver, displayed it, and replaced it.

Ann's mouth formed a little *O*, but Shields grinned. "Good for you, Wrangler. We may need that."

"I only fetched it out 'cause he told me," Wrangler said. "Back when Miss Lisa here and the other ladies was fixin' tea and coffee and suchlike, remember? He took me off to the side, sort of, and said he knew I'd lost my thirty-thirty, but did I maybe have another gun? And I told him, yep, I got this'un, it used to be my brother Bart's. Bart went off lookin' for gold in the Superstitions, and nobody ever did find him. But he left a lot of his stuff back home 'cause of not wantin' to load up too heavy, and this was part of it. It's a Smith and Wesson forty-four special, and you can drive tacks with it if you can hold it steady enough."

The battered Cherokee had been laboring hard to carry four people up the steep and narrow road, its manual transmission in second and its accelerator pedal nearly to the floor. Now Lisa eased back on it. "They're going to stop, I think." The brake lights of the Oldsmobile flared, and she swung onto the shoulder behind it.

In a moment more von Madadh was tapping at her window, and she rolled it down.

"We are here," he announced. "I have a flashlight, and I had planned to search for Mercedes's mysterious shortcut at this point; but I saw it as we drove up, so there's no need for that. Mr. Shields, Mrs. Shindler, Ms. Solomon—can any of you shoot? Do you know how to handle a gun?"

Shields nodded, and Lisa said, "I've shot a little skeet."

"Excellent. I didn't want to worry you before we left, but I've borrowed several weapons from Mrs. Howard. Her late husband was something of a hunter, it seems. I think it might be useful for anybody who understands such matters—I confess I don't—to have one. So if you would be so kind . . . ?"

Shields and Lisa got out. Bob Roberts had already unlocked the trunk of the Oldsmobile and chosen a bolt-action deer rifle with a telescopic sight. "I'll take this," he said, "if nobody minds. I gave it to Tom, and I know it's a good one."

The interior of the trunk was illuminated by a tiny bulb in the lid. Von Madadh said, "perhaps you should have the shotgun, Ms. Solomon. It's what's called a pump action, I believe."

Lisa nodded and took it, flicked the safety off, opened the breech enough to see that there were shells in the magazine but none in the chamber, and shut the breech again.

That left a semiautomatic twenty-two rifle for Shields. He jacked a round into the chamber and put on the safety.

"Mrs. Howard has agreed to drive as I direct," von Madadh explained. "But I have warned her that it may be frightening, and suggested that it might be better to have another, bolder, driver—"

Ann tapped his shoulder. "Willie used to drive in races."

"Really?" Von Madadh looked around at her. "Then if you wouldn't object to being separated . . . ?"

"Not if it's going to help get Mercedes back," Ann declared virtuously. Knowing it was her way of getting even with him for being wrong about the guns, Shields grinned at her.

Von Madadh said, "You must drive exactly as I instruct you, is that agreed? No matter how dangerous it may appear. I'll be sitting alongside you, and it will be just as dangerous for me."

Shields nodded, wondering whether it was really so.

Sally Howard's Oldsmobile was enough like his own Buick to make him feel that there was something subtly wrong about the location of its controls. Recalling what Mercedes had told him, it seemed possible it would not even start.

"Back out," von Madadh directed him. "The turnoff is a few yards back."

Shields put the Olds into reverse and backed out onto the road, hoping that no one was coming down from the summit fast. They crept forward in Drive until von Madadh pointed. "There! You see it?"

"No."

"Go slowly till I tell you to turn, then turn sharply."

From the rear seat, Roberts said, "He's going to be going down one heck of a steep slope."

Von Madadh glanced back at him. "See, Bob, you're afraid. Sally would have been, too."

Shields began, "I still don't—"

"Now! Between those big trees!"

There was no trace of any road that Shields could see, and the grade seemed close to seventy-five percent. He wrenched the wheel anyway, his foot stamping the brakes, and felt the Olds pick up speed despite them. There was bare clearance between the trunks; for a moment the right chrome strip scraped bark.

A track—very faint—veered to the right. Shields braked hard and threw the Olds into a skid-turn that brought the steel barrel of the twenty-two into painful contact with his elbow.

"Good!" von Madadh exclaimed. "Great!"

From the rear seat, Sally Howard called, "I don't know if they're following us. Yes! Here they come."

"That Solomon girl's got real guts," Shields said. To himself he added that she also had four-wheel drive.

The road appeared almost distinct now, but it seemed to him that it was less a real trail pressed by tires than an ephemeral pattern in the dew; dewdrops sparkled everywhere, shining in his lights like millions of diamonds. He assured himself that this was because it was the northern face of the hill, though he was by no means certain it was true.

"Careful!" von Madadh barked.

Slanted itself and running slantwise over the steep slope, slippery and ever at the point of vanishing, it seemed that the road could not get worse. Abruptly it did—but better, too, gaining a graveled surface as it plunged straight down the hill.

"Slower!"

Shields shook his head. "If I hit the brakes here, we'll skid and roll."

A sudden turn would finish them now; but if there were a sudden turn on this stretch, the road would be unusable—and it was plainly used.

Not a turn, a *Y*.

"Right!" von Madadh yelled.

Another swerve, another sickening skid with gravel rolling beneath the wheels. Then, suddenly, the road was almost level and nearly straight, dividing an ancient forest from an unfenced meadow.

Conversationally, Shields asked, "How did you know to turn right? Have you been here before?"

Von Madadh shook his head. "I could see that the left was sharper, that's all. I doubt that we could have made it."

Sally announced, "I thought they were going to turn over, but they're still behind us."

"I thought *we* were going to turn over," Shields told her.

Roberts said apologetically, "This's someplace I don't know at all, and I'd have sworn I'd walked over every acre for twenty miles around Castleview."

Von Madadh's smile was grim. "I don't think that this is 'wonted ground,' as we like to call it, Mr. Roberts. Here we're 'under the hill,' and if we hadn't gone between that particular pair of trees, I don't believe we could have come here at all."

Shields had lowered his window, letting in the night air as a living wind, although they had slowed to thirty miles an hour. It was as cool and damp as the air of the wooded hillside they had left behind; yet it possessed a quality that hinted that it was a different atmosphere altogether, purified, so it seemed, by a different sun—by a star younger or older than Earth's own, but whether older or younger not quite the same. It had owls in it, and bats rowed it with fingered wings; but these owls and these bats, Shields felt, might upon any given night join forces in some dark common cause.

A human hand running upon its fingertips scuttled across the road, briefly dead-white in the headlights. "This is the place, Rex," Shields said. "I don't understand how you knew, but you were right."

"I noticed the trees first," von Madadh told him. "Gnarled trees like those are generally called elf oaks or witch elms in the British Isles. Then I saw that the growth between them had been crushed not long ago. You're correct, I think—this is the place that our Institute has been trying to locate for more than twenty years."

Sally Howard leaned forward. "They're flashing their lights. I think they want us to stop."

Shields nodded. "Okay with me." He braked the Olds to a

gentle halt. There was no shoulder to pull onto here, but he doubted that they would be troubled by traffic.

Sally said, "Don't switch off our lights. Please?"

"All right." Shields himself had much the same feeling. Lisa's headlights grew in his darkened mirror, stopped, and winked out.

Roberts was already out of the car. "I'm going to wait in here," Sally announced.

Von Madadh nodded. "As you wish." He opened his door and joined Roberts.

Shields got out as well, though like Sally he would have preferred to remain in the car. He left the headlights on and the engine running, and he checked the safety of the twenty-two nervously as he walked back to the Cherokee.

Through an open window, Ann called, "We saw something, Willie!"

Shields smiled; Ann did not want to leave the protection of her vehicle either.

Lisa and Wrangler had both gotten out, Lisa carrying Tom Howard's twelve-gauge. Wrangler's right hand was at his side; his big revolver was in it, pointed sensibly toward the ground. Lisa blurted, "We saw a—well, a giant, if you want to call it that. A terribly tall man, or maybe a woman."

"Was he on horseback?" Von Madadh's voice cracked like a whip. "Where?"

Lisa shook her head. "No, he was standing at the edge of the road, about three-quarters of a mile back. He—it—was all hairy, we thought, and—"

Roberts nudged Shields, then von Madadh, and pointed.

To their left the forest gave way to a clearing of perhaps twelve acres, full of ferns and tall grasses dripping with dew and milky moonlight. On its farther side, barely beneath the first branches of the first trees, a large man—it was difficult to judge just how big he really was—sat a large horse. By some witchery of the moon, the eyes of both appeared to glow.

"That's him!" von Madadh shouted. "Shoot, Roberts! *Quick!*"

While Shields was still deciding whether to fire, he heard the snick of the bolt. Bob threw his rifle to his shoulder.

The shot and the horse's bound seemed to come at the same instant. There was a flash of polished steel in the moonlight, then horse and horseman were gone.

32

From Stone

shook his head. "A little girl. I've never seen him

low. Morales shout reuew." Seth shook the bars

JUDY DID not like the tall man. He was scary, as she phrased it to herself, and she did not want to go anywhere with him even if Sissy went too, especially not on any great big horse that stood up sometimes. Under her breath she said, "Well, *I* like ponies!" as she backed away. There was a funny bush growing out of the crack between two cobblestones, and she slipped behind it.

At once a voice hissed, "So you desire to leave them? Then come with me!" A blond lady not a lot taller than Judy herself laid a hand on Judy's shoulder.

"They'll see us," Judy whispered.

"They will not see you as long as you are with me," the lady assured her. "Come! Walk soft."

Quite suddenly Judy realized that the blond lady was right. For some reason, neither Sissy, nor the tall man, nor even the horse, would look where they were, though they might look all round them. "It's magic, isn't it?" Judy said.

Morgan smiled and nodded, and led her to a small door in the base of a different tower.

Seth had taken off one shoe and was using it to pound the bars of their cell door; the shoe was a rubber-soled Adidas and quite light, yet he managed to make a fair amount of noise.

Mercedes watched him for a while, then turned back to the window.

The cat was nowhere to be seen. The beach below was empty save for waves that marched in one after another to crash on the sand or smash against boulders. The dark, blue-green sea beyond displayed neither smoke nor sail. Mercedes counted more than a hundred waves before she gave up.

"He's going to bring us something to eat," Seth reported.

She turned away from the window. "Is it Dr. von Madadh?"

Seth shook his head. "A little guy. I've never seen him before."

"You know," Mercedes glanced away, back toward the bright rectangles of the window, "sooner or later I'm going to have to go to the bathroom."

"Sure. I won't watch, honest." Seth hesitated. "You want me to ask if we can't have separate cells?"

"I think . . ."

She was saved by the rasp of a key in the lock. The door flew open, kicked by a hairy dwarf balancing a wooden trencher; a still hairier giant lurked in the gloom behind him. "Here," said the dwarf. He set down the trencher, shoved it with a bare foot, and slammed the door.

"Okay," Seth said, "I'll ask him. But first let's eat."

Mercedes nodded, suddenly conscious that she was ravenously hungry, and eager for any diversion that would give her time to bring her emotions under control. "I like you," she told him. "Honest, it's not because I don't."

Seth held her uninjured arm as she sat down on the straw-strewn floor next to the trencher. "I know," he said. "I like you, too, Merc."

She looked up with tear-bright eyes. "My dad's the only one who ever calls me that."

"Your dad and me, we call you Merc. What'd they call you where you went to school before?"

Feeling better already, she wiped her eyes on her sleeve.

"The teachers said 'Mercedes.' I guess the other kids called me 'Hyphen' mostly."

Seth sat down beside her. "I like Merc better."

"So do I," she said.

There were rolls, a soft and somewhat runny cheese, a small pot of honey, and a dusty bottle. "No glasses," Seth reported, happy to change the subject. "No knife to spread the cheese and stuff with either."

"I guess we're supposed to eat with our fingers."

"That means I get twice as much." He grinned at her.

She tried to smile. "That's okay."

"No, we'll share out." He picked up the cheese and broke it into two, giving her the larger half. "You can have all the honey—I don't like it."

"All right, I'll take it." She broke her half cheese and gave one piece to him. "For your half."

"Okay." He gave her two rolls, keeping two for himself, then sniffed the bottle. "I don't like wine much, either, but that's all there is."

"Me neither. Is it sour?"

"I don't know—smells yeasty. You want to drink first?"

"Sure." She took the dusty bottle from him, held it to her lips, and tilted it back.

The wine was like a meadow in springtime. Every wildflower flourished there—buttercups and daisies, violets white or blue, dog rose, foxglove, a hundred more. She knew them all. A wren trilled in her ears, and a wind from the south ruffled her hair. Half afraid, she put down the bottle and wiped her mouth. The cell spun about her; Seth was a bronze giant with eyes torn from a summer sky; the bandages were unworthy of his face.

"Wow!" he said. *"That* good?"

"I guess I was thirsty."

Mercedes saw him raise the bottle, but only as she saw the light that streamed through the window and the dust motes that danced in that light. The odor of honey was intoxicating; she had never known how hungry she was, how hungry she had been all her life. She dipped a roll into the honey, and it was nectar and ambrosia.

The key turned in the lock, which squealed in climax. The heavy door swung back, and the cat entered with the key in his left front paw and a long gilded walkingstick with a gold tassel in his right. "Chère Mademoiselle," he began, bowing gracefully, "permit me please to introduce myself. I am none other than the celebrated G. Gordon Kitty, formerly of the FBI and the CIA, the protector and companion—the confidant, if I may say it—of Lady Judith Youngberg."

"Mercedes Schindler-Shields." Mercedes extended her hand to the cat, who kissed it. "This is—"

"Lady Judith's cousin; we have crossed swords in the past." The cat smiled the slight, superior smile of the victor and gave Seth a barely perceptible bow. "We have, I say, crossed swords; but the time has come to put petty disputes behind us. Blood is thicker than cream, as the aphorists have it. You must escape. We must rejoin Lady Judith and see her home. Are you ready? Or would you, perhaps, prefer to complete your collation?"

Lady Judy herself was brushing Queen Morgan's golden hair. "I don't understand about you," she said. "I don't understand about this whole place."

Morgan smiled. "While you understand your own place with a clarity of inner vision that is the despair of philosophers, I am sure."

"Huh-uh," Judy said, and Morgan laughed.

For a moment or three Judy tried to think of a good way to explain, and at last she said, "What I don't understand is how they fit together. Why this is here, and that's there."

"Blind chance," Morgan told her.

Judy brushed some more. It was supposed to be work—she was a Lady in Waiting, and this was one of the things Ladies in Waiting did—but she rather enjoyed it. Morgan's hair was so fine that an individual hair was completely invisible; it could be seen only when several hairs lay together. Judy knew her own was nowhere near as pretty, and she had an ill-defined feeling that if she brushed Morgan's enough, she might learn how to make her own nicer.

After she had lost count of the strokes several times, she asked, "Why did you want to hurt your brother?" though she knew that sisters usually did.

"I did not wish to hurt him," Morgan told her. "I wished to kill him—a very different thing. I only hurt him because he irritated me by remaining alive, or because I was trying to kill him in that way or this and did not quite succeed."

"But he died in the end?"

"Not wholly."

Judy continued to brush while she digested that. "I think you really loved him."

Morgan whirled so quickly it seemed a trick. "I did! Oh, yes, I did! Don't you know the legend of the three queens? Or the lady in the lake? Or the sword in the stone?"

Judy shook her head. "Are those stories?"

"Yes, wonderful stories! But first I must tell you how my brother and I came to be. Our father was merely a vulgar petty chieftain, one of those half-Christian Celts the Romans left in their wake like candy wrappers. His mother was a common duchess, but mine was a merrow. I doubt you know what a merrow is."

"You don't mean the gray stuff inside a soup bone?"

"Hardly." Morgan rose quickly (she seemed to do everything suddenly) and strode to the window, where she stood looking out at the water. "To explain I would have to tell you much more—how three brothers drew lots for the four quarters of this world from a helmet, and all that. Do you know anything about fairies, little Judith?"

"Not if you're one," Judy said.

"Well expressed. I was going to say that the merrows are sea fairies, and so we are. We are the Oceanids, descended of Tethys and Oceanus, and we live under the sea."

"You don't," Judy pointed out.

"Oh, but I do, little Judith, when I wish." It seemed to Judy almost as though it were the water itself who spoke.

"I have many homes; some are under the sea, others beneath lakes. But I meant to tell you that when my brother was a babe, a meteorite with a sword through it fell white-hot to earth. As you probably know, there used to be another world beyond the one your people have named for your god of defence. She died long ago, and her people perished with her, most of them. This sword was their work. It had become partially encased in molten rock, I imagine."

Judy said, "And only the Right King of England could pull it out! I know, I saw it on TV."

Morgan glanced back at her and smiled. "And yet some say children receive scant education these days. There was no such entity as England then—but that is another matter. Yes, my brother drew out the sword. He called it Excalibur, which means 'from stone.' It was the product of an advanced metallurgy, you understand, vastly superior to anything anybody has here."

Though she did not understand *metallurgy*, Judy said, "Uh-huh."

"He lost it, of course. You mortals have poor memories and you're horribly careless. I found it and threw it in my closet, and later I gave it back to him. Then when he had lost his last battle, in drowned Leonnesse where he was born, he sent it to me for safekeeping."

After a moment Judy shook her head. "I don't think that's a very good story."

Eyes wide, Morgan spun about. *"So all day long the noise of battle rolled, among the mountains by the winter sea; until King Arthur's Table, man by man, had fallen in Lyonesse about their lord King Arthur. Then, because his wound was deep, the bold Sir Bedivere uplifted him, and bore him to a chapel nigh the field, a broken chancel with a broken cross, that stood on a dark strait of barren land: on one side lay the Ocean, and on one lay a great water, and the moon was full."*

Very much frightened by all this, Judy shouted, "I'm sorry! I didn't mean to make you mad."

Morgan crouched until her lips were level with Judy's own, and whispered, *"Such a sleep they sleep—the men I loved."* Her voice was as lonely as the cries of the gulls. *"I think that we shall never more, at any future time, delight our souls with talk of knightly deeds, walking about the gardens and the halls of Camelot, as in the days that were. I perish by this people which I made—though Merlin swore that I should come again to rule once more; but, let what will be, be, I am so deeply smitten thro' the helm that without help I cannot last till morn. Thou therefore take my brand Excalibur, which was my pride: for thou rememberest how in those old days, one summer noon, an arm rose up from out the bosom of the lake, clothed in white samite, mystic, wonderful, holding the sword—and how I rowed across and took it, and have worn it, like a king; and wheresoever I am sung or told in aftertime, this also shall be known: but now delay not, take Excalibur, and fling him far into the middle mere: watch what thou seest, and lightly bring me word."*

Awed as much or more by Morgan's deathly solemnity as by her words, Judy mumbled, "I don't understand, Your Majesty. I don't know where it is."

Then Morgan led her to a cabinet and showed her the sword.

33

THE FURIOUS ARMY

SISSY AND Long Jim had put his sweat-soaked saddle blanket and heavy stock saddle on Boomer again. Sissy rode, with Long Jim walking at her stirrup. "I'm still worried about Judy," Sissy confessed.

"There's many more that bear the king's blood."

Sissy ducked beneath a limb. "You mean the old king in the Tower?"

Long Jim chuckled, a deep grating that made Sissy think of stones sliding upon stones, far beneath the ground. "Nope, not him. Viviane's brother."

"Is that Judy's father?"

Long Jim did not reply. If they were following any path, it was one Sissy could not see. They had climbed and descended stone-strewn hills, and traversed wide meadows pastured only by deer. Now Boomer's hooves were silenced by bright mosses, and trees rose before them and behind them, trees five and six feet through the trunk, trees that were often hollow and more often dead.

"Where are we?" Sissy asked after a long silence.

"On the border."

An east wind was rising, stirring and groaning, a cold wet wraith summoned from the world's night side by some necromancer. Its gusts sent damp leaves flitting forth like bats; one clung to Sissy's cheek until she pulled it off.

"This can't be the Canadian border. Can it?"

Long Jim shook his head, like a man awakened from a deep sleep. "Between your country and Viviane's." He stopped to glance up at Sissy, and Boomer halted at once. "Border's both places, like. They say they don't know where they are, 'cause when you're walkin' border land you're in the two together."

"I see," murmured Sissy, who did not. The lost wind sighed in her ears. She kicked Boomer with her heels until he resumed his slow walk.

They forded a creek, Long Jim leaping from rock to rock, Boomer wading in icy water as high as his knees and pausing in midstream to drink.

"I don't think it will hurt him," Sissy said. "He's pretty well cooled off now."

If Long Jim heard, he gave no sign of it. He crouched on the farther bank, bending to scrutinize the soft earth.

Sissy clucked to Boomer, slapped his neck with the reins, and dug her heels into his sides again and again. At last his head came up and he resumed the troublesome business of picking his way, in iron shoes, over slippery stones.

Safely across, she dismounted. Long Jim was standing again by then, but she bent to examine the overlapping hoofprints that he had been studying. After a moment she said, "Those were sure as heck a couple of big horses."

"He come across where we did. Went upstream there headin' for the lake."

"You know who it is?"

Long Jim nodded. "Green man."

"Mr. Greenman?"

"Don't matter to you," Long Jim told her, "and we're no goin' that way." Without a backward look, he plunged into the wood, moving at the swift lope of a backwoodsman in a hurry.

Sissy called, "Mind if I walk, too? I was getting chilly u there, and it'll give Boomer a rest."

There was no reply. She set off after him, half walking and half running, leading Boomer by the reins. The trees were smaller on this side and more thickly set. She reflected that riding would hardly have been faster, and she would surely have been badly scraped before they had gone half a mile. Briefly she lost sight of Long Jim as he detoured around a blackberry tangle, now largely leafless.

I don't care, Sissy thought. All I've got to do is keep headed this way.

She was jogging now, with Boomer trotting slowly behind her.

Then Long Jim was gone again, dropping down into some gulch or ditch. When she reached it—there was another stream at the bottom, one that had cut a twenty-foot cleft in the hillside—the banks looked too steep for Boomer, too steep, almost, even for her. She was forced to lead him a hundred yards down the slope to find a place where both could cross.

"We'd jump this, boy, if you were fresh," she told him, and knew she lied. Fresh, with an expert like Lisa on his back and a proper jumping saddle, Boomer *might* have made it; but Sissy herself would never have found the nerve to try it.

East, she thought. We were going east.

Earlier the sun had broken through occasionally to daub the underbellies of the thunder-haunted clouds with cerise and lend shadows to the moss-draped trunks. Then the wind had been in her face; now she tried to keep it there.

Once she thought she heard a truck, and she veered in that direction; but after a quarter mile or less the woods became an impassible tangle.

It was dark by the time she turned back. "I wish I'd eaten more carrots," she told Boomer. "And I wish I had a carrot here to give you."

He nodded in the dark. She could not see his head, but she felt the motion of the reins.

Again it seemed to her that she heard an engine and the hum of tires. She recalled the castle, abandoned, as it had seemed, save for flitting figures glimpsed at a distance, the lost girl, and the aged king. It came to her fully now for the first time that the castle had not belonged in the reality she knew at all, that such a place could hardly exist anywhere, and certainly could not exist here, in this forgotten and countrified corner of upstate Illinois.

At length it occurred to her that from Boomer's saddle she might be able to see the lights of the vehicles she had heard. She mounted and found that his night vision was better than her own; he threaded the tree trunks at a slow walk, seldom making an error. She watched for headlights but saw none; nor did she hear the sound of a car or truck again; the wind was quartering now, and she did not dare rein Boomer around to face it. Horses were supposed to have a wonderful sense of direction. A horse, or so she had been assured, will always find his way back to the stable, back to oats and corn and water. Sissy hoped fervently that it was true.

She had been riding for what seemed like an hour or more when she heard a familiar voice: "Sissy, you are lost? I too am lost."

"Sancha! Is that you?"

"I am here. I see you. Can you not see me?"

Boomer caught the smell of another horse and whinnied. The other replied—old friends happy to have met again.

"Sancha, where are you?"

"You are coming toward me, do not concern yourself. But you do not know the way back?"

"I've been giving Boomer—" Abruptly he shied, and Sissy was nearly thrown.

"It is the blood, Sissy. The smell disturbs him."

"Are you hurt?"

There was no answer.

Tired as he was, Boomer broke into a nervous trot. Sissy tried to rein him up, but her right leg slammed into a tree, and for a moment the pain was so intense she thought she might faint.

Then Boomer stopped, as it seemed, of his own accord, head tossing, dancing sidewise. A second or two passed before Sissy realized that Sancha had hold of his bridle.

"You must dismount, Sissy. I wish to kiss you."

She had been only frightened before, alone and cold, afraid that she might walk and ride all night without ever finding her way back to Meadow Grass. Suddenly she was terrified. She had been a child, trembling in the dark; now the tiger had come. As violently as she could, she slapped Boomer's haunch. He reared, pawing air, so high it seemed that he might fall backward.

A cold hand touched her own, and the reins fell from it. Someone—Sancha?—was kissing her knee, kissing the spot where some stub of limb had torn her skin, kissing away her blood.

Light stabbed the trees, wandered away, returned to pick out Buck nibbling at a fern, his reins at his forefeet. Sissy jabbed her heel into Boomer's side with all her strength. He wheeled, and the shaft of yellow light stabbed Sancha's blood-smeared lips and cheeks.

Long Jim rumbled, "Well, well. Look what's here."

For an instant Sissy thought he meant Sancha; but it seemed he meant himself, because he turned his light upon his own face; it appeared unchanged, save as any man's face will change when lit from below, yet surely there was some horror in it. Sancha screamed, a high, uncanny wail of dismay and despair . . .

And was gone.

The light vanished too, and Long Jim's face with it. Sissy heard Buck's saddle creak as Long Jim settled himself. At last she managed to ask, "How did you find me?"

"By lookin'. With a horse an' all I figured you'd keep up. After a while I seen you weren't behind me and turned back." He clicked his tongue to Buck.

Sissy said, "Just a minute, I've got to find the reins."

"He'll steer you better'n you him."

"You're probably right. Okay, I'm ready. Can I ask you where you found that flashlight? I don't think you had it this afternoon." Buck, Sissy sensed, moved off at a fast walk, his steps scarcely audible; a twig snapped as they brushed past it. With her knees and heels, she told Boomer that he might go too.

"Out of a car. Figured I needed it worse'n they did. You know I used to work at the track? Stable hand and so on. Been a long time since I been on a horse, though. Viviane wants me to drive for her, mostly."

"You must know what it is I want to ask you," Sissy said. "What will you do if I ask it?"

"Answer you, I guess, if I can."

"All right then. What was the matter with Sancha? I know her, or I thought I did, and she's never been like that before. And why was she so afraid of you?"

It was a long time before Jim replied. They turned at the bottom of the hill. The trees were larger again now, as well as Sissy could judge from their loom in the dark. Certainly the ground was more nearly level here.

"You a church-goer?" Jim asked at last.

"No, not really."

"I never was neither. They don't believe what they preach — that's what always sent me huntin' or fishin' instead. I was married awhile, and once the minister come over. Some of it's right, though."

For a moment, the moon broke through the clouds. Sissy saw Long Jim slumped in the saddle, ten feet ahead of Boomer's nose. "What do you mean?"

"A livin' man has got a soul, a spirit in him. One anyhow, an' maybe two or three. You believe that?"

"I don't know," Sissy admitted.

Long Jim sighed, or perhaps it was merely the wind. "I do. That's the difference between us, see? Now suppose a person — what'd you call her?"

"Sancha. Sancha Balanka."

"Suppose she was just about dead, some way. Maybe a doctor might think she was. Sometimes a heart will beat so slow that a doctor listens and goes away before it ever does. Flesh cools down like a snake's. He signs the paper then, nowadays, and the person goes to the undertaker's. He drains out the blood—they do that—and pumps in embalmin' fluid, and that kills 'em. In the old days they'd have to dig 'em up an' burn 'em, or cut off the heads, or maybe stake 'em down."

Sissy shook her head. "I can't believe we're talking about this. Taking it seriously."

"You asked me. You want to hear or not?"

She shrugged. "Go ahead."

"All right, that's what happened to your friend, only she ain't got to the undertaker yet. What you seen wasn't her, or anyhow not all of her, just the part that wants to stay alive no matter what. Now you're goin' to ask me what a thing like that would need a horse for."

"Yeah," Sissy said. "I guess I am."

"Really it don't, but it wants to think it does. It wants to think it's the whole girl, see? So it'll ride a horse if it can, or maybe drive a car, and act like it was the real person, the body and everythin'. Only if somebody holds up a mirror to it, that makes it face up to what it is, and it'll skedaddle."

"I'm not buying a bit of this," Sissy told him. "I'm not buying any of it. But why—"

The crack of a rifle interrupted her. It was neither near nor far, neither loud nor faint, but a distinct flat report, the sound a soldier hears when he is fired upon by a sniper half a mile off. After it, faintly at first, came the drum of hooves, followed by the snarl of engines.

"It's him!" Long Jim shouted. "By God, it's him!"

"It's who?" Sissy asked. "Is it Greenman?"

The quick tattoo of Buck's gallop was the only reply. She urged Boomer forward, and he went willingly, not galloping but trotting with surprising speed, dodging trees that Sissy herself could hardly see.

Another shot, its hollow boom nearly lost in the hysterical keening of the engines. A different gun, Sissy thought. So now there's somebody else shooting—it's a shoot-out at a drag strip and why the hell am I riding into it?

She struggled to rein Boomer up, but the edge of the woods was already far behind them, and the yellow glare of headlights lit the open ground before them like a stadium. A huge man upon a far bigger horse than Boomer came thundering down on Long Jim and Buck; twice she saw the flash of Long Jim's automatic before the horses met like linemen in the closing seconds of the final quarter of the hardest-fought football game ever played and Buck was thrown back end-over-end, spinning and rolling and tumbling like a kicked puppy.

It seemed that the lead car, a shiny blue sedan, was going to strike poor Buck as well; but its driver must have seen him. At the last possible moment it swerved to one side.

(Boomer was galloping now, dashing along like a race horse with the bit in his teeth; and no pressure from the reins would slow him.)

Something terrible rose upon its knees from the place where Long Jim had fallen. As nightmares fasten on some single detail to present immutable to the horror-stricken gaze of the sleeper, Sissy beheld its decayed and skull-like face, its skeletal hands outstretched as though to ward off the second onrushing car.

Then it was gone, and they too were caught up in the chase, Boomer galloping like a fresh horse, Boomer flying like a steed bewitched or enchanted, Boomer flying, a transfigured horse —he was Pegasus now, he was Alborak! Sissy's frenzied shout was of triumph as much as fear, when wrapped in rain, wind, and biting hail they burst into Castleview.

34

CHINA KNIGHT

THERE WAS LSD in that wine, Mercedes thought. None of
this is really happening. It can't possibly be.

She felt as though she were floating. Someplace behind or
below (directions were exceedingly hazy) was the cell in which
they had been confined. Someplace else, someplace on the
other side of the woods and the other side of the pounding sea,
was a hospital bed, a room in the Red Stove Inn, her own room
back in Arlington Heights in the home Mom and Dad were in
the process of selling. In some sense she was still in all those
places, and in some senses she was in them all much more than
she was here now.

Absently, she glanced down at the sword in her left hand. It
was long, slender and double-edged, and its blade was not as
bright as she expected the blades of knives to be; it reminded
her of a new nail. She tried to imagine herself sticking it in
somebody's chest and could not.

The cat, who had been directing them with almost theatrical
stealth, turned to face them now and made a speech.

"We're come," the cat announced, "to what may well prove
the most difficult and dangerous part of this initial phase of our
entire escape—the steep stair."

"The steep stair," Mercedes repeated under her breath.

"Purcisely. You may indeed have need of your swords—but

certainly you shall have need of your hands. Sir, I suggest you put your weapon through your belt. I sincerely regret that it proved impossible to procure sheaths and baldrics. Like this."

He took Seth's sword, pulled out Seth's belt, and slid the blade between the belt and the waistband of Seth's jeans.

Mercedes said, "I'm not wearing a belt."

"I had observed it, my lady; there remains a second method. Allow me." The cat held out the elastic waist of her own jeans and thrust the sharp point of her sword through the denim. "You must think of yourselves as having steel tails," he warned them. "Imagine yourselves cats, for example—the fancy may encourage you. But cats having steel tails. Should you turn quickly or thoughtlessly, your steel tails will clash against the stones of these walls, quite possibly summoning a gaoler or someone else whom we should not wish to meet. Is that understood?"

"Too good," Seth agreed vaguely. The tower had begun to rock, and Mercedes, leaning against the wall to steady it, did not risk a reply.

"How'll you manage the stick?" Seth asked the cat owlishly. "You don't have any sword and you can't stick that through your skin."

"As for a sword," the cat slipped a paw beneath the fur of its chest and drew a large automatic pistol far enough for them to see it. "I have chosen the Browning *Grand Pussance* for this mission. It was my grandsire's, and I am sentimentally attached to it."

Mercedes nodded understandingly.

"I have, I concede, a Glock 17 beneath the other arm for emergencies. As to my badge of office, I shall manage it as I have so often managed it before. Now follow me!"

The "steep stair" proved to be a ladder with rope sides and frighteningly slender wooden rungs. The cat slipped his foreleg through the gold cord that held the tassel and swarmed up this ladder like a monkey. Rather more circumspectly, Seth followed him; Mercedes, her right arm nearly useless in its plaster

ast, brought up the rear more circumspectly still. After a score
of rungs the swinging ladder climbed through a lightless shaft
of smooth, chilly metal that might have been the casing of a
well. Mercedes's fingers told her at each new grip just how small
the ropes were; she was very glad (or told herself she was) that
she could not see them too.

Through the narrow parting in her drapes, old Mrs. Cosgriff
watched Sally Howard's windows. Somebody was in there; a
shadow moved against Sally's curtains from time to time, first in
one room, then in another. Mrs. Cosgriff itched to know who it
was. Not poor Mr. Howard—he was dead and buried. Not the
Howard boy—the Howard boy was missing and wanted by the
sheriff, so Mrs. Cosgriff had heard. Not Sally herself, or that
handsome doctor who was (perfectly disgracefully if you asked
old Mrs. Cosgriff) staying with her—they had gallivanted off
together in Sally's big Oldsmobile, leaving poor, dead Mr.
Howard's Chrysler in the driveway.

"It's that little dark fellow," Mrs. Cosgriff muttered to
herself as a taxi pulled up in front of the Howard house. Mrs.
Cosgriff had not seen the little dark fellow for some time, but
she had always suspected a little, darkly, that the little dark
fellow was still there whether she saw him or not.

The front door opened, there was a wholly coincidental clap
of thunder, and her dark little suspicions were amply confirmed. Dressed in a three-piece suit and carrying a leather
briefcase, the little dark fellow emerged from the house,
pranced down the porch steps, and sprinted along the front
walk through the first big drops of the storm. Mrs. Cosgriff
watched him get into the taxi and watched the taxi pull away.

The question was who to call? Who was likely to be home,
and to whom would she enjoy relating this most and discussing
it afterwards? Old Mrs. Cosgriff was very close to settling on
Annabelle Peters when a—a *something*—a whole lot of *some
things*—came rampaging up the street. There was—she
had—a confused impression of horses and dogs, of men and

women whirled along by the wind, of lightnings shot like
arrows and lightnings thrown like spears.

One of the women was Sally Howard.

Old Mrs. Cosgriff jerked her drapes shut, tottered over to
her nice cowl-back chair, and sat. The telephone stood ready
on the end table, but all of her speculations about the little dark
fellow were flown. Old Mrs. Cosgriff imagined herself calling
Annabelle Peters to say that she, old Mrs. Cosgriff herself with
her very own eyes, had seen ghostly Indians on the warpath
here on Pine Street in Castleview. Annabelle Peters would be
certain she was both out of her right mind and stark, staring
mad; but old Mrs. Cosgriff discovered that she did not much
care as long as she could tell *somebody*, leaving out all that about
Sally's being in the wagon. That was, so old Mrs. Cosgriff
judged from long experience, the touch too much, the straw
that would break the camel's back.

Rain and hail rattled on her roof, on her porch.

She would call Annabelle Peters soon. Call just as soon as she
felt a little better.

Fortunately, Phyllis Sun had worn her London Fog, and she
kept a plastic babushka in the pocket. With the babushka drawn
tightly over her sleek black hair and the coat buttoned to the
neck, she struggled against the storm, lips set and eyes nearly
shut. In China, she told herself, a thousand women were facing
similar storms in raincoats of straw; she wondered whether they
ever thought about her, decided that they did not, and
attempted to suggest tactfully to whatever god might rule that
those women would not be required to welcome and seat
patrons at the finest Chinese restaurant in this part of the state
when they got where they were going.

If the Heavenly Emperor heard her, he rejected her implied
suggestion, sending blasts of rain, wind, and hail that seemed
more than sufficient to overturn any truck. Phyllis staggered
backward two steps, bowed lower still to the wind, clenched her

teeth, and struggled forward again, wishing wholeheartedly that she were back in jail.

There, Hwan Lee—when eventually they had let her in to see him—had been extravagantly grateful. His little cell had been warm, clean, and dry, and she had sat on his bunk while he stood respectfully, his eyes aglow with thanks, and resolutely refused to make any sense at all. Phyllis reiterated her arguments to herself as she struggled along, both because she hoped to find some flaw that could be corrected on her next visit, and because it distracted her somewhat from her present misery. Pear Street—three and a quarter blocks to the Golden Dragon, and three and a quarter blocks under such nightmarish conditions as these were the equivalent of twenty miles on a fine day. No, more.

"Hwan Lee, we've—"

A taxi whizzed past, its tires raising plumes of rainwater. Phyllis waved frantically, shouting against the roar of the wind and flourishing her now-sodden best purse; but there was someone in the rear seat, the roof light was dark, and the taxi slowed not one whit. She would have resented the spray from its wheels if she had felt it; but it struck her no harder than the driving rain and was if anything less densely wet.

"Hwan Lee," she had told him, "we're going to get you Len Turner, the best attorney in Castleview, and H. Richard Wang is coming out from Chicago."

"Thank you velly much!" Hwan had said, exactly as though he had just gotten a good tip.

"H. Richard Wang is Bob Chen's son-in-law, so we feel that we can trust him. But it's better to have a local man, too; a Caucasian."

"Ah, wise!"

Phyllis had found herself desperately wishing she knew more than a few hundred words of Chinese; it would do her little good now to urge Hwan to hurry up, or to warn him that he might shortly become a very crispy duck indeed. "But neither

Mr. Turner nor Mr. Wang can help you at all unless you give them your complete cooperation."

Hwan had stared at her blankly. And she, assuming that he had not understood *cooperation*, had added, "Work with them, tell them what you know."

"Oh, yes."

She had hurried on. "It isn't just a matter of attempted murder, Hwan Lee, although that would certainly be bad enough. Because they know you were trying to stab that man, and there isn't any connection between the two of you that they can come up with, they think you may have stabbed other people—stabbed people at random. There are unsolved murders here; I suppose everyplace has some. Some were committed with knives. They're going to try to blame you for those."

Hwan had said, "Okay, I tell. First time, no bull."

"That's good. That's very good! But why? Why did you do it?"

There had been a lengthy pause, during which she had been forced to bite her lips to keep from repeating *why?*

And at last Hwan had said, "They tell me."

"They did? Hwan, who are they?" She had asked it over and over again, threatening and pleading, rephrasing the question in every way she had been able to think of; but there it had ended. No words she had found would drag a name or any other indication of identity from Hwan. She had spoken of the difficulties that he was creating not only for her and for their family, but for all the other Chinese-Americans in Castle County, and at last in desperation of the fall-off of business at the restaurant. Hwan had received word of both with oriental stoicism.

Next time her brothers could damned well go themselves.

A hailstone struck her full in the mouth, and she wiped her lips and examined her hand in the light from a shopwindow to see whether she was bleeding. There seemed to be no blood but it was possible the pounding rain had washed her hand at once; she probed the place with her tongue.

The light from the window flickered, then kindled anew.

Another two and a half blocks to the Golden Dragon. Phyllis fought her way forward in defiance of wind and rain, one hand grasping her purse, the other clutching the edge of the plastic babushka.

All the lights flickered. For an instant the streetlights and all the lights in all the stores—stores implacably closed that nevertheless maintained illuminated displays calculated to engender an acquisitiveness they were unwilling to satisfy—were gone, and only the pandemonium of the storm remained.

In a second or less they came back on, some of them, but with sadly diminished strength, yellowish and feeble, no longer uniting into a spurious day but as isolate as the fixed stars, guttering candles wrapped in twilight.

Above even the howling of that raging storm, Phyllis heard the two-fold hoofbeats of Sleipnir, though for a moment more she did not know what it was she was hearing.

Horns wildly blowing, they raced toward her; they were the soul of the storm. And for one burning instant before darkness fell, she glimpsed him astride the eight-legged stallion, beheld that wide-horned helm and the dwarf-forged spear, and worst and best of all, never to be forgotten, his single, blazing eye.

I've seen it, she thought; this is the Savage Course. This was the Riding.

The babushka was gone, her hair was sopping with rain, and her purse had fallen to the rain-scoured sidewalk. She had been going somewhere and she had been coming from someplace else, but none of that mattered any more. She had witnessed the Wild Hunt and lived.

"You not Mr. Turner," Hwan Lee said. "You Mr. Fee."

The gentleman thus addressed nodded. "Per'aps you've been wondering why you're still alive."

Hwan said nothing. If he had been wondering anything at all, his features betrayed no trace of it.

"You were warned that if you failed to take the life of the

261

man we pointed out to you, your own would be forfeit. Had you wounded him, we might per'aps have forgiven you and offered you a second chance. You did not so much as draw blood, however." Opening the lawyer-like briefcase on his lap, Mr. Fee took out a long-barreled target pistol.

Hwan's small stature, eager waiter's manner, and ignorance of English combined to give an impression of simplicity and even timidity—this though no simple, timid man could have succeeded, as he had, in reaching Hong Kong from the People's Republic, or in entering the U.S. from Hong Kong. In reality he was neither timid nor simple; he was both shrewd and complex, and when his reason indicated it necessary, the master of an almost infinite reserve of cool fortitude. The long barrel was in his left hand before it could be leveled at him. The heel of his right struck Fee sharply on the chin, and the back of Fee's head struck the concrete wall of the cell more sharply still.

As night vanishes with the raising of a blind, Mr. Fee was gone. His clothing remained, but in that clothing was a large-headed being with three pairs of eyes and pipe-stem limbs. It pressed its hands to its head and blinked its largest pair of eyes, night-black ovals the size of eggs. Mr. Fee reappeared, wavered, and vanished again.

Hwan transferred the target pistol to his right hand. He had never handled a gun before, though guns had been pointed at him more than once. He found that having the gun in his own hand was a considerable improvement. "Be Mr. Fee," he said. "You not Mr. Fee, I shoot."

The many-eyed being rolled its larger pairs as though to judge whether Hwan was serious, and Mr. Fee returned.

"Call police, say unlock door, you go home."

Mr. Fee called, "Guard! You can let me out now."

The turnkey was more than a little surprised by Hwan's gun; no one had broken out of the Castle County Jail in twenty years. Hwan locked him in the cell with Fee and trotted out of the jail into pouring rain, with Tom Howard's target pistol tucked into his waistband and concealed by his shirt.

35

HITCHHIKERS

FAR ABOVE Mercedes the cat called, "Here we are!" A tiny square of light appeared, winked out as he (presumably) stepped through it, and reappeared again.

She climbed with renewed determination, and succeeded well enough to bump her head on Seth's heels. For a minute at least—an actual minute by the clock—she feared that the bright door would close before they got to it, shutting them somehow in this dank tube of iron forever. Then Seth was through, and she heard him say, "*Judy!*" He had mentioned a Judy while they sat side by side sipping Coke in his mom's car at the scenic view; Mercedes knew a brief pang of jealousy before she recalled that Judy was his cousin. A little cousin, she seemed to remember. A child?

Four more slender rungs, and the door was hers as well—but the last snapped beneath her foot. She squealed and grabbed the side ropes. Swaying, the ladder thumped her against the rounded wall until her swordblade chimed like a bell; the tube seemed to spin around her, and she felt she was about to be sick.

Desperately groping, her toes reclaimed the rung below the broken one. With one foot on that, she got the other onto the next sound rung and pulled herself up, keeping her feet well out toward the ends of both, away from their fragile centers.

She nearly collapsed as she stumbled through the bright door. Seth caught her, and the feeling his arms brought was brand new, whispering of wonder.

"Easy," he said. "You okay?"

"A step broke. I thought I was going to fall."

"Easy," he said again, and squeezed her. His hand brushed her hips as he released her. She felt like backing into it to make it brush her harder. I'm not drunk any more, she thought. Maybe I'm in love, but I'm not drunk, and the cat's still up on his hind legs, and he carries a cane.

"This is my cousin Judy," Seth told her. "Judy Youngberg. Judy, this is Mercedes."

"Hi." The little girl nodded shyly. "This's my cat, G. Gordon Kitty."

"I know," Mercedes told her. "He brought us here. He's a wonderful cat."

"He's not always as wonderful as now," Judy confessed, "but he's always a really good cat."

The cat bowed. "Who urges you to fly this phantasmagoric palace. Here we stand in the very apartments of the sorcerous queen. She has departed upon some urgent errand but may return at any instant."

Judy nodded her agreement. "Only first we better shut that door 'fore somebody down below sees it's open—Queen Morgan said for me not to open it 'cause I might fall down. Then I have to show you the sword."

Mercedes closed the bright door, discovered that it could be bolted from their side, and bolted it.

"I've got a sword already, Judy," Seth objected. "So does Mercedes, and you're too little."

"It's real *important*. Look." Judy trotted across the fey room to a tall cabinet, painted and coarsely carved, standing in a shallow recess. It seemed to Mercedes that she heard a faint, clear hum as the cabinet door swung back.

For a moment the object within did not seem a sword at all, but such a cross as she had seen in pictures of ancient and holy objects hoarded in museums, its hilt and scabbard glowing with gems. She blinked and saw that there were none, and that there was little light in the cabinet for gems to catch. Instead both sword and scabbard were of some silvery metal greater than the silver she knew, a silver full of starlight, faceted, polished and pierced almost to filigree. Mercedes had breathed, "Oh, isn't it *beautiful!*" before she realized the voice was hers.

With some effort, Judy lifted it from the cabinet. The tip of the scabbard had rested on a shabby little leather book that fell to the floor as she took the sword out. Mercedes picked up the book, but had eyes only for the sword.

"There was a battle a little while ago," Judy explained, "and the wrong ones won. This is how you make it go the other way."

As each fresh vehicle approached, Hwan Lee turned to face the street and made the thumb-out gesture of begging a ride. Each drenched him with stinging spray that left him no wetter than he had been already.

Yet it did no harm, Hwan reflected, to beg thus. Those who ask others many questions seldom question beggars, being anxious to escape their importunities. And who could say with certainty that no car would stop?

He was trying to hold that thought for the thirteenth time when one did. It was a black Cadillac, nearly new; the driver who motioned for him to get inside was a big man with a coffee-light complexion and a wide black mustache. Smiling, grateful, and sodden, Hwan sank into the upholstered luxury of the front seat.

"Leeve here?" the driver asked. "Know dees town?"

Hwan tried to guess which answer was desired, decided on the affirmative, and nodded.

"Meadow Grass—you take me to dat, okay?"

First vaguely, then precisely, Hwan's memory reproduced the conversation he had overheard while eavesdropping on Ann and Shields. "Ol' Penton Load," he stated confidently. "Know how get there?"

The driver shook his head. He had taken a cigar from the breast pocket of his yellow suit; he offered it to Hwan, then lit it with the dash lighter.

"You go," Hwan said. "I show. See light? There turn."

The big car floated smoothly ahead, and for a second or two Hwan permitted himself to relax; he knew where Old Penton Road began, and they had only to follow it to find this Meadow Grass. Should they miss it and go too far, so much the better—he would get out when the driver turned back. "Two block more. Go that way, Sick'more Avenue. Sick'more get new name, be Ol' Penton Load when get out of town."

Rain blinded the windshield, drummed upon the steel top of the car. Puffing pungent smoke, the driver leaned forward and swung the car sharply around.

"That light," Hwan told him. "Easy now. Leal soon Meadow Glass."

"Somebody shoot *minha irma*—my seester." Thinking Hwan had not understood, the driver made a pistol of his hand. "Beeng! I jus' see my seester een 'ospeetal, *compreendo*? She ver' bad. I go see dees woman was dere."

White clapboard houses were edging apart to make room for more trees. The flashing VACANCY of the Red Stove Inn appeared and drifted away through the rain.

"*Polica* say ma'be they got heem, but I do' know. We leeve Brazeel so ma'be dey don' care, eh? Ma'be we mus' do someteeng, I teenk."

Abruptly, the driver touched the brakes. A girl, pale and insubstantial-looking, had emerged from the woods that lined the road, her hands outstretched and imploring, her pale hair awash in rain. The driver glanced at Hwan, who understood that he was wishing Hwan were not there.

As it happened, it was a wish that Hwan himself heartily seconded. "I get out," he suggested quickly.

The driver smiled. "Okay."

Almost skidding, the Cadillac came to a stop. Hwan sprang

out into the pounding rain and held the door for the blond girl, who flashed him an appreciative smile. "Please get in back."

He wanted to slam the door or to flee without slamming it—to run away into the rain, never stopping until he reached China once more.

"In back," the girl whispered. "Immediately!"

Helpless, Hwan slid between the post and the back of the front seat. The door closed behind him, seemingly of its own volition.

The driver was grinning like a tiger beneath his big black mustache as he introduced himself. "*Meu nome é* José Alvarez Martim Basílio Bonifácio Balanco, *senhorita*. From Brazeel— before I say dat you guess already, no? José Alvarez Martim Basílio Bonifácio Balanco, hees *carro*, dey yours."

The girl favored him with a heart-melting glance. "I am Viviane Morgan. And your friend?"

"I don't know hees name. I fin' heem een thees rain, like you, *Senhorita* Morgan."

Morgan looked back at Hwan as though they had never met. He said hurriedly, "I Eddie Sun, please know you." Eddie Sun had been the youngest and friendliest of the cooks at the Golden Dragon. Hwan made an effort to give his final sentences extra emphasis, always a difficult thing to do in a language foreign to one's thoughts. "I do whatever you ask, lady. Anything you want, say me."

"Oh, I hope you mean that! Thank you both—thank you very, very much." Morgan's regard returned to José. "Some— persons," she hesitated and appeared to choke back a sob. "They are in my house, doing the most terrible things. I got away—that is why I was running through the rain."

"Dey break een?" José's scowl would have shaken Cochise.

Morgan nodded, her face a plea. "I have servants, but—but they are not strong like you. Could you help me, please? Force these persons to leave me alone?"

José grinned and patted her shoulder. "You wan' da best een

da whole worl'? You got heem. Jus' da good luck, you come out, stop da *carro,* an' een it da best. Da angels, dey watch over you, *senhorita,* or ma'be you a angel yourself."

"It is not far," Morgan told him. "Right there, see? That little dirt road. I do hope your car will not become mired."

After half a mile it did. José opened the trunk, removed his luggage, got out the jack, and showed Hwan how to raise the car with it. While Hwan was jacking up the car, José opened a suitcase and got out a huge knife with which he lopped branches from the evergreens beside the road. When the bottoms of the front tires were higher than the ruts they had made in the mud, he put the branches under them, and the Cadillac crawled forward once more. "Now we all wet," he said, grinning. "*Tres amigos,* eh? Da tree drown meece." He handed Hwan the knife. "Better we keep heem een here. Ma'be need heem again."

Morgan assured him that she was very, very sorry indeed and touched his hand. He kissed her fingers, saying *"Igualmente."*

Little by little the rain slackened; there was no more hail and no more thunder, until at last José was able to switch his wipers from the fastest speed to the intermittent setting. Once Hwan glimpsed an antlered buck standing under a large pine some distance from the road. Something that might have been a child or a bedraggled doll rode the buck's back, and waved as though giving a signal as they passed. Hwan blinked and tried to tell himself he had been mistaken, although he knew he had not been. The gun he had taken from Fee gouged him painfully just below the ribs; as carefully as he could, he inched it toward a more comfortable position, hoping all the while that José could not see him in the rear-view mirror and keeping his shaking hands well away from the trigger.

Morgan said, "It's been a weary way, going so slowly over the mud, but we are nearly there. My home is just around this next curve."

"Muito obrigado, Senhor Deus."

The trees were larger here, and yet so thickly set that it

seemed that the land itself had once been larger, and had shrunk until no tree or stone had room to breathe. The trees had built domes and arches across the road long ago; now all the thousands of colonnaded spans bore so heavy a load of wood and rain that Hwan felt they must soon fall, crashing down upon the car under their centuries-long accumulation of squirrels' nests and half-ruined birds' nests, their innumerable rotten limbs and autumn-wearied leaves. A horned owl as large as the black firepot for *kur loo op* studied the car, half hidden behind dripping foliage on a low branch. As Hwan met its orange eyes, it pronounced his name distinctly: "*H-w-a-n L-e-e. . . .*" Neither Morgan nor José appeared to notice.

It had seemed to Hwan that the curve would go on forever, a coiling line that never closed, drawn through an endless forest. At last it halted so abruptly that their bumper nearly struck a gate of thick and rusted bars set in a dripping stone wall whose top was lost among the trees. A dull-eyed, exhausted horse and two empty cars—a battered Jeep Cherokee and a shiny Oldsmobile—waited there beside the road.

"Thees ees your house?" José looked at Morgan with new respect.

"Just a moment," she told him. "I will open this, and you can drive on through."

She got out but did not walk to the gate, merely standing beside the car before resuming her seat. From beyond the wall (or perhaps from within it) there came the grinding of iron on stone, the grate and clank of huge chains, and the slow hammer-taps of an immense pawl. The rusted bars shuddered, so that it appeared for a moment that the gate was somehow dying; then it began to crawl upward.

"*Amigo*, my machete, my beeg chopper—you got heem? Geeve heem to me. I teenk ma'be I need heem real soon."

Hwan passed the three-foot knife up to José.

Beyond the gate of bars, beyond the wall, lay the wide and weedy court from which Sissy Stevenson had ridden with Long Jim. It was no longer entirely empty, though the very presence of two disparate groups (as bizarre as the throngs half seen in dreams) made it appear more deserted still, as a cathedral or basilica intended for thousands is made to appear the more desolate by a handful of worshipers, votaries vastly outnumbered by saints in marble, limestone, and stained glass. Unseen ghosts of fear and fight, of oath, ordeal, and the eventual Judgment of God were evoked by the very presence of Wrangler and Lisa Solomon; Will E. Shields, Ann Schindler, and Mercedes Schindler-Shields; Sally Howard and her son, Seth; Sissy Stevenson, grim old Bob Roberts, the tough yet elegant G. Gordon Kitty, and little Judy Youngberg. They were fewer than a dozen all told, and the thronging ghosts made that very few indeed.

The group that faced them was only somewhat more numerous, and many among it appeared spectral themselves, whether called ghosts or goblins, ogres or elves—this though von Madadh, with his red-gold beard and cigar, might have dominated a convention of the American Medical Association, and the erect and nearly human apes who flanked him were as solid as gorillas in a zoo.

"Stop here," Morgan instructed José; she touched his hand, and the Cadillac halted abruptly, as though its brake pedal were beneath her feet. "Follow me, both of you."

She got out, and José opened the door on the driver's side and joined her; together they strode toward the spectral cluster headed by von Madadh.

Hwan left the big car more slowly, and for a moment stood staring from one group to the other.

Ann exclaimed, "Mr. Hwan!"

He turned to look at her, and after a second or two walked toward her. Morgan glanced back and whistled to him as if to a dog, but he did not appear to hear it. "Now war?" he asked Ann.

"I'm afraid so. We were chasing a man on a horse—shooting at him, even. Then we found out *he* was chasing that woman who whistled—she was the one who got Mercedes into so much trouble, we think, so we started chasing *her*. Then we found this—"

Wild and clear as the sea-wind across the waves, Morgan's voice silenced her. "My brothers! We have summoned you, your lemen, your knights and ladies to battle, for we will take you fairly if we can. Choose your champion. Who is the bravest you breed? The strongest and most skilled?"

G. Gordon Kitty bowed. "Though modesty—"

But the time was already past. It seemed to Shields that he himself did not advance; rather, Ann, Mercedes, and the rest fell ever farther behind him while Morgan and her fay hench-men drew nearer without taking a step. There was a centaur in armor there; a squat brute with six hands held a long knife in each.

Shields leveled the rifle that von Madadh had given him, and pushed off its safety.

36

The Land of Apples

HWAN HEARD the sharp report of Shields's rifle echo and re-echo between the beetling walls and the slanting, unearthly towers until it seemed it must shake the sky. The brown-haired lady gasped; but if the bullet struck von Madadh, he gave no sign of it, grinning like a wolf. "What's this, Will? Would you shoot an unarmed man?"

"It's a whole lot safer that way," Shields told him. "But I've a feeling you're not unarmed, and you're certainly not a man." He fired again as spoke. Before he could get off a third shot, von Madadh was at his throat. As Hwan drew Tom Howard's pistol from beneath his shirt, they fell to the lichen-gnawed stones together.

The boy with the bandaged face shouted, "Here!" and tossed a flashing silver sword to the pale little man (he was scarcely taller than Hwan himself) whom Hwan had once been ordered to kill. The boy produced a second sword as he ran.

The cat-man dashed after him, a pistol in either hand. The pale man raised his shining sword, and his big revolver boomed. An ape dropped as though clubbed; the second charged him.

Others were charging as well, nightmare shapes dashing from Morgan's side to join the fight. Though he did not understand its sights, Hwan trained his pistol on José like a sensible man and pulled the trigger.

"The king is dead!" Von Madadh sprang up, his once-golden beard red with blood. *"The king is dead—and the world lives! The end is not yet!"* Morgan's high, uncanny voice joined his: *". . . will live again!"*

Their echo did not die away, but swelled to the rattle of iron-shod hooves. His green cloak billowing, a huge rider on an eight-legged horse thundered into the courtyard, followed by a wild-eyed, riderless hunter who looked small only by comparison. Phantom and specter scattered like bats before them, so that for a moment Hwan supposed the battle won.

Yet there was a single, stooped figure that did not flee. Slowly, it straightened until its snowy beard hung no farther than its knees; and Hwan saw that it was crowned, and what he had first thought a staff or crutch was in fact a long straight sword. King Geimhreadh's cracked voice was nearly lost in the immensity of the courtyard. "You are come at last."

"Blood-bought, I am here to die," the green-cloaked giant acknowledged; he pointed to Shields. "To die, so that you and many another may live." Throwing his great horned helm to the cobbles, he leaped from his eight-legged horse to kneel before the old king. "Strike me, as in time I shall smite you."

The long sword rose and flashed down. Green-faced beneath —then above—its olive hair, the giant's head tumbled over the stones to rest beside his helm. It had not yet ceased to roll when the first snowflakes fell.

"What happened to the Chinaman?" Roberts asked. He was driving his daughter's Oldsmobile; she sat beside him.

From the rear seat Seth muttered, "He shot the guy with the big jungle knife, the man who came with him and Ms. Morgan—just shot him down."

Sally said, "He's a murderer, then, like whoever it was who killed Tom. He wouldn't have taken a ride back to town."

Roberts asked, "You think it was von Madadh?"

From her place beside Seth, Judy said, "It was the man that wanted your house. Morgan told me."

Her aunt nodded. "Mr. Fee? Yes, I suppose it was. It would be just like him."

Seth felt very tired, and the deep glass-cuts in his cheeks and scalp loosed yellow waves of pain across his mind; still he asked, "Where's your cat, Judy? He saved us. Did he go in the Cherokee with Merc?"

Judy shook her head. "He'll come back by and by. He always does."

"I'll bet. Won't he be just an ordinary cat, though?"

"He's my cat," Judy said. "He never is."

Sally sighed. "That's the part I don't understand. How could Judy's cat talk? How could he help Seth get away from them?" When her father did not reply, she added, "I saw it, too, when they were going to fight us. It walked on its hind legs like a man."

Roberts gunned the engine as the car slowed on a hill that seemed as steep as many stairways. "Things aren't the same in fairyland. When you and Katie were little, I used to read you stories about it. Remember 'Puss in Boots'? You used to love it."

Sally shook her head. "It was Kate that liked it so much, Dad. But fairyland? You don't mean that. There isn't any."

"A lot of people have believed in fairies. That's where those stories came from to begin with."

"That's the sort of thing Dr. von Madadh used to say."

"Right. And maybe he was trying to tell us something. You ever think of that? He was the best of 'em."

"He was the worst! He was the one who killed Mr. Shields."

"I know." Something dark bounded across the road. Roberts blinked, then decided it was only a rabbit. "Sally, he was the one they sent out to fight for them. They asked us to pick out a champion, remember? The best we had. So we sent Mr. Shields. That cowboy's still pretty weak; so's Seth, and Seth's too young anyhow. I've got too darned old now, and I didn't see none of you women comin' forward. But he did. The cat would have gone in a minute or two, but Mr. Shields, he stepped forward as soon as they said it. You don't send the worst at a time like that, Sally. You pick out your best, and von Madadh was the one they picked. Recollect how I was in Germany for a while right after the war?"

"Sure, Dad. You've told us about it."

Seth was half asleep, but Judy said, "Not me. You never told me, Grandpa."

"That's right, I guess I haven't. Well, Judy, all my life I'd heard about this place called Germany, and I knew as well as a man can know anything where it was and that the people who lived there were the Germans. We'd been fighting them for four years. I'd seen dead Germans and German prisoners, and I'd seen German planes fly over a few times. But when I got there, I found out it wasn't Germany at all. They called it *Deutschland*, and they were *Deutsch*. Germany wasn't any real place. It was just like fairyland."

A strip of black asphalt speckled with snow appeared in the headlights. Roberts had to wait for a pickup that left ghostly, serpentine tracks before he could pull the Oldsmobile out onto the road.

In the Cherokee, Sissy said, "I sure hope she makes it."

Wrangler, who was driving, nodded solemnly.

"Boomer's Lisa's horse, and if anybody can get him out, she can, I guess. I tried to tell her how it is there—to watch out for Sancha, and so on."

Mercedes glanced at her mother. "I thought you said that Sancha was in the hospital. Didn't you and Dad take her?"

"Back home, she's in the hospital," Ann told her wearily. "Here I don't know. Neither do you." Dry-eyed and grim, Ann stared straight ahead at the back of Wrangler's head.

Mercedes swallowed to summon courage, and at last said, "We should've taken Dad's body."

"They wouldn't let us have it."

"We could've fought them for it." Mercedes spoke with an intensity that surprised even herself. "I've got this sword. Some of you have guns."

Sissy slid around in the front seat. "So did they, or some of them. Long Jim had a gun."

Ann told Mercedes, "We could have fought them for it, and more people would have died—more and more, until there weren't enough left to carry all the dead away. You might have died, Mercedes, and you're all I've got left."

For a half mile no one said anything more; then Mercedes began to sing, hesitantly at first. "*'Twas just about a year ago, I went to see the queen . . .*"

Louder and stronger then, until her vibrant young voice filled the car and spilled from the open window through which Wrangler thrust his elbow.

> "*You've heard o' Cleopatra,*
> *The serpent o' the Nile,*
> *An' how she conquered Tony,*
> *Wi' one allurin' smile.*
> *She tried to conquer Ireland,*
> *But we would not give in,*
> *An' we beat her off wi' cabbage leaves,*
> *From the town o' Magheralin.*"

After he had dropped Ann and Mercedes at the Red Stove Inn and driven back to Meadow Grass, Wrangler emptied the old trunk from which he had taken his dead brother's revolver. He wrapped the bright sword Seth had thrown him in a horse blanket and laid it at the bottom, covering it with folded jeans and faded work shirts. When everything had been put away again, he locked the trunk and went to the kitchen to make coffee.

Sissy had been there before him. He filled a cup from the graniteware percolator and carried it into the lounge.

Sissy had built a fire as well, and sat staring at the new flames from the kindling as they licked the split logs.

"Coffee's done," Wrangler said.

"I'll get some after a while."

He sat down, choosing a chair rather too big for him, with

road wooden arms and leather cushions. "You oughta go to bed. You must be beat."

"I'll wait," Sissy told him.

"Boomer was done up," Wrangler said. "She'll probably walk him most of the way. She won't even try to make him trot."

"You think they'll let her out, really? Not try to hurt her somehow?"

He sipped his coffee, still too hot to drink. "They said they would, and they let us out. If they don't, I'll tell you I'm goin' back to see about it."

"I don't think you could find the way back."

"I've got that sword," he told her.

For a moment, Sissy turned her attention from the fire to him. "Do you trust them, Wrangler?"

He shook his head.

"Me neither."

Sissy was sound asleep on the sofa, under the cheerful red and yellow Indian blanket he had drawn over her an hour before, when he heard Buck neigh. He walked out into the softly falling snow, and for a time he and Lisa embraced without speaking. At last he said, "You go in. I'll see to them."

"I'll help you," Lisa told him; and when he had lifted off Boomer's saddle, she led Boomer to his stall, saw that Wrangler had already forked down clean bedding straw, slipped the bridle from Boomer's head, and shut the stall door. She heard the big horse lying down before she had taken a step away.

"Going to have to get some new doors before hard winter," Wrangler told her. "That Mrs. Shields did for the old ones."

Lisa nodded wearily, thinking of money and insurance they did not have. The telephone rang in her office in the lodge, a faint, insistent buzzing through the thermalpaned windows.

"We better get that," Wrangler said. "Sissy's sleepin' in front of the fire."

Lisa nodded again; and they went up the steps together, she holding the railing because she was so tired and the treads were slippery with snow. He opened the door for her, and she walked softly to her old wooden desk and picked up the handset, saying, "Meadow Grass."

"'Ello? Lisa? Eet's me! I 'ave not get you out of the bed?"

"Sancha!"

"I am not die, you see. My nurse, she say you seet weeth me long time, always come back, no? Now I am wake up, but Lisa, I am the most terreeble dream!"

When Lisa had hung up the telephone, Wrangler said, "She's goin' to pull through."

Lisa nodded, and even smiled a little.

"It's all over now, and we'll pull through, too, Miss Lisa. Know that big pine up on the bluff? Tomorrow I'll take it down and slab out boards with the chain saw. I'll open stack 'em in the barn till Christmas, and they ought to season in there pretty good. Before January I'll make new doors—I can use the hardware off the old ones, it was only the wood got broke. Come spring, there'll be more campers. Sissy'll come back sure, and maybe not go home at all. Then come spring, we'll get married. You'll marry me, Miss Lisa, won't you?"

She could only weep and nod and hug him. "Oh, Wrangler," she whispered. "Oh, *Artie!*"

Back home in the big old house that had been Tom Howard's, Seth awoke from an uneasy sleep and went to the kitchen for a glass of milk. As he returned to his own room, he heard soft voices from his mother's bedroom and stopped to listen. As soon as he was certain of the other voice, he returned to bed; he too had liked the doctor, Seth reflected, as sleep crept once more across his mind. Still, he wondered what his half brothers and sisters might be like, if there were any. Should he tell Merc?

Epilogue

Shields awakened in a high, wide bed in a wide, dim room. band of watery gray light shimmered between heavy brocade apes, and once he saw a hammerhead shark drift past, nging motionless in the current like some pale hawk. A pale wk also was the silver scabbard that hung motionless above m, suspended, as it seemed, from the canopy.

A woman bent above him, her hair falling upon his still hands floods of heavy gold. "Sleep," she whispered. "Rest you, O y lover. Sleep, O my brother, and be well."

GREG BEAR

☐	53172-8	BEYOND HEAVEN'S RIVER	$2.95
☐	53173-6		Canada $3.95
☐	53174-4	EON	$3.95
☐	53175-2		Canada $4.95
☐	53167-1	THE FORGE OF GOD	$4.50
☐	53168-X		Canada $5.50
☐	55971-1	HARDFOUGHT (Tor Double with	
		Cascade Point by Timothy Zahn	$2.95
☐	55951-7		Canada $3.95
☐	53163-9	HEGIRA	$3.95
☐	53164-7		Canada $4.95
☐	53165-5	PSYCHLONE	$3.95
☐	53166-3		Canada $4.95